Iowa
Exposed

Published by Bob Bancks
Blue Grass, Iowa
www.iowafarmboy.net
bob.bancks@gmail.com

Dedication

It is time to recognize my lovely wife, Jane, for her patience and encouragement while I write. She is my first editor and reviewer. She was the person who encouraged me to publish my first novels, and she continues to support my habit of dreaming up new stories.

Preface

Despite the tranquil scenery of waving corn and soybean fields, there was a sinister underground criminal faction unseen. A small town newspaper reporter accidentally exposed the illegal business and a corrupt sheriff department. Here in the small of Wapello, Iowa was a big city organization. Bobbi and Dan Dorman, two of the DCI's best agents, were given the task of exposing Iowa.

Map of Iowa

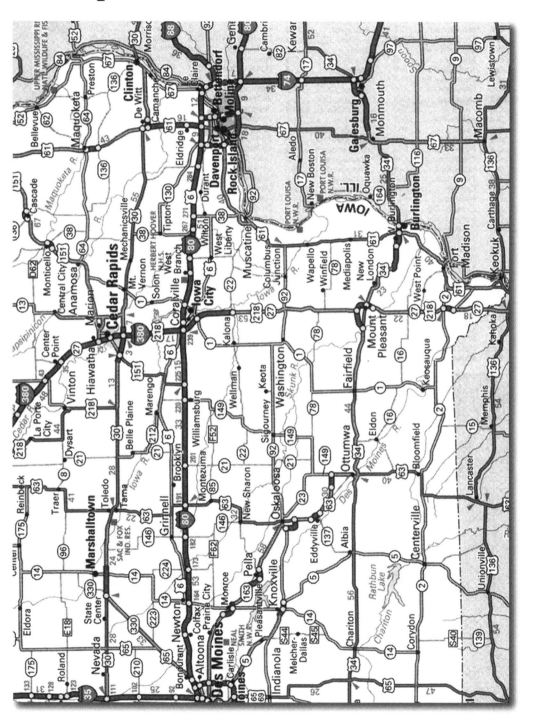

Table of Contents

Chapter 1

Wednesday, March 26

It was dark in the little room; Karen thought it was probably a broom closet, because it smelled of waxes and cleaners. She wondered how long they would keep her locked up in here against her will. She fumbled around in the darkness and discovered a broom and mop handles, a couple of buckets, and a hammer. She realized she was probably making a racket, but making noise wasn't her concern right now. In fact, she hoped someone on the other side of the door would hear her and let her out.

"Maybe I can beat the door down with the hammer," she thought.

Then she heard voices outside the closet.

A woman's loud and irritated-sounding voice hollered, "I don't care how you do it, but make it look like an accident. Don't undress her like the others. I want her fully clothed. I don't want any suspicion placed on the plant or my husband's business. Understand?"

"Yes, Mrs. Boss," a deep male voice answered. "Freddy and I have a foolproof plan. Nobody will place any connection with Acme. Where is the bitch now?"

"Jake locked her in the broom closet. Be careful, she may have some weapon like a broom handle. As soon as I see the truck pull away, I'll call the sheriff in Muscatine County, so you won't be bothered by competition. He does what I ask. He is putty in my hands. I contributed a large amount to the sheriff's campaign coffers just for times like this. Now it is payback time. Understand?"

Karen was ready if and when the door opened. She had a firm grip on the hammer. The door opened. She swung, but because of the bright light, she swung wildly. Before she could recoil, a giant of a man grabbed her arm and painfully whipped it behind her. She screamed in pain. She turned to lash out at him with her free hand; her fingernails found his face. She gouged a groove across her assailant's cheek.

He swore and hit Karen across the side of her face with the back of his hand. She was temporarily stunned. As she regained her senses, her head throbbed, and she realized her hands were bound behind her back. She tried to move her legs, but they were tightly secured with ropes to the table on which she was sitting. The table was cold because it was stainless steel. The room was white and austere with bright florescent lights overhead. Across the room was a dark figure of a man. He had dark hair and a big mustache. Judging by the tone of his skin, he was Hispanic. This didn't seem unusual; there were many Hispanics working at the plant. He was holding a handkerchief against his cheek, but it didn't stop the blood trickling down into his mustache.

Karen started to speak, "Why am I here? Where am I? Why am I tied to the table? Who are you? Why don't you let me go home?"

"You ask a lot of questions, lady," the man answered. "The reason you're here is because Mrs. Boss said so. You are in what we call the autopsy room or specimen room. It is where the veterinarians bring in suspect meat and innards. You are tied to the table because you struck me and scratched my face, so I tied your hands. I didn't want you to run away, so I tied your legs to the table. If you try to run, you will fall on your face. Who am I? I'm Rick. I work for Mrs. Boss. I do what she tells me. I'm the enforcer for Mrs. Boss. I don't ask questions of why or who. I don't know why you can't go home. I only know Mrs. Ping is angry, and Mrs. Boss said to keep you here until she can figure out what to do with you. I don't know what might have upset Mrs. Ping."

"Upset Mrs. Ping! I don't even know a Mrs. Ping! All I know is when I went to see Mr. Johnson, the plant's owner and manager, in his office, I went to his door and knocked, but no one answered. I turned the knob, and let myself in, which is when I began telling him I was quarantining today's production because I thought I saw a human arm in one of the containers. He had a surprised look on his face. Then he made a quick phone call. I couldn't hear what he was saying, because he held his hand over his mouth. He told me to follow him. We exited through a back door in his office, and he led me down a long hallway with several door openings. He opened a door into a darkened room where I heard what sounded like women talking quietly. Mr. Johnson motioned for me to follow him inside," Karen told him.

"Did you see the women?"

"Yes, I saw about twelve to sixteen young women who were all clothed in short dressing gowns."

Then from somewhere in the room, a woman's voice called out, "Is this the woman?"

Mr. Johnson answered her right way, saying, "Yes, she's the government inspector who worked the last shift. She's the one who found the body in the bin and quarantined the whole day's production until she had other inspectors check into the bins. I'll try to have the men find the bin and exchange it or dump it in the incinerator. We can't get arrested for placing an empty box in the stack."

With a cold tone of voice, the woman commanded, "Get rid of her then and make it look like an accident. Tell Freddy to keep his filthy little hands off of her. Understand?"

Before I knew it, someone grabbed me from behind and a cloth sack was shoved over my head. A hoarse woman's voice yelled, "Get her out of here!" I was bear hugged from behind by someone's arms. He lifted me off of my feet and then dumped me into this broom closet. I've been there until you found me."

Rick shook his head, rolled his eyes, and then told Karen, "I'm sorry to tell you this, lady, but you have seen Mrs. Ping's girls. No one sees or knows about Mrs. Ping's girls except Mr. Johnson, Mrs. Boss, and Rosa, my girlfriend. Rosa got me my job. Although I work for Mrs. Boss, everyone answers to Mrs. Ping, even Mrs. Boss. You are in big trouble."

"But I didn't do anything wrong. I'm innocent. Can't you tell Mrs. Ping my story?"

Rick paused a moment, then continued, "You stated you saw a girl's arm in one of the containers?"

"Yes, but I didn't know it was a woman's arm. Maybe I was just seeing things. An arm could look like a roll of hamburger. But it had fingers! I just wanted to check it again tomorrow and report it. I thought Mr. Johnson should know. That's why I told him. I figured he'd call the authorities. I can rescind my order. You don't have to get rid of me. I can keep my mouth shut. I promise I won't tell anyone. Please, please don't kill me. I have children and grandchildren."

"Now I know why you were captured, and you are in big trouble, but as I said, no one talks to Mrs. Ping. I don't even know who she is or where she lives. She is a mystery woman. All I know is whatever she says, I do. I've seen her punish her girls when they do something wrong and it is not very nice."

The door to the room opened a crack and a woman's voice

said, "Have you a plan yet, Rick?"

"Yes, ma'am. I told you, Freddy and me have a foolproof plan."

Karen strained forward so she might get a glimpse of the woman behind the demanding voice, but the woman wasn't revealing herself.

"Can you tell me?" the woman demanded.

"In a minute, ma'am. I have to gag the lady first. I'll be out in a minute."

"Okay, hurry, time is wasting."

Karen blurted out, "Let me talk to her, please, I beg you and why do you have to gag me?"

"Sorry, I can't let you speak to her face to face. I have to gag you, because maybe you will scream and attract attention. I don't want that to happen, especially when Mrs. Boss is here. Now open up your mouth."

Karen refused.

Rick repeated his command in a much louder voice, "Open your mouth now!"

Karen still refused.

He grabbed her jaw and squeezed. She started to scream, and the minute her mouth opened, he stuffed his handkerchief into her open mouth.

"There, that's better. Now sit still until I get back."

Karen slammed her feet against the table legs in her outrage as she watched Rick disappear through the open door, but all she could do was squirm. Her feet were securely tied to the legs of the table she was sitting on. Karen heard several people involved in a heated conversation and then someone slammed the door shut. She sat quietly, not knowing what would happen next, but fearing the worst.

The door reopened and she heard, "I'll be back in twenty minutes, and you, the lady, and Freddy better be gone."

"Yes, ma'am, I assure you we will be gone. Freddy is after the wrecker as we speak."

Rick entered the room and cautiously closed the door. He looked nervous, Karen thought, as he glanced at his cell phone and then at his watch.

The door opened again. This time, a stylish-looking Mexican lady stepped into the room. She was dressed in high heels, tight black slacks and a colored T-shirt top. Her clothes looked as if she had been poured into them. Karen wondered if she had to have help getting into her slacks. The woman's hair was a wavy shiny black. She had long painted fingernails and toe nails which protruded from her toeless shoes. Karen glared at the woman, but said nothing.

"Rosa, why are you here?" Rick demanded.

"Mrs. Ping told me you had a woman in custody. I need some new clothes for several of the girls. Since I know where this woman is going, I also know she won't need the clothes she's wearing."

"Rosa, this lady keeps her clothes on. Mrs. Boss wants it to look like an accident. It won't look like an accident if she is naked. Now would it?"

Rosa walked around the shackled Karen. She scanned her up and down.

"Look at her boots. I could get $85 for them."

She walked behind Karen and pulled her jacket and blouse away from her neck.

"Hmmm, Coldwater Creek. These would bring Rosa $50 apiece. Look at her jeans, L.L. Bean. They're $100 if they are ten. Come on, Rick, honey. Let me have her clothes."

"No, not a stitch."

Karen watched as Rosa wrapped her arms around Rick and kissed him. She rubbed her body up against his and cooed, "Please, Rick, baby."

"No."

Rosa backed away and approached Karen from the front. Rosa started to unbutton Karen's blouse. Karen shook her head, no.

Rick grabbed her hand and said, "I said, no. Now, back away."

"But I just want to see what kind of bra she is wearing. Rich women wear fancy bras and not one from Wal-Mart," she whined.

Then she disregarded Rick's words and continued to unbutton the blouse. She pulled Karen's blouse open.

"See, she's wearing a lacy bra. I'll bet it's a Bali bra."

"I don't care if it came from Saks Fifth Avenue, you are not taking her clothes!"

"I'll make you a deal. You pay me $200 for not taking her clothes. I'll take $100 for me and I'll use the other $100 to buy new threads for the girls. That will make the girls happy, and they won't have to know where the new clothes came from. Deal?"

With that being said, Rosa pulled Karen's blouse off of her shoulders and down to her elbows. She ran her fingers along the back and pulled up the tag.

"See, it is a Bali. I never had a Bali bra. It is even one of those convertible bras where you wear it several different ways like a halter, or crisscross, on the shoulder. They are expensive. Can I have her bra, Rick? It is easy to take off. See these little loops on the edge where the straps hook? I don't even have to cut the straps. I mean, I could take it off and re-button her shirt and no one would ever know. What do you say to that, Rick? I'll even wear it for you later tonight. Then you can take it off of me. Please, Rick, Sweetie, just this once?"

Rick rolled his eyes and relented, "Oh, okay, what's it going to hurt? But hurry before Freddy gets here."

"Oh, thank you, thank you, honey. I'll be quick as a bunny."

Rosa unhooked the back of Karen's bra, then unhooked the shoulder straps. Karen's bra easily slid off. Karen was mortified, but what could she do? She sat there naked to her waist. Karen looked over at Rick. He had turned his face away. He wanted no part in Rosa's antics. Rosa held up her prize and quickly stuffed the bra into her purse.

She gazed at Karen's chest and reached over to take each breast in her hands and lifted them up.

"You sure have nice tits, honey. Rick, look over here. Doesn't she have nice tits?"

Rick slowly turned and looked at the humiliated woman sitting on the table.

"Yes, she has nice tits. Now hurry and button up her blouse before Freddy gets here."

Rosa pulled Karen's blouse up over her shoulders and began to button her shirt. The door flew open. It was Freddy.

"The wrecker is ready, Rick. I got it all hooked up and everything. What do we do next?" Freddy's voice trailed off, "Wow! What do we have here?"

He shoved Rosa aside and pulled open Karen's blouse again,

popping two buttons off. He proceeded to rip her blouse off her shoulders and stepped back to view the scene.

"Man o' man. You've got some fine tits, lady. I don't get to see tits like those every day."

He reached over and fondled Karen's breasts. Karen burst out crying. You could hear her moaning inside. Her tears flowed down her cheeks. Freddy was about to bend and suckle her breast when a big right hand caught him and sent him sailing across the room into the sink.

"I said leave her alone. Can't you see she's hurting enough already?"

"But, Rick, you have to admit she does have nice tits. Just give me fifteen minutes alone with her, and I'll see if the rest of her is the same. You can watch if you like. They don't call me 'Fast Freddy' for nothing."

Karen tried to gasp but couldn't. Rick could tell by the way her chest was heaving she was crying on the inside.

"No, you little idiot, we don't have time. You just keep that little dick inside your pants today. There will be no extras."

Rick's phone rang. He answered and listened to the voice speaking to him. Then he ended the call and faced Rosa.

"That was Mrs. Boss. She'll be here in ten minutes, and if she catches you and me still here, we're fired. Now let's get going. Rosa. Will you please, for the last time, put the lady's blouse back on?"

"I guess, if you put it that way, but her..."

"I heard you. She has nice tits. Now hurry. After you're finished, find some gauze and tape. We'll have to blindfold her. Freddy, you bring a box cutter and some cardboard. I'll carry her out to her car."

Rick easily picked up Karen and threw her over his shoulder like a piece of meat.

"Get the door, Rosa."

They exited to the outside where the air was cool. March can be fickle. You start the morning warm and finish the day cold. Rick had Freddy open the car door. He gently placed Karen behind the steering wheel.

"You climb in the back and hold her while I work with her feet," he ordered his partner. "Rosa, put the sun shield in the front window and begin to cut out cardboard to cover the side windows. Don't ask any questions. Understand?"

Freddy crawled in the back seat behind Karen and put his hands around her shoulders and held her back. Soon his hands found Karen's breasts. He fondled her mercilessly while Rick worked on her feet.

Karen endured Freddy's fondling as best she could. She heard a chuck-a chuck-a sound. It was like someone squeezing a caulking gun. She felt Rick grab her foot and place it on the floor. He held it there for a few seconds, and then he did the same with the other foot.

"Cut her hands free, Freddy. Rosa, if you are done, put the cotton and gauze over her eyes. I don't want her to see this. "

Freddy shoved Karen against the steering wheel so he could reach her hands behind her back. He pulled a knife out of his jacket pocket and cut the plastic ties which held her wrists. He released his hold and let Karen bring her hands forward. Karen instinctively rubbed them together. Before she could react, Rick grabbed her right hand. He pumped some cold goo on it. He formed her hand around the steering wheel and held it tight. With his free hand, he pumped some goo onto the steering wheel itself. He grabbed her left hand and pressed it into the cold paste. Rosa finished with placing patches over her eyes and bound them with some stretchy tape she had discovered in a drawer in the autopsy room.

"Okay, we're ready to go, Freddy. Winch the car onto the wrecker. Rosa, you go home. I'll see you tonight, and you had better be wearing that confounded bra you said you needed so much."

"*Si, senor*," Rosa cooed.

Karen felt her car being pulled up the incline of the tilt bed wrecker. The whine of the cable winch stopped. The bed settled down to a horizontal position. She tried to adjust her feet. They wouldn't move. She tried to remove her hands from the steering wheel, but they wouldn't release. It felt like she was glued to the floor and the steering wheel. When she tried to wiggle her feet, she realized she WAS glued tight. Maybe she could get one foot free of her boot. They must have used some sort of quick setting epoxy glue. The wrecker started to move. Karen tried to remember the stops and turns they made. She rode in darkness for many miles. The chilly air was getting to her. She began to shiver and wondered if she had really seen that arm in the box of meat or had she been dreaming?

Why, oh, why, do I have to be so inquisitive? I must have seen something or I wouldn't have run to Mr. Johnson's office. Then I had to follow him down to that, that, room. Her thoughts turned to Darren, her daughters, and grandchildren. Would she ever see them again? Emotions were running high. She may never see Cassie's baby boy. He was to be the first boy in the family.

At the top of her lungs, she wailed, "Oh, God, please save me. I don't want to die."

* * *

Mrs. Boss waited in her car outside the gate until the wrecker passed loaded with a car. She reached for her cell phone.

A cell phone buzzed in a drawer in the sheriff's office.

The man reached in and answered, "Joe Ward, is this an

emergency? This is my private phone and I'm on duty."

"Hello, Sheriff Joe, this is Rita Johnson. I need a favor."

"Yes, go on."

"There's a yellow and blue tilt-bed wrecker heading your way. It is going to place a car on the railroad tracks west of Walcott. I believe that is still your domain."

"Yes, it is."

"I need you to make sure the same wrecker picks up the vehicle after the accident."

"What accident? Is there a person involved?"

"Yes, but no one you know."

"That's homicide. I can't promise I'll help."

"Sheriff, how much did I contribute to your re-election campaign?"

"$50,000."

"Sheriff Joe, did you and your buddies enjoy the New Year's Eve party I threw with my girls?"

"Yes, they were lovely young ladies."

"I didn't want to have to say this, but I'm sure you do not want it to be known you attended my little get-together."

"That's blackmail."

"I know, but I do have connections and if JJ gets elected, I'm sure I can get some Federal funds headed your way, or if you don't cooperate, he might order a review of your department."

"Okay, what do I have to do?"

"Just be sure you are the first on the scene and my boys get to retrieve the wreck. You take care of the body, if it doesn't burn in the crash."

"By taking care of the body, does that mean destroying it?"

"No, no, I mean just make sure the funeral people get it and give her a proper burial."

"So, it's a woman."

"Yes."

"I won't be involved any more than that?" he questioned.

"No, my good sheriff."

"Okay, I'll do it."

"Thank you, Sheriff Joe. It is nice doing business with you. Oh, by the way, the two men in the wrecker are Rick Sanchez and Freddy Rodriguez. They are employees of mine. Good men."

* * *

The truck slowed and Karen could tell they were driving on a gravel road. The truck stopped and began to back up. She heard Rick's voice give a command.

"That's good. Let's raise the bed and get this over with."

The bed tilted again and her car rolled back. Soon it was level.

"You pull away, Freddy. I'll see how she is doing."

The passenger side door opened. She heard a rustling of paper and cardboard. The door slammed shut. The driver's side door opened. She felt the blindfold being removed. She opened her eyes and right in front of her face was Rick Sanchez. His eyes were full of tears. He pulled the gag from her mouth.

He spoke quietly, "I'm sorry this had to happen, lady. You shouldn't be here. I've done a lot of jobs for Mrs. Boss, but this is the worst. If it makes it better, I know you're innocent, and God above knows you're innocent. Tonight, I'll pray to the sweet Mother Mary to accept your soul. I know you will be in heaven soon and I, well, I will be in Hell."

Rick moved close to Karen's face and kissed her on the cheek. He placed her purse in her lap and closed the door. Karen's eyes were just focusing on her surroundings. She tried again to tear her hands from the steering wheel. She looked to her left and discovered she was sitting in the middle of a railroad track out in the country. A train horn sounded. Karen could now see a locomotive rounding the slight curve just east of Durant. She franticly pulled and tore at the steering wheel. The engine blew its horn longer and longer. It was getting closer. A big bang came from the train as the engineer had set the emergency brakes. Sparks flew from the locked up wheels. Karen freed her left hand by tearing her skin from her hand and leaving it on the wheel. She worked her feet free. With her left hand, she tore away at her glued right hand. The plastic wrap of the wheel pulled free. She looked out the window. It was too late. The engine was just feet away from impact. She screamed and put her bloody hand on the window as if she could try and stop the collision. WHAM!!!! It was over.

The locomotive hit the driver's side door with its huge knuckle coupler. The car exploded in fragments of glass and a cloud of dust, but fortunately not fire. The car was forced up on the front of the engine and carried another mile to almost the next crossing. The engineer scrambled out and called 911. He walked away from the wreck for a second to be sure there wasn't going to be a fire. He had heard of engineers sitting in their cabs and being burned alive by the exploding gasoline from the car.

After waiting a bit, he slowly crept up to the damaged vehicle and looked into the windshield. He could tell the victim was a woman, and he could also tell she was not alive. He looked toward

Walcott and could hear the sirens. Then he saw the blue and red lights leaving town. He also saw a truck parked about one-quarter of a mile to the north. It was blue with a yellow stripe across the door.

The first emergency vehicle to arrive belonged to the sheriff, which seemed odd. This was Muscatine County, but Muscatine was miles away. How did he get here so fast? Who called the emergency vehicles? The fire trucks arrived, and the ambulance roared in from Durant. They hooked a chain to the car and to one fire truck. The engineer backed the train away. The wounded car peeled from the engine. It took the Jaws of Life to extricate the body.

Rick and Freddy were parked about 1000 yards away in a field driveway. They had front row seats to the accident. Rick sat silently, while Freddy whooped at the impact.

"Boy, that Chevy made a splash. Too bad it didn't catch on fire. It would have burned her to a crisp. Well, now all we have to do is wait for the sheriff to call. That was easy, huh, Rick?"

Freddy laughed as he hit Rick on his shoulder.

"Shut up, you little pest. If I didn't need you, I'd kill you right now and leave you for the buzzards," Rick snapped back.

He had tears flowing from his eyes.

"What's the matter, Rick? Getting soft in your old age?" he teased.

"Oh, shut up. We wait until the ambulance leaves, then we just show up, check with Sheriff Joe, load the wreck, and take off for Washington. We unload there and hurry home. I want to put this out of my mind as soon as possible. Maybe I should take a vacation."

"Ah, Rick, as soon as you get to Rosa's and all she has on is the crazy bra she wanted, you'll forget all about today. Just like before."

"Yeah, I guess so. There goes the ambulance. Here we go."

Rick fired up the engine of the wrecker and shoved it into reverse. He backed onto the road and headed for the accident scene. Sheriff Joe was patrolling the road and was standing next to his cruiser as Rick pulled alongside.

"You guys sure got here fast," he said with a smirk. "Well, I guess the early bird gets the worm. There's no one else close, therefore, the rules state you get the business. I guess you know where to deliver the wreck?"

"Yes, sir, we know exactly where to take it. Now let me and Freddy get'er loaded and we'll be out of your way. Thanks for the business."

Sheriff Joe smiled and said, "No problem. Anytime and anything for Mrs. Johnson."

Freddy attached a cable to the mangled piece of metal which used to be a Chevy Impala. Rick threw the winch in gear, and the car slowly screeched and groaned onto the tilt bed truck. The pair attached a couple of log chains to the back bumper and secured the load. With a wave of their hands and a thumbs-up gesture, they drove away from the scene. The firefighters washed down the tracks and the surrounding embankment before heading back to the station. It was fairly chilly, and because it was a volunteer fire department, the men had jobs to return to.

Freddy and Rick headed for Washington. Freddy lit a cigarette. He reached in back of the seat and pulled up Karen's cell phone and her laptop. He flicked the phone on and accessed her photo gallery app. Within seconds, he scrolled through several family pictures.

"Can I have this smartphone? My niece would love it. How about the laptop? I know a guy who can get into computers and make them work for him. I know he could clean this one out and sell it."

"No, these have to stay with the truck for a couple of weeks.

Then when the heat is off, we'll see if you may have them. I'm sure the boss lady won't mind. You just can't take them right now. Understand?"

"I guess so. Hey, the lady had some kids, good lookers, too. If these are her daughters, they are real knockouts. I'll bet they have tits like the old woman. Hey, here's one of her with some children. Grandkids, I bet. Do you want to see them, Rick, old pal?"

"No! You just don't get it, do you, Freddy? We just killed a good-looking wife, a mother, and a grandmother, and all you can think of is her daughter's tits. Don't you ever think of anything else? I'm getting tired of this business. I'd quit if I could, but the only way that will happen is if I shoot myself. I'm going to hell anyway, so I might as well keep on trucking."

Freddy kept oo'n and ah'n at the snapshots scrolling across the screen, until a photo of a very pregnant young woman appeared.

"Hey, the little lady was going to be a grandma again. Too bad, she won't be here to see the baby," Freddy announced.

"Give me that phone, you knucklehead. I don't want to hear any more about the lady or her family."

Rick grabbed the phone and shoved it into his shirt pocket. He was about to give Freddy a swift backhand, but then thought different. He needed Freddy to help finish the job. They continued their trek to the recycling yard in silence. It was 4:30 when they arrived at the recycling yard gate. Rick stopped at the guard shack.

"Hello, Pete. How are you doing? I got a wreck, and it needs to be processed right away. Mrs. Boss's orders. She wants everything ground up. Don't take the time to remove any tires, the engine, or insides. She claims it will all mix up later and no one will know."

Pete replied, "It's almost closing time. It will have to wait until tomorrow. You dump the wreck right in front of the chipper. I'll have the boys do it first thing in the morning."

Rick drove to the other side of the yard. There were stacks and stacks of worn-out pickups and automobiles waiting to be ground into small pieces and dumped into waiting rail gondolas. Rick knew afterwards, the scrap from the cars would be sent to the various mini steel mills for reprocessing. Who knows, Rick thought to himself, maybe they would become cars again in their next life. What he did know was after the vehicles went through the chipper, no one could tell what they had originally looked like, because the remains were all the same.

Rick backed up the wrecker and raised the bed. He released the cable. The black Impala slid to the ground with a crunch. He pulled away and let the bed settle down.

"Well, Freddy, we're done. We can go home. I don't know who you are shacking up with tonight, but I've got my Rosa."

It was like a big weight had finally been released from his shoulders. He waved at Pete as they drove by. Pete was already closing the gate before they made the highway. Soon, they would be back in Wapello.

Freddy answered, "Yeah, your Rosa with her new Bali bra. I'll bet it won't stay on long. Kiss her tits for me, Rick."

Rick's phone rang. It was Mrs. Boss.

"Yeah, we dumped the car. It should be dust tomorrow morning. Yes, we will hide the truck at Mr. Johnson's. Yes, the laptop and phone will stay with the truck."

There was a long silence on Rick's end. Mrs. Boss continued her instructions. Freddy could hear part of the conversation. His eyes moved toward Rick when Mrs. Boss told him they must become scarce for about a month. She suggested they stay somewhere in Texas and they would be traveling by bus. That way, car licenses couldn't be checked. Freddy was instructed to tell his live-in he would be going to visit a sick grandmother. Mrs. Boss had arranged everything in advance, and Rosa had already bought the bus tickets.

They would leave at 7:00 in the morning from Burlington. Rosa would drive them there. That was it. The phone call quickly ended.

They drove the truck into a shed located on the backside of Mr. Johnson's acreage. It was almost hidden from the house and definitely hidden from the road. Rosa arrived minutes later. She said her instructions were for the three of them to stay at her apartment until morning.

* * *

At five o'clock the next morning, Freddy was watching the news on television. A reporter told of a bad train-car accident in which a local woman was killed. Rosa was in the shower. Rick was sulking in the bedroom. The door to the bath opened and Rosa stepped out wrapped in a towel. Rick's mood changed. He smiled a big toothy grin as Rosa came to him. Just about three feet in front of Rick, she loosened the towel and let it fall. All she was wearing was the Bali bra. Rick quickly stood and grabbed his beautiful, nearly naked, Rosa.

"I'm gonna miss you, Babe. It will seem like forever until I can come back."

"I'll miss you too, sweety. I hope you don't forget what I look like. Close the door. We have time for a little loving. Freddy won't bother. He understands," she whispered softly in his ear.

She reached behind her back, unhooked the Bali bra, and let it fall. As she pressed her large breasts against his chest, she worked on unbuttoning his jeans. They fell into the bed and made love.

Sometime later, Rick told her, "There's no way I'll ever forget you, Rosa. When I get back, we'll get married. Now hurry and get dressed. Me and Freddy have a bus to catch."

They made Burlington in plenty of time. The trio had a quick breakfast at a café just across from the terminal. Rosa kissed Rick goodbye and waved as the bus headed south toward Fort Madison.

* * *

October, One Year Earlier

Phil Robbins is a reporter for a weekly small town newspaper. He actually writes for a couple of papers and does radio news casting on a part-time basis. He originally started working for a large tractor manufacturing company. He worked there for fifteen years before he fell from some scaffolding and broke a leg, a couple of ribs, and crushed his hand. He spent several months in rehab, but soon the company realized he would never be able to return to work. He received a call from his boss asking if he would consider a buyout from his job. Well, push came to shove, and the company offered him a chance to get a college education and a new career path. That is how Phil became a reporter.

He laughs at his slow writing because his right hand refuses to cooperate and it hits the wrong keys. He found he liked writing and reporting for a small newspaper took the pressure off because there were few deadlines. Phil read the headlines of the daily papers and tried to find out what was behind the news. He liked to think he was an investigative reporter. He investigated people-to-people stories, local events like Walcott Days and The Long Grove Strawberry Festival. The most fun for him was checking out the many church suppers and Lion's club fish fry events. There was always a ton of events going on all the time and few people ever knew about them. That is where Phil shone.

The craziest thing he ever did was while interviewing a stock car driver at the track in West Liberty. Right before the races were about to begin, the regular announcer for the night became ill. Someone knew Phil had done some radio work and was related to the race association president. The president approached Phil and asked if he would call the race.

Phil said, "Sure, but I don't know much about the cars or drivers."

They gave him a program for the night. This started his career as a stock car racing announcer. It was fun and paid fairly well. He and his wife, Sherry, traveled all over the Midwest calling races.

* * *

Phil was reading today's news about the recall of millions of pounds of ground beef which were found to be contaminated by E. coli bacteria. Several hundred people were affected. The price of beef cattle plunged. He called a farmer friend, Darren Hellzer, who raised beef cattle. Darren was also a director on the Iowa Beef Association Board. He had a good knowledge of the beef industry. Phil asked if he could come to his feedlot and home to interview him.

"Sure, Phil. Come on out. This E. coli runs deeper than just a few bugs in some hamburger," he told him.

Phil scheduled a time for the upcoming Monday. He planned to take photos and tape the interview. When he arrived, Darren and his wife, Karen, were waiting for him. They immediately led him to their large feedlot.

"There's a quarter of a million dollars' worth of beef out there," Darren said as he pointed to lot of fat steers. "Since the E. coli scare, we've lost nearly $20,000. The market lost ten dollars a hundred last week. That's a hundred dollars an animal. Multiply it by 200, and you get $20,000. All this happened because some small packing plant was sloppy or negligent. There are hundreds of good, clean, well run packing plants, but all it takes is one bad one and the media is all over it. I'm sure the market will recover, but it will take time to renew the customer's confidence."

"You indicated there are other factors associated with this problem?" Phil asked.

"Yes, there is and it is not easily solved. Many of these bacteria problems are due to the lack of meat inspectors. Big operations employ full-time inspectors and are generally contaminant free. It's the small packers who have the problems. First, there are so many little packing houses and very few government inspectors, state or federal. There just aren't enough inspectors to go around. The plants either kill only on certain days or self-inspect, which is dangerous. Why do the large plants have the better inspectors? They pay more. It's steady work and there is no travel."

"Does everybody get inspected?"

"Yep, even the little butcher shops like the ones in Durant or Bennett. Of course, they usually kill once a week and not every day. Very few sell product to the public, and they only butcher individual's animals. Their inspection is usually scheduled and basically is for cleanliness. It's the small packers who target a specific market like Acme Pack in Wapello. They only kill cutter and canner cows. A cutter or canner is usually an older animal, dairy, or beef, which has outlived her usefulness. They slaughter the animal, strip the meat from the bones, and grind it all into hamburger. We need plants like Acme to have a place to get rid of older stock. They have a place in the market chain. Basically, Acme caters to schools, nursing homes, and hospitals. Those places are the ones needing cheap meat. Most businesses don't use only Acme beef, because it is too lean and has only a little flavor. They mix better quality meat with it to stretch their supplies. The only trouble is Acme has had bad reviews prior to the time when the Johnson family bought it."

Phil asked, "I never heard of Acme Pack. Where is it and who are the Johnson's?"

Darren replied, "The plant and its investors were lured here by the governor and his staff. They promised tax breaks and other incentives. All he looked at were the potential jobs it would create for the local people. The plant was poorly managed from the git-go. Soon, it was evident it was going to fail, and all those wonderful jobs would be lost. In order to save his reputation, the governor had one of his wealthy supporters bail him out. J. J. Johnson of Washington bought the plant at pennies on the dollar. The original owners lost a lot of money. If you haven't heard of JJ, he owns several car dealerships, a John Deere dealership, and a metal salvage yard in Washington, named J & R Recycling. His wife, Rita, is a realtor and inherited big bucks from her parents, who owned a gypsum mine, until they sold for millions to US Gypsum. To top it off, JJ put the Acme plant in her name and his son, Jacob, as CEO. A note about Jake, he is an only child and a playboy. He drives Porsches and Ferraris. He has his own house on the banks of the Iowa River, which I am told, is patterned after Hugh Hefner's Playboy mansion. You know, hot tubs, swimming pool, mirrored bedrooms, and girls. Just last year, he applied for an extension on the TIF money for the packing plant, so he wouldn't have to pay the extra property tax. The bumbling board of supervisors, under pressure from Des Moines, relented and gave him ten more years. You can be pretty sloppy with your management if you don't have to pay taxes, and you bought the plant for less than a quarter of its value."

Phil couldn't write very fast, so he scribbled the facts in his reporter's notebook which he considered the most important. He could verify Darren's statements later by searching the internet.

"As for the violations, someone isn't reporting them, or they are being paid off to keep things quiet. It's funny how the governor's office controls all the agencies which were designed to protect us."

"So, what about the jobs the town was promised? There are certainly jobs at a packing plant, right?"

"Oh, there are jobs, but very few for anyone who lives in the immediate area. There are some white collar jobs for the local population, but most of the real work is done by Hispanic or Southeast Asians. They are the only ones who will work in such terrible conditions. I've been there and so has Karen. It is hot, humid, all concrete, and stainless steel. There's open gears and chains and, of course, sharp knives and saws. It is a dangerous place to work."

"Aren't all meat packing plants somewhat dangerous?"

"Yes, but the larger plants have a lot of safety equipment and shields. They mostly have larger spacing, and the hours are better. At Acme, when they wanted to expand production, instead of enlarging the building, they went to a ten or twelve hour day. The workers are very tired at the end of the day. There are more accidents there than the average."

"My next question is how do you know all of this?"

"I have an excellent source. Two years ago when this inspector shortage began to occur, Karen and I decided to help out. Karen has a degree in animal science, and she was on the meat judging team at the university. She applied for an inspector's job, and after spending six weeks at the large Morrell plant in Ottumwa as an intern, she became licensed as a government inspector for the state of Iowa. Karen inspects several local butcher shops plus she fills in at Acme. She has never worked at Acme for more than a few

days at a time. She never had to fill out reports on the plant as she does on all the little locals. She has, however, recorded many violations at Acme and reported them to the supervisors. It seems that is about as far as it goes."

Phil was about finished with his interview when Karen called us from the house asking if we would like some iced tea. Phil didn't refuse, because he knew there would be cake, pie, or cookies to go with the beverage.

As we sat at the table, Darren asked Phil how much he was going to write about their conversation.

Phil told him, "Just your comments on the beef industry and the lack of sufficient meat inspectors. I wouldn't be able to write anything about Acme, because it would be called *heresay*, because there wouldn't be enough facts to base any accusations."

"Good," he said, "I was hoping you'd say that. It could be a case for liable suits. I wouldn't want you to get in trouble."

Phil wrote his story and got it published. The local people read it and told him they liked it. His paper did put it on the "wire," but it was only picked up by a few big papers. Phil also received a letter of thanks from the Iowa Cattlemen's Association for his interest. That was about it for this story. He continued to interview others depending on various events, and he even wrote for several other papers as a freelance writer. It would be a year before Phil would meet Darren again, and it would be under much different circumstances.

In his new role as a reporter, Phil thought it was strange how names and places popped up after an interview. The Iowa Primaries are in June. The congressman from the southeast Iowa district decided not to run again. He had been Iowa's representative for thirty years and was a good congressman. Now there were candidates vying for the job. Both parties had several good candidates.

It just happened to be that J. J. Johnson was one of those men. His wife, Rita, was really the pusher behind his campaign. She was a diligent worker for the party, but didn't have the credentials; therefore, she talked JJ into running. Being a congressman's wife would get her into all the right circles in Washington—Washington, D.C., that is. She loved the glory and glamour of politics. Phil's boss wanted someone to attend a debate between the candidates. When he asked Phil, he jumped at the opportunity. He would be seated in the front row of seats and be allowed to ask questions.

The big night arrived. The debate was held in Mount Pleasant at the college. The crowd wasn't as large as Phil anticipated. There were other reporters, some college professors, and a representation of locals and students. Phil was intrigued by the intense questions. The toughest question asked was by a reporter from the Des Moines Register. It was directed at Mr. Johnson.

"What are your views on immigration? I see you own a packing plant which hires Hispanics and other ethnic groups. Are you sure there are not illegal persons working in your plant?"

He adjusted his tie and said, "First, let me correct you. The Acme plant is owned by my wife, Rita, and it is operated by my son, Jacob. I have nothing to do with the day-to-day operations. Second, the plant provides many jobs for many people and adds to the local economy. Sure, there may be Hispanic and other ethnic people, but they all buy food, clothing, houses, and cars. Third, to my knowledge, all the workers are citizens of the United States. Most have just moved from the southern states because of the unemployment situation in that area."

The questioning continued on immigration reform and illegal aliens. It was clear Mr. Johnson was not comfortable. Phil never got a chance to ask a question, but he was satisfied to be able to sit with the big paper reporters. Since the North Scott Press is a weekly paper, the actual debate would be old news. He wrote about the body language of all the candidates and their comments at the reception after the debate.

Phil was typing his story when Sherry walked into his office.

"Do you want to hear Rita Johnson speak?" she asked. "I received two tickets from school to hear her speak on 'Human Trafficking.' I guess she is some kind of an expert. She spent time in Southeast Asia and Central America on fact-finding trips. I asked Carol Spencer, but she was busy, so now I'm asking you."

"Sure, is there food afterwards?" Phil replied.

"Oh, Phil, is that all you are concerned about? But, yes, I think there is a reception after the meeting."

Phil had never met Mrs. Johnson. He was surprised by her knowledge of the subject. She told of slavery and child brutality in foreign countries. After speaking for twenty minutes, she opened up for questions from the audience. The very first question was about trafficking in the U.S.

"Most definitely, there is trafficking in America. It is mainly located in the larger cities. The largest offenders are pimps who sell sex to everyone. Their girls, as they call them, must be able to return a certain money figure every night. If they don't produce, they are punished or sold to someone else. The prostitutes or call girls are in a desperate situation. If they fail at sex, they are sold to sweat shops or sold as house laborers. There are laws to prevent this from happening in the U.S., but the perpetrators are difficult to catch and prosecute."

"Do you know of any cases here in Iowa?" Phil asked.

Mrs. Johnson stared coldly at Phil.

She said, "Not that I know of. Iowans wouldn't tolerate such hideous crimes. Iowa doesn't have a big enough population to support a major call girl operation."

Sherry and Phil visited with Rita Johnson afterwards. She was very cordial and friendly. She thanked him for his question about Iowa trafficking.

"I hope my speech alerts more people to the problem. We have kept it out of our great state, and if my husband is elected to Congress, he is going to write legislation with others, of course, to stiffen the laws already on the books."

"Thank you, Mrs. Johnson," Phil said. "I hope you'll like my comments about your speech which will appear in our local paper."

Chapter 2

March 28

Several months passed before Phil met Darren Hellzer again. This time, it was at his wife's funeral. It seems her vehicle got stalled on a rural railroad track and was hit by a freight train. Phil had been at the accident scene, because he was a volunteer firefighter for the Walcott Fire Department. At the time, he helped cut her body from the wreckage, but he had no idea of who she was. The sheriff identified her from the driver's license and ID cards found in a wallet in her purse. Phil couldn't sleep that night. It was a recurring problem being a volunteer fireman seeing humans suffer or die. He sometimes had to deal with friends and relatives in those tragic cases.

The line was long at the funeral visitation. When Sherry and Phil finally made the receiving line next to the casket, they offered their condolences and started to move on for there were still many behind them.

Darren leaned over close to Phil and said, "Could I see you

later this evening after the visitation?"

Phil gave him a funny look, but said, "Sure, you set the time. I'll be there."

"Ten o'clock. The family should be gone by then."

Phil took Sherry home and drove out to Darren's. When he arrived, the only other persons there were his two daughters. He said his hellos. Darren motioned him to his office in the back of the house. His office was a converted hired-help girl's bedroom, which was a flashback to a time when women were hired just to keep house. The other problem was, Darren told Phil he had three brothers and no sisters. His mother needed help. A couple of the hired girls actually became part of the family because they married his brothers.

The office was not large, but comfortable. There were two big leather swivel chairs and a huge desk covered with papers and on one end a computer monitor. He had another small TV which never shut off. It gave updates on the markets and weather reports.

Darren leaned back in his chair and looked at Phil with piercing eyes.

He said, "I think Karen was murdered, or put it this way, I think she was planted on the tracks against her will."

Phil gave him a quizzical look.

"You are about to ask why I feel this way."

Phil nodded.

"First, Karen seldom used that particular crossing, because she felt it was dangerous. Second, at the time of the accident, she would be coming home and driving south over the crossing. Her car was headed north. Third, a deputy interviewed the engineer of the train, and he told them he could see the car from about a mile down the track. It looked as if someone was trying to load the car onto a flatbed wrecker. Instead, it dumped the vehicle there and drove off.

His associate in the cab with him said it was a blue and yellow wrecker. That's all. It took them almost a mile to stop. He also mentioned the car seemed to explode, but did not catch fire on impact. This was because the deputy told me the muffler was not hot neither was the key in the ignition. There were no sparks to ignite the gasoline. Fourth, Karen was thrown from the car and the authorities claimed she was not wearing her seat belt. Karen always wore her seat belt. When the EMTs recovered her body, they noted the skin on her hands had been ripped off. They were skinned raw. The steering wheel was bent by the force of the collision. The fake leather wrap of the steering wheel was torn and in her hand. It was as if she was glued to the wheel. Fifth, neither her cell phone nor her laptop was ever found at the scene. Sixth, about an hour before the accident, she texted this message to me. 'At Acme, found body. Look in box. Got caught. Love you. Call pol.' That was the last message she sent. I suspect whoever had her in their custody took the phone away from her. I can't prove anything, but I have a feeling good old Sheriff Joe Ward is sand-bagging and he isn't being entirely truthful."

"That's a lot of unexplained evidence," Phil said quietly.

"The last thing was the strangest. When they found her, Karen was braless. Someone had removed her bra. My wife sometimes worked at home without wearing a bra, but she never would go to work braless. So, what do you think? Do I have a case? Can you help me?"

"Darren, I'm only a reporter. I'm not one of those big fake stars on television or in the movies who pretends to be a detective or a lawyer. I don't know if there is much I can do, but I do know a private detective, who is very good. He does things by the book. If he finds enough evidence to support your claim, he will call in the local people or maybe the DCI."

"Thanks, Phil. I know it is just a hunch, but I strongly feel this way. I also know we must keep this as quiet as possible until enough evidence is found. You tell your man, I'll pay his fees whether the result of his investigation comes out good or bad."

Phil got home about eleven o'clock. Sherry was ready for bed. She claimed she was tired. As I told her the story, her tired feeling disappeared.

"I think you should call Ron right away. This sounds serious," she said.

"But it is after eleven. I hate to call him now."

"Oh, come on, Phil, he'll still be up."

Seeing he'd better follow his wife's orders, he dialed his friend, Ron Puck. Ron had been an MP in the Army. When he finished his tour of duty, he became a policeman for the Davenport Police Department. While checking on a routine family dispute, he was blindsided by an enraged husband and shot in the knee. He did recover, but his patrol days were over. The department gave him a desk job, but it drove him crazy.

He resigned and became self-employed as a private detective. He spent most of his time investigating insurance frauds and domestic disputes. Because of the sporadic jobs available for PI's in Iowa, one of the odd side jobs Ron had was selling and installing security systems. Ron considered the job to be a good supplement to his cop job. In fact, Phil had just helped Ron on a job at Jacob Johnson's place. Jacob was the son of JJ Johnson.

His alarm system wasn't operating correctly. The alarm would sound without any reason. The repair job required extra hands to replace the unit. As they arrived, Jacob and another man were carrying a young woman to a car. She was wearing a red bikini and had a distinctive tattoo of a serpent winding up the right calf of her leg. When Ron asked if he could help, the reply was, "She's okay. She had a little too much to drink and we are taking her home."

It did seem unusual, because one would think they would have wrapped her in a blanket or towel to keep her warm. We continued doing our job figuring it was none of our business.

Phil dialed Ron's number and he picked up immediately.

"Ron, this is Phil Robbins. I think I have a job for you. Do you remember the car-train accident which happened last week?"

"Yes, I read about it in the paper. It was very sad, and she was so young."

"Well, her husband, Darren, feels she was murdered. He claims her car was set up, and she was either dead before the accident occurred, or she was bound in such a way she couldn't free herself from the car. He would like to hire you to investigate and see if he is right."

"Wow, he is making quite an accusation, but he must have reasons. How come he doesn't work with the authorities?"

"He has, Ron, but he thinks the sheriff is sandbagging or is being paid off. If I were a detective, I'd help him myself. I'll help you as much as possible, if you take the case. Her funeral is tomorrow."

"Where does this man live? When can I see him? May I talk to him yet tonight? I may want him to delay the burial."

Phil gave him Darren's phone number and address. He told him that Darren might still be up. He had had a big day, but sleep was going to come slow. Phil didn't say anything, but he wondered why Ron thought it was so urgent.

* * *

Sherry and Phil attended Karen's funeral which was shortened, because there was not going to be any graveside service. The explanation was a great friend was delayed getting to the service and the graveside service would be set at a later date. Ron evidently made his point.

Chapter 3

March 29

It was seven o'clock the next morning. Sherry was getting ready to go to work at the school library. Phil was sipping his last cup of coffee and planning his jobs for the day. His cell phone rang. It was Ron.

"Say, Phil, could you meet me at the accident scene in about an hour? I need to check for overlooked evidence and take some photos. Mr. Hellzer will be there also. If we find anything, I want him to be able to identify it."

"Sure, Ron, I can be there in ten minutes. Where are you now?"

"At the truck stop having breakfast."

Phil told Sherry where he was going. She told him he should wear a jacket and gloves for it was a chilly gray March morning, March 29 to be exact. He fumbled around in the hall closet for a coat. He knew Sherry was never wrong about the weather.

He met Ron and Darren at the crossing. Ron started snapping pictures right away. We walked down the tracks to get to the final stopping place of the accident. The dead grass was scorched. Truck tracks along the embankment were still visible. Quite possibly, it was the wrecker retrieving the vehicle.

"We will start looking for anything which might remotely be related to the accident. If you find something, don't touch it or move it. I will photograph the article and flag it. If we find something significant, I will call the DCI of Iowa. I have a good reputation with the bureau, and I don't want to tarnish it."

They started walking slowly back to the crossing. Darren stayed on the tracks; Phil took the right side, and Ron took the left. We weren't fifty feet away from the scene and Ron stopped. He reached down with a weed stem and poked away some grass.

"I think I found something," he shouted.

Phil hurried over to his side. Darren was already kneeling down.

"What is it?" Darren asked.

"The black material is the wrapping from the steering wheel. The grayish, plastic looking material hanging on it is, I believe, skin. Possibly, your wife's skin stripped from her hand. It looks to me as if they are glued together. If that is the case, maybe you are correct, Mr. Hellzer. This isn't just an accident. Maybe your wife was not able to escape the car, but was tied or glued to her position. I think this is definitely a homicide. I'm going to call Des Moines."

Ron was about to place his call when Phil heard him say, "Oh, no, here comes trouble."

Phil climbed the embankment again only to see Muscatine County Sheriff Joe Ward's squad car pull up. Ron hurried down to meet him.

"Well, well, well, what do we have here?" the sheriff commented. "Is this a citizen's investigative team or some men doing community service?"

"Hi, Sheriff, no we are just doing the research in case something was overlooked. Oh, by the way, I'm Ron Puck, private investigator. Mr. Hellzer hired me to help him clear his mind. He's going through a tough time right now," Ron answered and extended his hand.

"I'm well aware of whom you are, Mr. Puck, and I don't like you snooping around into my business," he grumbled.

Darren butted in, "I hired him, Sheriff. I wanted to see the accident scene for myself to try and figure out just what happened to Karen. I thought maybe it would ease my mind to get a second opinion."

The sheriff backed off a bit from his gruffness and said, "That's all right, Darren. I don't care if you get a second opinion, but we did investigate this scene thoroughly. My boys were very careful."

Darren then dropped the bombshell. I could see Ron's face cringe as he spoke. Evidently, Darren was not a fan of Sheriff Joe.

He said, "If your deputies were so thorough, then why did they miss this piece of evidence we just found?"

A look of disgust and surprise came over the sheriff's face at the same time.

"What do you mean, Darren? I thought you were satisfied with the investigation. What important piece did my boys forget and this two-bit PI found?"

Darren led the sheriff to the first flag and the steering wheel fragment.

"The two-bit PI, I hired suspects the leather and the skin or plastic hanging from the leather is glued together. If it is skin, it is probably my wife's. This indicates to me she was somehow trapped inside the car and could not escape. I personally feel this is a homicide, and the case will cover more than Muscatine County. Therefore, I would ask if you would call in the DCI to help investigate."

The sheriff sputtered and coughed, "You certainly are not going to call in the DCI over this little piece of evidence, are you?"

Darren answered, "Sheriff Joe, you have this county in the palm of your hand. You may do anything you want. This evidence plus the fact we found Karen's purse alongside the road and a tube of glue in the ditch tells me your deputies did not do a very good job. Now are you going to call the DCI, or shall I have Ron do it?"

The sheriff was very quiet, as if he was weighing his options. Maybe he thought, "I should try and keep this case as low key as I possibly can and avoid any more damage. The body is already buried and the vehicle is on its way to the scrap yard to be shredded. In a couple of days, all the evidence will be gone and forgotten."

"I'll call the DCI as soon as I return to the office," he told Darren.

"Why don't you call from right here?" Ron chimed in. "I have my cell phone and their number."

"Yeah, why not?" Phil commented, but then he wished he had stayed silent.

"Who's this idiot?" the sheriff growled.

Darren saved Phil's butt and responded, "He's a friend of mine. I asked him to come and help."

It seemed to satisfy the sheriff. He grabbed Ron's phone and pushed the send button.

"Cal, this is Sheriff Joe Ward of Muscatine. In my

investigation of a train-car accident, I feel there is cause to suspect a homicide. I'm asking for your help, because this may cross county lines."

There was a pause and some more conversation followed by a, "Thank you, Cal."

The sheriff turned to Darren and said, "I guess you're lucky. The head of the DCI plus two of his best agents are just a few miles away. They are having coffee at the I-80 truck stop. They will be here in a few minutes."

Turning to Ron, the sheriff said, "I'm going to leave for a minute. I've got to check in with the office. I'll be back."

The rotund sheriff waddled back to his car and flopped in. The big Crown Victoria roared to life and took off, throwing rocks and dust for about a block.

"It seems the great sheriff is a little perturbed," chuckled Ron. "Thanks, Darren, for bailing me out. The great sheriff is probably trying to contact his buddy, the county attorney. He is most likely wondering what his next step should be."

"No problem, Ron. He is a poor example of an officer of the law. If you have money, he's your friend. If not, look out. I know the children of the rich and influential of Muscatine get away with a lot more than we poor folks."

They all had a good chuckle and returned to their search. Two cars approached from the north. Phil assumed it was the officers of the DCI. The first car carried one person, the second two. A tall, dark-haired man emerged from the first car. He motioned for the occupants of the second vehicle to follow him. The three walked over to Ron's side of the tracks.

Phil was surprised to see one of the three was a woman. She was petite and way over dressed to be walking on a railroad track. High heels don't lend to crawling up steep embankments or walking railroad tracks.

"Good morning, gentlemen. I'm Cal Stender, Captain on the Department of Criminal Investigation for the State of Iowa. These are my agents, Roberta Stroud, or Bobbi as she likes to be called, and this is her partner, Dan Dorman. If we have a case here, they will be assigned to investigate. I must say, they are two of my best agents."

Ron introduced Darren and Phil. After a little chit chat, the group got down to business.

"Tell us, Ron, what have you found?"

Ron explained the steering wheel cover and the purse. He also told Cal we had discovered some cigarette butts in a driveway just a quarter mile down the road. The agents downed some gloves and carefully collected the evidence.

"Where's the vehicle now?" Dan asked.

"I honestly don't know, but I was told it was loaded onto a tilt bed wrecker from Washington," Ron answered.

"Washington, you mean, Washington, Iowa?" Bobbi blurted out. "That's an hour away from here. Why did they get the job?"

"Hmmm, that is strange. I'll ask the sheriff when he returns," answered Cal.

"It seems maybe the sheriff isn't really doing his job. If the wrecker was from Washington, it is out of his jurisdiction. Ladies and gentlemen, we have a case for the DCI. Ron, since you seem to know the most, I'm going to ask if you will sign on as a special agent for the bureau. Will you accept?"

Ron smiled and said, "Yes. What about my friend, Phil?"

Phil jumped right in on that statement.

"I'm a reporter and not a cop. I don't like being shot at or being a shooter. I don't even own a gun anymore. I used to hunt with my brother and Dad, but that was long ago. I'll be satisfied if Ron clues me in once in a while. I don't want to get in the way. If you need someone to write a story, I'm your man. Thank you."

"Thank you for being candid, Phil. You're one of the few media folks who don't want to be in the thick of a case. Ron will be in touch, if anything breaks."

Then Ron announced, "Now we have to finish this search, because it looks like rain and I'm sure we are all getting chilly. I have to leave soon, but I want to wait for the sheriff."

He didn't have to wait long. The sheriff arrived shortly in his big cruiser. Ron met him by his car. In the quiet air, the conversation was quite terse.

"Sheriff Ward, I feel there is enough evidence to merit the DCI becoming involved. There is enough evidence here which your men did not find or attempt to find."

"Are you accusing my men and me of not doing a thorough investigation?"

"I think you could have done better or maybe you just didn't want to."

Now the sheriff was becoming red in his face. He took a breath.

"I don't understand why you feel this way, Captain. I ran a good investigation, and I detest you big boys from Des Moines messing around in my business."

"I figured you say that, so may I ask you a few questions?"

"Sure, shoot."

"I am told a tilt bed wrecker from Washington, Iowa picked up the damaged vehicle. Doesn't it seem odd a wrecker from so far away would be here so soon after the accident? I was told they were here within ten minutes. I also read the accident report and discovered the truck came from J & R Recycling and not an auto salvage yard. Do you know what the difference is?"

"Yes, at an auto salvage, they tear apart the car and resell the usable parts. At a recycling plant, they grind up the cars into small chips and sell the scrap to a recycling foundry or a mill."

"Exactly! You, Sheriff, let a chipper take this car, which is evidence and without any restrictions. It is possible the car may have already been turned into a pile of chips. Do you agree?"

"Yes, I suppose it is possible, but what does this have to do with me?"

Cal was trying to restrain his emotions with the now smiling Sheriff.

"Since the vehicle in question may have been destroyed, we may have lost a valuable piece of evidence. Because of your inept investigation, you let it go. I'm going to called Des Moines and have them issue a search warrant for the J & R yard, and if that car is not there and has been demolished, I will personally file a complaint and have you arrested for tampering with state's evidence, obstructing justice, and anything else I can think of. I'll see you are disposed and impeached. Do you understand?"

Sheriff Joe stood quietly as if in shock. He acted as if what he had just heard was baffling. He turned around and left. Again, his big Ford threw rocks and gravel down the road for a block.

Captain Cal turned and spoke to the rest of us who were stunned by the action we had just witnessed.

"We'd better get somewhere for some food and warmth. I have to call Des Moines and then the Sheriff in Washington County. Hopefully, the vehicle in question is still in one piece."

Cal left. The five of us looked at each other.

Phil spoke first and said, "First, I want to know, whom is the leader of the group, since the captain is gone now?"

Evidently, it was a stupid question. Both Ron and Dan smirked and pointed at Bobbi. What an ignoramus he was! Sure, why not? It didn't take long for him to find out.

"Phil," she asked, "where is the best and closest place for lunch with a small room for just us?"

He thought a moment and replied, "Walcott Coliseum. They have a small room off the kitchen. If it is not busy, I'm sure Beth will let us use it. I could call right now if you want."

She smiled at him and said, "Phil, you're a jewel. I'd like nothing better than some home cooked food and a quiet room. Call Beth."

Phil called the Coliseum. There was a room available. We headed for town. Darren opted out. He claimed he didn't want to be too close to the investigation, and he needed some rest. Ron thanked him for his help and Darren headed home.

We entered the bar and grill and wound our way to the back room. The main room was filled with local farmers and business people who were mostly men. It was a place where diners could acquire neighborhood gossip plus the food was good. Beth and her helpers were all good cooks. We did draw some stares, but the conversations didn't stop. Beth showed us a small room in the back. It was warm and cozy.

"This is great!" commented Bobbi as she started to remove her big down-filled jacket.

It was then when Phil realized she was a knockout. She was dressed in black slacks and a white blouse, and she wore a blue denim jacket over her shoulders. She was about five-foot-six and trim. Her dark brown hair was cut short and wrapped around her ears, which were decorated with gold and diamond earrings. She weighed no more than 120 pounds soaking wet right out of the shower, which he was trying to imagine. Her figure told him she worked out, maybe a runner, and probably because of her job, she wore a black belt in karate. She was impressive even with her hair in a mess, because it had been crunched under her stocking hat all morning. Let's be honest. The woman was hot!

Dan was almost the opposite. He was six feet tall, lanky, and raw boned. His face was craggy and his hair was sandy and unkempt. No movie star was he. He wore blue jeans and a worn sports jacket over a plaid shirt. He seemed to be a quiet person. Maybe that was because Bobbi was very vocal.

Beth took our orders and sent them to the kitchen. When she returned with water and some coffee cups, Bobbi asked her if she would point out the way to the powder room. She needed to freshen up.

Beth took one look at her and said, "The restroom is in the basement, but let me take you through the back way. If I let you walk through the bar, looking like you do, I'll be mopping up the floor because of all the coffee and beer they'll spill. Those old guys out there will lose their appetites, for food that is. They haven't seen a woman like you in years. Follow me."

Bobbi left the table and disappeared through the kitchen door. Phil figured by the time she and Beth returned, Beth would have filled Bobbi in on all his family and what he did for a living.

Sure enough, the first words out of Bobbi's sweet mouth were, "Beth tells me you have three sons, you are from Davenport, and married a farmer's daughter. Her name is Sherry, and she is a school librarian."

"Yup! That about wraps it up. Not much else to tell."

"Well, I hope Dan and I can have some children someday, but right now, we feel is not a good time, two cops raising kids. One cop would be enough. But we are going to have some, aren't we, honey?"

She ran her fingers through his auburn hair. Dan just looked at her and smiled.

"You two are married?" Phil blurted out.

"Yes, for two years. It really saves on finding the right accommodations for the two of us. It saves the taxpayers money, too," she giggled.

Phil watched, aghast. How did this common looking unkempt man happen to catch a babe like her? They say love is blind, and I'm sure under the covers, he must be appealing. Lucky guy!

A few minutes later, our piping hot food arrived at the table. Bobbi placed her cell phone next to her plate as if she was expecting a call.

Chapter 4

Meanwhile, as they warmed up and ate, Captain Stender was busy at work in his car. He was supposed to be in Iowa City by one o'clock to meet other detectives who were on another investigation. He was already late. He would grab a sandwich later. First, he placed a call on his car phone to his office and had Evelyn, his personal assistant, find a judge who would issue a search warrant for J & R Recycling. Next, he phoned the sheriff of Washington County.

"Sheriff's office. Sheriff Tom Peckenschnieder here. Just call me Sheriff Tom, please."

"Tom, this Captain Cal Stender of the DCI. I need some immediate help from your department."

"I'll do as much as I can to help. What do you need?"

Cal explained the situation and how important the wrecked auto would be to the case.

Tom told him, "The junkyard is open until twelve on

Saturdays. Only the gate man and a couple of men to unload are there. I'll be glad to drive over and see if I can locate your car."

Twenty minutes later, Cal's Bluetooth phone rang. He punched a button on his steering wheel.

"Cal Stender speaking."

"Mr. Stender, this is Sheriff Tom Peckenschnieder. This is your lucky day. I visited with Pete at the gate before he closed. He informed me the car in question might still be here. The chipper machine broke down last Wednesday, and they are still waiting on parts to make their repairs. He doesn't know if the car was destroyed or not, but he said we may have a look around. His only problem is all vehicles to be sent through the chipper are inventoried. He has to have the right count at the end of his day."

"Thank you, Tom. I'm going to send a couple of agents to Washington. Is there a possibility they could meet you at the yard tomorrow morning? It might help if the gateman sees a familiar face before letting us in there."

"Can do, Mr. Stender. Either I or one of my deputies will be there, say about 8:00 a.m.?"

"Eight will be fine. The two detectives are Dan Dorman and his wife, Bobbi Stroud. They're some of my best personnel."

"Did I hear you say Dan and his wife?"

"Yes, they are married, but Bobbi decided to keep her maiden name while working for the department. I'll have them there at eight sharp."

Cal called Bobbi as soon as he got off the phone with Tom. Bobbi was halfway into a piece of apple pie when her phone flashed. She looked at the screen. It was Cal.

"What's up, Captain Stender?"

"I need you and Dan to be at J & R Recycling in Washington at eight tomorrow morning. The sheriff informed me there is a possibility Mrs. Hellzer's car is still there. The gateman informed the sheriff the chipper machine broke down early Wednesday, so maybe the car did not get processed. You and Dan need to confirm its existence, and then find a way to get it out of the yard."

"Can't we just get a court order?"

"Yes, but I want to use that as a last resort. I don't want to tip off the people responsible for this crime. The yard man must crush as many cars and trucks as he has in his inventory."

"What if we could exchange a vehicle to replace the one we need?" Bobbi suggested.

"Great idea, Bobbi. Do you think you can find a match?"

"I don't know if I can, but I'll bet Ron's friend, Phil, has connections. He works the sound booths and calls many stock car races in southeast Iowa. I'll put Ron and Phil on the job. Dan and I will find a place to stay tonight. We'll be in Washington at eight sharp."

They were listening to Bobbi's side of the conversation.

After she hung up, Phil asked the obvious question, "What connections do I have to help in this case?"

Bobbi replied, "We need another wrecked black Chevy Impala to substitute for Mrs. Hellzer's car. I know stock car people depend on salvage yards for parts. Which yard would you recommend we start looking in for a substitute car?"

Phil thought a minute.

"Ernie Van Dyke's Salvage. He deals in only late model vehicles and probably has the largest yard in Iowa. He's located in Oskaloosa. If he doesn't have what you need, he has a network of other dealers who might have what we're looking for."

"Great, will you and Ron handle it for us?"

"Yes, I've got a few days before I have some assignments," Phil told her.

This was most exciting, actually working with the DCI, Phil thought to himself.

"I'll put a call into Ernie right away."

Phil could see Bobbi called the shots. Dan just agreed. Bobbi pulled out a map of Iowa from her purse. She marked Walcott, Washington, and Wapello in red. Next, she put crosses on Wapello, Columbus Junction, and West Liberty.

"It looks like Muscatine should be our center point, maybe the south side of Muscatine. Are there any motels or efficiency units on the south side, Ron? It looks as if Dan and I will be in the area for a few weeks, and we need a good place to chill out."

"There are a couple of old motels in the south end. There is even a small apartment complex in Fruitland. They may have a furnished apartment available, because they cater to the Monsanto plant," Ron answered.

"Okay, now here's the plan for the rest of today and tomorrow morning. Phil, you and Ron locate a replacement Chevy. I don't believe color is very important as long as it is fairly dark. It must be a totaled car with the front end smashed. You call me as soon as you have one located. Dan and I will locate a place to stay for tonight and maybe longer. We are to meet the sheriff of Washington County at the recycling yard at eight. If you have any problems acquiring a car, we may have to go to plan B, get a court order, and impound it. Captain is hoping to avoid that scenario, since it might tip off those responsible for her death."

The late lunch broke up. Bobbi and Dan headed for Muscatine. Ron and Phil drove the three blocks to his home. Phil booted up his computer to find Ernie's website. He had two late model wrecked Impalas. Maybe this was going to be easy. Phil called the yard. Ernie answered. The two cars he had were both white, but he'd get on the network and see if he could locate a black one. Fifteen minutes later, he called back.

"I got a black late model Chevy Impala in Keosauqua. It was a new graduation gift. The young girl took it for a spin in the rain and lost control. She rammed a light pole. Luckily, the air bags deployed and she walked away with a few scratches and bruises. The car was totaled, a lot of front end damage. It could be the car you're looking for."

"Sounds like a match. Keosauqua. The only junk yard I know in that town is Grumpy Gus's."

"You got that right, Phil. He's a tough nut to crack. I've dealt with him many times. Take plenty of cash. If you need a tilt bed, I'll rent you one of mine. Good luck."

* * *

Keosauqua

Phil quickly looked up Gus's number. This guy had the personality of a grizzly bear. The only reason he knew him was his son raced stock cars, and Phil had met him while interviewing his son.

The phone rang several times. Finally, someone answered.

"What do ya want? It's almost closing time."

"Is this Gus Gustofersen?"

"Well, it ain't Queen Elizabeth. Who are you and what do you want?"

Phil had to make up some kind of a story and fast.

"I'm Phil Robbins. You know, the guy who calls the stock car races in the summer. I'm looking for the rear fender and trunk lid for a 2010 Chevy Impala. My son was rear ended by a pickup and smashed up his mother's car. I'd pay cash for the car, because I want to keep his record clean. Ernie in Oskaloosa said you might have such a vehicle."

"Yep, I do. Ernie offered me $1,500 for it as she sits. I turned him down. I want $2,000. If you got $2000, you can have the back end."

"I would like the entire car, Gus. Who knows what else might be damaged."

"That'll cost extra."

"How much extra?"

"I'd be happy with $2,500, and you haul it."

"Deal! Is it all right if I have one of Ernie's men pick it up?"

"I don't care, but I've got to have the money in my hand before they leave, and I want cash."

"Keosauqua is about 110 miles from here. We'll be there around nine."

Phil turned to Ron and asked, "Now where am I going to get $2,500 cash by tomorrow morning? I've only got a couple hundred around the house."

Ron shrugged his shoulders and said, "I probably can come up with $500."

Sherry walked in the door. She saw the long looks on our faces.

"What's the matter, boys? Why the long faces?"

"We need $2,500 cash to get a replacement car for Mrs. Hellzer's car. If we don't come up with the money, her car goes into the grinder, and we lose a lot of precious evidence. Between us, we have maybe $700. We need another $1,800."

"Do you get paid back?"

"Most definitely by the DCI, but it may takes weeks."

"I have some cash stashed away for a new sewing machine that I'll probably never get. You stay here while I see what I have. I don't want Phil to know where I hide it, or I'll have a computer instead of a sewing machine," Sherry said with a smile.

She quickly headed upstairs. They could hear her opening some drawers and doors. When she returned, she had a hand full of bills.

"Here's $2,000. Consider it a loan. If it helps solve Karen's murder, it will be worth it."

"Thank you, hon," Phil said, thinking to himself how much his wife was always full of surprises.

He left a message on Ernie's phone that tomorrow was a go. He and Ron decided to leave at 6:30 to get to Grumpy Gus's on time. They decided not to call Bobbi until they had the car loaded and were on the road. They needed to take the chance the car in question was still at J & R and hadn't been destroyed.

* * *

At eight o'clock sharp, Bobbi and Dan were outside the gate at J & R Recycling. A sheriff's car pulled in behind them. Bobbi and Dan hurried to the officer's car. After showing him their credentials, they discussed their next move.

Sheriff Tom claimed he knew the gatekeeper well. He would first attempt to have him let the three in without any warrant. Junk dealers are strange people and cops are not their favorite visitors.

Bobbi watched as Tom spoke with Pete. They watched as Tom slapped Pete on his back and they were laughing. This was a good sign. Tom motioned for the pair of DCI detectives to enter. They were instructed to leave their vehicles outside the yard. Pete furnished a golf cart for them to ride to the chipper.

"That was easy. What did you have to promise the gateman?" Bobbi asked, knowing there was some kind of bribe.

"Old Pete likes raised doughnuts. His wife won't let him have any because of his heart. I told him if he would let us look around, I'd take him to the Kalona Bakery, and we would get a dozen donuts between us."

The trio reached the chipper. There were, at least, twenty wrecked cars piled in front of the machine. Bobbi went right to the car in front. She could tell it was a black sedan, but couldn't get close to be sure if it was Mrs. Hellzer's. Sheriff Tom motioned to the only other worker on duty. He told the worker that Bobbi and Dan were insurance investigators. They wanted to make sure this was the car from the accident. All they needed was the VIN number and they would be gone. The forklift driver shook his head. He rammed the forks under the auto and lifted it away from the pile. Dan waved and began to search the windshield area for the number. The forklift driver said something to Tom and left.

"We've got about fifteen minutes before he gets back. It is his coffee break time," Tom told the pair.

Dan found the VIN number. It matched. Bobbi poked around the wrecked auto. She looked inside and gasped.

"Look here! Inside on the floor," she said excitedly.

Tom and Dan hurried around to what had been the driver's door. It had been torn off while trying to free it from the locomotive. There on the floorboard was a brown boot. Bobbi found a broken radio antenna and reached in to poke at the shoe. It wouldn't budge.

"Her shoes were glued to the floorboard. She couldn't

move."

Bobbi's attention moved to the bent steering wheel. Pieces of the vinyl were torn off. There was a piece of what looked like human skin still hanging from the right side.

"She had her hands glued to the steering wheel. She was trapped. She never had a chance, the poor woman. Good God, help us find this evil person who did this to an innocent woman."

Ron and Phil were pulling through Mt. Pleasant when Ron's phone rang. It was Bobbi. They had checked the car. It was the right one.

"Phil and I are outside Mt. Pleasant and heading for a matched car. We think. We have to go to Keosauqua. Phil's friend, Ernie, is providing a wrecker for the pickup. We should be able to be in Washington before noon."

"That's great news, Ron. We'll see if the sheriff can keep the help preoccupied while we exchange cars."

"There is one problem," Ron told her.

"What's that?"

"The car cost us $2,500 cash. Thanks to Phil's wife and her sewing machine fund, we have the money. I told her the department would reimburse her. I hope that is true."

"Well, it is a little unusual, but under these circumstances, we'll find a way to cover it. Call us when you are about ten minutes away."

Ron and Phil arrived at Grumpy Gus's at nine. He was in his usual nice mood.

"Where's your wrecker?" he grumbled.

"I've been thinking. I feel $3,000 would be a better price for the car."

Ron sighed. Now he raises the price. Phil looked old Gus right in the eye.

"Gus, you old grumpy so and so, you agreed to $2,500 cash. I have the cash. Now don't go changing your mind, or I will inform all the drivers and sponsors that you reneged on a deal. I'll make sure no one deals with you or your son. Now show us the car. Then I'll give you the cash and you walk away. We'll load it ourselves. Understand?"

The old man knew Phil meant business, and he counted on the stock car drivers for selling them parts. He knew if Phil had to carry out his threat, he would lose a bunch of business.

"Okay. Okay. $2,500 cash will do. Give me the money and I'll go home. You be sure to shut the gate when you leave."

Ernie himself was driving the tilt bed. He hopped out of the truck and greeted us.

"Phil, how have you been? I hope this car is worth the trouble. Who's your friend?"

Phil introduced Ron as a special agent for the DCI.

Ernie blinked his eyes and said, "This is more than a car exchange, isn't it? May I ask what's up or is it a secret?"

Ron answered, "It is sort of a secret, but I can tell you this much. The bureau feels they have enough evidence to rule a case a homicide. We have found the vehicle involved and it is in J & R Recycling. Our only problem is the yardman is afraid if we confiscate the car, he will not be able to prove his inventory count. Therefore, we are exchanging similar vehicles so he will be safe. If someone connected to the crime is present at the destroying of the auto, they will be satisfied it is gone. We hope they won't check the VIN number."

"Boy, this sounds like real cloak and dagger stuff. I deal with JJ Johnson quite a bit. He always seems like a nice guy."

"Well, maybe he is, but someone wanted that car processed immediately. We don't know who or why. Maybe we'll find some answers in the car."

We loaded the car and headed for Washington. By 11:30 a.m., we were just a few miles out. Ron dialed Bobbi.

She answered, "Come in through the gate. The sheriff conveniently took both employees to Kalona for coffee and donuts. We have forty-five minutes to exchange the cars."

Ernie pulled his truck in by the chipper and dumped his load. He hurried around to the other side and winched on the black Impala.

"Where to now?" he asked.

"Des Moines. I'll give you the address. Dan will ride with you, and I'll follow along behind. It's not that we don't trust you. We want to make sure no one stops you or causes some kind of diversion. I also have alerted the highway patrol of our route. This car is a valuable piece of evidence, and we have to make sure it arrives in Des Moines."

Bobbi turned to Ron and Phil.

"You two may go home for now. I'll contact Ron on Monday. The lab should have some results from the autopsy by that time. If you hear or see anything, give me a call. Here's my business card. See you on Monday, Ron. Phil, Ron will keep you informed. I promise if anything breaks, you will be the first to know."

Chapter 5

Dan and Ernie headed for Des Moines with Bobbi following close behind. Ron and Phil headed back to Walcott. Our day was over and Phil needed some rest before Sherry and he attended the St. Paul's chicken sandwich and soup supper.

Phil didn't know if it was the long day or just boredom, but Ron started to tell him his life story. Phil knew he had been married and had two children, both of whom were older. His son was in the Navy and his daughter was married and lived in Minneapolis. He told me his ex-wife, Laurie, and he seemed to be happily married until she started working full-time again. She designed and sold kitchen cabinets. Pretty soon, she was calling and saying she had to meet with a client. Then, it was a concert in Iowa City with friends. Finally, she told me she didn't want me sleeping with her anymore. They tried marriage counseling, but the lady leading the discussion could sense my ex wasn't interested in repairing our marriage. Ron claimed he didn't have a clue of what was going on.

A neighbor at a PTA meeting, which he was attending

without his wife, let it slip. She asked Ron who was the gentleman Laurie was with at the Iowa basketball game. Of course, it was news to him. She had told Ron she was seeing a client in Iowa City. He wouldn't believe it until his investigative nature took over. He just happened to be in the neighborhood when she was exiting a new house and right behind her was the carpenter. It didn't appear to be an unusual situation until she turned and kissed him good-bye.

He followed her to another house which was for sale. She parked in the driveway and entered the home. Ten minutes later, the carpenter arrived with supper. Ron said he waited and watched. Eventually, the kitchen lights went out, and the bedroom lights upstairs turned on. He watched as the pair embraced and disappeared. He said he wanted to go in and expose both of them, but he was afraid he might shoot one of them or both. Instead, he patiently waited until they were finished. The carpenter left first; therefore, when Laurie appeared several minutes later, he stepped from his car and met her in the driveway.

All she said to him as she brushed by was, "Well, now you know. I want a divorce and soon. Good-bye, Ron."

Phil looked over at Ron. He had tears flowing from his eyes. Evidently, he still had feelings for his former wife.

"I'll call you in the morning. I'm sure the DCI agents will want to interview Mr. Hellzer again," Ron told Phil as he exited the car.

Sure enough, at eight the next morning, the phone rang at Phil's.

"This is Ron. Bobbi and Dan want an interview with Darren Hellzer. I called Darren and he will see us at ten o'clock. Do you want to ride along? I'm sure they won't mind."

"I'll be ready, but I will also bring something to read just in case I'm not wanted."

"Suit yourself, but I don't see a problem."

Ron arrived at 9:30. When they got to the Hellzer place, Bobbi and Dan were already there. The traffic on I-80 was light, and they had made good time.

"Can Phil come along for the interview?" Ron asked.

"Only if Mr. Hellzer approves, but he will have to be just an observer."

Phil stayed in Ron's Jeep while the trio went to the door. After a short conversation, Ron motioned for Phil to come in.

"Mr. Hellzer," Bobbi started.

Darren held up his hand, and said, "Please call me, Darren. I think this is an informal setting."

"Okay, Darren, what makes you feel your wife was set up? You have already given us your reasons for why she was in the car at the crossing, but did she have vital information that management wouldn't want the public to know?"

"Well, I have been lucky enough to tour the plant with the Iowa Beef Producers. The place is run fairly well. Yes, they overwork the employees, but all in all, they are about average. It was an interesting tour especially in their freezer department. They keep their inventory stacked according to the day's run. This way, a box or two of meat wouldn't become aged and unsellable. If the freezer space got close to capacity, they'd try to sell the meat at a discount. Sometimes, when a big food chain like HyVal or Farway needs some meat to put on sale to draw in customers, they can purchase this almost expired meat at a discount to add to their supply. The meat is always good, but it is better to lose a little on a small batch than have to dispose of it entirely. At Acme, they store it in long columns of boxes. Each day is marked at the beginning of the column. It is an easy way for the warehouse managers to keep tabs on their product. It also keeps each day's run separate from other days just in case something went wrong. The shift manager is responsible for the columns' contents. If he wants to keep his job, he will make sure every box is clean and stacked properly."

"I wonder," Bobbi pondered out loud, "if the meat packaged on the day when your wife worked there would still be on the premises? If it is, maybe we can examine the box or boxes your wife was texting about. How do you think we could find out if the box is still there?"

Silence filled the air, and then a few weak ideas were tossed around. It was Phil, the mild mannered reporter, who had been very silent, who came up with a bright idea.

"I could try doing several stories about the packing plants in the area and the workers they employ. I could have Dan pose as a photographer, and we could interview workers, plant managers, and owners about their respective operations."

Bobbi almost shouted, "That's a great idea, Phil. How soon could you work it into your schedule?"

"I probably could do it next week. I'll have to run it by my editor," Phil answered.

Dan spoke up, "I do have a big camera. I could look professional. I'm sure the Captain will agree with your idea."

"I think Dan and I should print business cards to make us look official. Dan could be a freelance photographer with his own studio in Clive. I'll work for Prudential Mutual as a troubleshooting investigator and live in Urbandale."

"I can print out a few business cards on my printer at home. I do all mine," Phil interrupted.

With the idea being kicked around a bit more, it was decided Phil would start with either Tyson Foods or West Liberty Foods. That way, there would be less suspicion on Phil or Dan.

Phil called his editor, and he was okay with the plan. His

only comment was, "Be careful, I don't want to lose a good reporter."

"One more thing before we go, Darren. Your wife's phone, could you describe it to us? Are there any markings on it, or is it an unusual color?"

"Her cell phone was a bright yellow-green with the initials K. H. on the back. Her laptop was issued by the Department of Agriculture and was nothing special."

"Thank you, Darren. I hope we find them and solve this case for you," Bobbi said with a smile.

It was noon when they finished their interview with Darren. As we walked out to our cars, Ron suggested we all go to the best Mexican restaurant in eastern Iowa, "The Mexican Rose" in Conesville.

"But isn't that quite a distance away from here?" asked Bobbi.

"Well, yes, it is. Maybe we should go to the Creamery Restaurant in Durant for lunch and hit Conesville tonight," answered Ron.

Ron added, "The Mexican Rose" is run by a true Mexican lady by the name of Lola Ortegas. Today is her sixtieth birthday, and tonight she is throwing a party at the restaurant. Besides, I wish you all could meet my friends. Maybe they can throw some light on who might have done such a dastardly deed. Phil, why don't you bring Sherry? She speaks a little Spanish. Do either of you speak Spanish?" he continued looking at Bobbi and Dan.

"Bobbi is fluent in Spanish. I can barely say "Si," Dan replied.

"Good, but there's one thing I must insist on. I don't want any of you to reveal your true identity or my friends may clam up. So, Dan, you are Phil's personal photographer from the North Scott

Press/Wilton Advocate. Bobbi, you're an insurance fraud investigator. You work for Prudential in Des Moines. Sherry, she is just Phil's wife. They all know me. Let's meet outside the cantina at 6:00 p.m."

Everyone agreed it would be a nice change of pace and maybe someone had some information to share.

"Dan and I have to do some shopping. The agency located a furnished apartment in Fruitland. All we have to do is furnish our own food. Also, we'd like to tour Wapello a bit and study the countryside around town. Maybe we could drive by the Acme plant. Sometimes knowledge of local roads is a plus. If we're lucky, we might even sneak in a nap. We didn't get to bed very early last night. Then it was an early get-up this morning, but we'll be in Conesville this evening."

Chapter 6

Conesville

Ron, Sherry, and Phil rode together in Ron's old Jeep. They arrived in Conesville a little before six. Bobbi phoned saying they missed the road in Columbus Junction and would be a little late. Judging by the number of vehicles parked around the café, there was little doubt it would be filled to capacity.

Ron said we would wait for the late couple because of the crowd, and he wanted everyone to sit together. The lost couple arrived. Dan wore a dressy western shirt and jeans with cowboy boots. Bobbi was all decked out with tight fitting black slacks, a flowered yellow top buttoned up to her neck, a red bolero jacket, and black boots. Ron led the way inside.

The group no sooner had passed through the door when they heard, "Hi! Ronnie, I see you brought some friends. I've got your table already reserved. You are just two rows from the front."

A man gave Ron a big hug and continued, "Lola and I are

glad you could come. It's her big sixtieth. All the kids are here."

Ron turned to the group and introduced the friendly man.

"This is Luis Ortegas. He is Lola's husband. Together, they own and run this restaurant. They have the best Tex-Mex food in Iowa. I come here often."

"*Si*, my friends, any friend of Ronnie's is our friend. Did he tell you he also is sweet on my youngest daughter, Julia?" Lu kidded Ron and slapped him on his back.

Ron's face suddenly became bright red. Very few people outside of Conesville knew Ron was dating.

Phil said, "Now I know where you are going all the time. I call your sister, and all she says is that you are away."

Sherry softened the kidding by saying, "I think it's great. You need someone to take care of you. Tell me all about her."

"At a later date," Ron replied. "Let's get to our table first."

The five sat at a table for six, which was not far from the little stage where a small band was getting set up. Soon, a very pretty waitress appeared at their table.

"My name is Julia. I'll be taking care of you tonight. Oh, hi, Mr. Puck."

Everyone chuckled.

Phil blurted out, "Mr. Puck! How about Ronnie, dear? or maybe sweetie?"

Julia gave Phil a dirty look and scowled. Then she looked at Ron.

"It's all right, hon. your dad spilled the beans. Everyone here knows."

"Spilled the beans? I don't know of anybody spilling any beans here at the restaurant. What do you mean, Ron?" Julia quizzed.

Now everyone at the table was laughing. Ron smiled and pulled Julia down to him and explained.

"Spilling the beans means your papa told everyone in our little group about you and me dating. So now, you don't have to be so formal. You can call me, Ron."

Julia's face lit up and a big smile came to her lovely face. She sat down in the empty chair next to Ron and gave him a big kiss.

"Oh, Ronnie, I'm glad we don't have to keep secrets anymore. I love you."

Everyone at the table clapped and laughed. It was a good start to the evening.

Julia snapped back up and said, "I'm supposed to be your waitress for the night along with three other tables. What would you like to drink? We have Corona beer, iced tea, soda, and wine. Tonight the food is free, but Lola asks that you take what you can eat and no more. Since it is free, there will be no take homes. There is a buffet in the other room with tacos, burritos, enchiladas, and tostadas. Just serve yourself."

The group placed their orders for drinks and headed for the food line. Lola had not scrimped on the food and everything was delicious. The noise from so many people talking made it difficult to talk across the table.

At eight o'clock, the band began to play. They were very good. Soon, Lola appeared and took the microphone.

She started out by saying, "I'm so glad everyone could come tonight. It is nice to have so many friends to help celebrate my birthday. First, the band came all the way from San Antonio, Texas. This is my nephew's band. He brought his whole band up here to cold Iowa just for my birthday. Isn't he great?"

Loud applause filled the room.

"Also, my entire family is here tonight, all twenty-one of them. I'll introduce them later, but first I want to tell you how happy I am to be here. When I was ten years old, my papa crossed the border, legally I must add, and began to work in the groves around McAllen, Texas. We were there for ten years before he got a job in San Antonio at a fruit warehouse. I got a job at a restaurant as a waitress. Luis was the cook there. Pretty soon, he asked me for a date. Next thing, wouldn't you know it, we were married and having little *bebes*. We needed more money and there were jobs in Iowa at IBP Packing in Columbus Junction, Iowa. So, we moved north. Luis worked there until he was having such leg pain he couldn't stand anymore. As the good Lord above would have it, Mr. Tieg was ready to retire and close this bar and grill. He gave us a good price and contract, and we bought it. Isn't America great?"

Everyone in the place began applauding and cheering.

"Now, I would like to introduce my family."

Lola introduced each son and daughter and their children. She did well until Julia came up.

"Julia is my youngest. She and little Mike live with us. Her husband worked down in Wapello at the Acme plant. One night, he didn't come home. We asked but were told nothing. One of his friends said the last time they had seen him was right before he went to talk to Mr. Johnson, the manager. Hopefully, someday we will find out what happened. Tonight, we will try to forget our big Mike and have a good time. So, everyone, it's my birthday, and I want you to have a good time. Be sure to say hello to all my six children and ten grandchildren before they have to go home to bed."

The crowd applauded.

Camilia, the middle daughter, stepped forward and said, "Mama, you are soon going to have eleven grandbabies," as she patted her expanding belly.

"Oh, praise the mother Mary of Jesus. I'm going to be a grandma again," Lola screamed.

Everyone laughed.

The band leader took the mike and quieted the crowd.

He said, "Tonight, we have a treat for you. Rosanna Mendenez is going to sing a few numbers. Let's give a nice hand to welcome Rosa."

A dark haired lovely woman in her thirties stepped on the stage. She was dressed in tight jeans, a yellow flowered top, and a red bolero jacket. The only difference between her and Bobbi was her four-inch high heels of gold, and she was more endowed. She went to the mike and nodded for the band to start. She had a lovely voice. She sang some upbeat Mexican tunes and finished off her set with a slow and touching rendition of "*Vaya Con Dios*." The crowd gave her a standing ovation.

It wasn't until after the music had stopped when Bobbi decided she needed to find the ladies room. She went to the bathroom and was standing in front of the mirror putting on another application of lipstick when Rosa came out of an adjacent stall and stood beside her.

"I guess we have the same tailor," she said while smirking at herself in the mirror. "Are you trying to be a Mexican woman?"

Bobbi answered, "No, not really. I just like this outfit."

"Well, if you're going to please your man, you must dress like one of us. Here, let me show you."

With that being said, Rosa reached over and unbuttoned several buttons on Bobbi's blouse, exposing some cleavage.

"There, that's better. You never catch a man all buttoned up to your neck. Men like to see a little tit once in a while."

"Sorry, I'm not looking for a man. I've already got one, and he seems satisfied," Bobbi snapped back while re-buttoning two of the four buttons.

"You're married to who? Is it that tall, sandy haired fellow out there?" Rosa spouted as she pointed to the room beyond the door.

"Yes, and I love him very much, thank you. Now if you will please leave me alone, I'll join him and my friends. I must say you do have a beautiful voice. Do you sing professionally?"

"No, I tried, but I have a better paying job at Acme Pack. Maybe we will meet again. Remember to keep your blouse unbuttoned even if it's just for your man. Why do you think we Mexican gals wear these low scoop tops?" Rosa answered with a touch of sarcasm in her voice.

Bobbi returned to her table. Lola had taken her seat beside Ronnie, so she sat in the chair across from the pair. She could tell they were discussing Julia. The rest of the people at the table didn't seem interested in what they were saying. Then, Bobbi realized Ron and Lola were holding their conversation in Spanish, and because she was fluent in Spanish, she could easily understand them. She quickly entered into their conversation. Sherry, who was sitting at the end, was not having any fun. She could understand some of the conversation next to her but not all. Bobbi invited her to join them. When Sherry looked perplexed, the others would stop and explain their conversation in English.

Phil and Dan sat at the other end of the table watching the steady stream of well-wishers congratulate Lola, and they also thanked Ron. The pair was becoming bored.

"My enchiladas need some cooling off. How about you and I retire to the bar and grab a beer?" Dan asked Phil.

"Sounds good to me. Looks like there are a couple of stools

at the end of the bar."

Phil motioned to Sherry where he was going as he and Dan left the table. Their spots were soon filled by Julia and a couple of the other waitresses. The dinner hour was almost over, and their work was about finished until everyone left. Lola walked through the crowd at the restaurant greeting more of her guests.

"What will it be, fellows?" asked the bartender.

"A couple of beers, neither one of us is driving tonight."

"You friends of Ronnie Puck?" he asked.

"Yes, I've known him for a long time," Phil replied.

"He is a great friend of all of us. You know he coaches a little league team in West Liberty."

"No!"

"Yes, when big Mike went missing, he took over Mike's job as coach. The kids love him. That's how he met Julia. The two of them run our team. Julia runs the food stand, too."

"What do you know about what happened to Big Mike?" Dan asked.

"No one knows. All we know is he went to report a breakdown on the line to Mr. Johnson and never came back. We suspect foul play, but without a body, how can you prove it? Many of the workers at Acme suspect he walked in on Mr. Johnson doing something illegal. His bodyguards, Rick and Fast Freddy may have done him in. We don't know and maybe we'll never know. The cops have given up looking. They never found a body in the river. There is a possibility they put him in the cooker and he became tankage. It is really difficult to get any information when you're of Mexican descent."

"Has anyone contacted the DCI?" Dan continued.

Phil gave him a kick.

"I mean, doesn't the sheriff do anything for this community?"

"Ha! The sheriff. Sheriff Ward hates us. He is at us any time he can find a reason. That's why he and Ronnie don't get along. Every time he arrests someone over here, Ronnie comes to our rescue. Sometimes, it is legit, but most times, it is something he has drummed up. Ronnie has saved our butts many times. Here are your two beers. Nice talking to you."

Phil turned to Dan and said, "I'm not the one to challenge the Sheriff of Muscatine County, because I live in Scott County, but I do believe I have a story of racial profiling here. I will write an editorial about the subject. Our papers do reach many people in Muscatine County. I won't mention the sheriff by name. I'll rely on general terms."

"Sounds like a great place to expose the department. The press does have a lot of influence sometimes, and you are a respected news reporter," Dan answered.

The party continued until Dan sensed a subtle stirring among many in the crowd. Everyone was staring at the entrance. A man and a woman who looked like bodyguards appeared. They said something to Luis Ortegas. Luis pushed his way up to the front and asked for the microphone.

"Ladies and gentlemen, we have esteemed guests entering our restaurant. It is Mr. and Mrs. J. J. Johnson from Washington, Iowa. Mr. Johnson is running for congress from our district. Now, I don't care what your political agenda is, but please treat this man and his wife with respect. He is here to talk to you and meet you. He did not ask to speak. He just wants to meet some of his constituents personally."

JJ and his wife, Rita, entered the room. There were a couple of cheers, but mostly polite applause. They quickly split and worked the room separately. Rita happened to stop at the table with Ron and his friends. Bobbi politely rose to greet Rita. They were about the same height. They shook hands and Rita asked Bobbi what her occupation was.

"I'm an insurance adjuster and fraudulent claim agent. I work for Prudential Insurance of Des Moines."

"That could be a very dangerous job for a woman, but somehow, I feel you are able to handle it well."

"Thank you, I try," answered Bobbi as she studied Rita's face and voice.

She detected a slight lisp in Rita's speech. It was not noticeable except for certain words with double s's. The skin on her face revealed she was not a young woman, maybe in her early fifties. She had tried to conceal a mole on her upper lip with makeup. Her hair was short and dark brown, obviously dyed recently. Worst of all, she had a bad case of halitosis. Bobbi discovered Rita was bilingual and her ability to speak Spanish to the patrons seemed easy. Rita stayed at their table for only a few minutes, and then she moved on.

The pair of politicians stayed for only fifteen minutes. The media they had accompanying them took a few photo shots, and then they and their bodyguards were gone. The party resumed. It was just about 9:30 when red flashing lights in the parking lot were begging for everyone's attention. Soon, the great Sheriff Joe Ward entered the restaurant with his bevy of deputies.

He waddled up to Lola and asked, "How many guests do you have here tonight, Lola?"

"I don't really know, Sheriff. I couldn't take a head count, because they were coming in and out."

"Well, I bet there are 150+ in here right now, if there is one."

"Could be!"

"Well, the sign says 'Capacity 146.' You are over the limit, so I'll have to close you down for the night."

"What? You wouldn't close me down on my birthday, would you?"

"The law is the law, Lola. I'm shutting you down. I want everyone out of here in thirty minutes, or I'll haul you and Luis off to jail. I'll be back in thirty minutes, and this place better be empty."

Ron stepped up to engage the sheriff.

The sheriff sneered and shouted, "What are you doing here? You, little two-bit detective, you're not going to stop me tonight. Now get out of my way."

"But Sheriff, this is discrimination. There is nothing illegal going on."

"There are too many people in here and that's against the law."

"Sheriff, it is just your opinion. Maybe there are only 146 people here. You didn't count."

"Listen, you crippled cop, I run this county, and what I say goes. Now clear this place out."

Ron wanted to say more, but he caught Lola shaking her head, no. This time, he let the sheriff have his way. Someday ol' Sheriff Joe Ward will slip and all his walls will tumble down.

Chapter 7

It was 9:50 p.m. when Ron and his friends exited the restaurant. Since tomorrow was Saturday, little would be done on the case. Even the autopsy would be delayed. Bobbi and Dan followed Ron to Nichols. They both turned east on Highway 22. Phil noticed the sheriff's car parked at the Catfish Place. He probably was free-loading from the owner. At the junction of Highway 22 and 70 east of town, Ron noticed two deputy's cars sitting on the side of the road.

"Uh, oh, they're laying for some poor fool to drive drunk back to West Liberty. I feel sorry for that guy," Ron commented.

Little did Ron know, but the poor fool they would catch would not be some drunken smuck, but it would be the Gomez twins. They were two of the most attractive women in West Liberty. They were twenty-two years old and both held good jobs. Anita worked at West Liberty Foods in the bookkeeping department. Juanita worked at Tyson Foods as an assistant to the manager. They had attended Lola's party. Anita had but one beer, because she was to be the designated driver. Juanita had a few more but still was under the limit of being intoxicated. The pair left the party ten minutes after Ron. They arrived at the stop sign on Highway 22. Anita reached over to tune the radio and did not come to a complete stop. She wasn't a hundred feet away from the sign when the lights on the deputy's car flashed. She immediately pulled to the side of the road and waited.

The officer approached the side window and asked for her license. He could smell a little liquor coming from inside the car.

"Have you two been drinking?"

"I haven't, but my sister had some," Anita answered.

"I'll have to ask you to exit the car and take a breathalyzer test."

Anita sighed, but didn't say anything. She knew both would pass easily. It was just an annoyance by the sheriff. Juanita also got out and walked around to the front of the car. They were both dressed alike, tight blue jeans, a red top with a scoop neckline and satin jackets. The only difference was Anita wore red high heels and Juanita wore black heels. By this time, the second deputy arrived. He was Sheriff Joe's right-hand man, Keith. He took one look at the twins and let out a whistle inside his car.

"What do we have here, Don? A pair of drunken ladies?" he asked.

"No, they ran a stop sign, that's all. They are not even drunk."

"That's a shame," quipped Keith. "I'll call the sheriff and see what we should do."

Anita sighed again. This was just a traffic violation not an arrest. Why would he have to call the sheriff?

Keith went back to his car and spoke on his radio.

"Sheriff, this is Keith. Don has a pair of Mexican beauties stopped for a traffic violation. It looks as if they just came from the party. We could have some fun tonight if we could just get them arrested."

"Who are they?"

"I think they are the Gomez twins. They are clean as a whistle."

"Say, aren't they the pair of gals who had a petition out to have me recalled?"

"I think there the same ones. They sure caused a stink for a while."

Well, my old man, Keith, haven't you got some of the stuff you sell to the kids? Slip some in one of the girl's purses. I'll be out in a minute. Me and Alvin are just finishing our catfish. I'll send him on ahead and have him get Betty out of the office. I'll have her check out a domestic abuse call in Montpelier. Boy, this could be a fun night. We haven't had to search two ladies in a long while."

Keith walked back to the scene on the passenger side of the twin's car. He reached into the open window and grabbed Juanita's purse. He slipped a small bag of white substance into it.

"Well, well, well, what have we here?' he chuckled as he emptied Juanita's bag on the car hood. " It looks like we have crack or coke."

Juanita was speechless, but not Anita.

"You just planted that and you know it. We don't do drugs," she screamed.

She wanted to say more, because she knew old Keith was selling drugs to the students at West Liberty High.

"We'll just sort this out down at the office."

"What about our car?"

"I'll call Kelly's in West Liberty and he'll store it at his garage. You might be able to pick it up tomorrow. Now let's get you into the squad car."

The women calmly got into the rear seat of Keith's cruiser. The sheriff's big cruiser arrived. He looked into the back seat. He showed a wicked smile and almost drooled. He had Alvin driving ahead to get Betty out of the station. It is the law that female officers search or care for female prisoners, but if they are not available, those officers who are available may do the interrogation.

Betty Winters was one of three female deputies on the sheriff's roster, and she was the most outspoken. She knew the law and quickly realized Sheriff Joe Ward made some of his own laws and bent others. She was in her early thirties and had a little girl. Her husband worked at Stanley Engineering as a draftsman. Betty stood about five-foot-eight and had long brown hair, which she wore in a bun while on duty. Her trim figure was due to the fact she was a runner and biker. Most everyone in the department liked Betty with the exception of the sheriff himself and the sheriff's right-hand man, Sergeant Keith Waters. To them, she was a thorn in their side. They had to tolerate her because the state required at least three women officers in each department.

Alvin arrived ahead of the rest of the group. He told Betty she was to head for Montpelier to check out a domestic abuse call. Betty thought the order was bogus, so she checked with the dispatcher. He had had no reports on his docket, but she kept quiet. She slowly prepared to leave the station. She sat in her squad until she saw the two squads enter the parking lot. The first was Deputy Waters' vehicle. Betty watched as he let two young women out of the back seat.

"Now I know why he wanted me out of here," thought Betty. "He wants to play with these women, and he knows they will not protest because of his position."

Betty exited the yard just as Sheriff Joe's cruiser was coming around the corner. She made sure he saw her leaving. The sheriff slowed his entry into the parking lot to make sure Betty headed south on Walnut Street. He smiled as she disappeared in front of the courthouse. Now he and the boys could have some fun with the lovely twins and no one would disturb them. He would give orders to the jailer to turn off the surveillance camera in the interrogation room and drunk tank.

Betty turned left on Mulberry instead of right. She proceeded to Fifth Street and turned back toward the jail and the sheriff's office. She parked her car a block away and walked to the back door. She buzzed the jailer.

"Who is it?" he asked.

"Betty Winters, Jim. I need some new batteries."

"Why didn't you come through the front door?"

"The sheriff and his crew are down there, and I don't think they want me around, if you know what I mean."

"Okay, come on in."

Betty made her way to the jailer's office.

"Hi, Jim," she said cheerfully.

"Why am I honored with such a visit on such a dull night?" he asked.

"I think your dull night is about to change. Can you turn on the camera down at the drunk tank?"

"Not supposed to, Sheriff's orders. What's up?"

"Well, I think your boss is about to do something illegal."

"In that case, let's see what he is up to."

Jim switched on the camera. It showed Deputy Waters just entering with the Gomez twins.

"What do you think he is going to do?"

"I don't know for sure, but he wanted me out of here."

"Boy, I'd like to stick it to that son of a gun."

"I know. So would I," Betty replied.

Jim Smith was and has been one of the county jailers for five years. The pay was not that good, but it was a job. He worked four, twelve-hour shifts one week and three shifts the next. On his off days, he worked as a house painter. He hated his boss, the sheriff, because of the sheriff's attitude toward the Hispanic population. Jim's mother was a Mexican-American from San Antonio. She met his father while he was stationed at Fort Hood, Texas. She was the real reason he continued to work at the jail. He knew about the abuse the sheriff and his deputies had given his friends and family. Jim tried to make sure every prisoner was treated fairly.

Betty watched over Jim's shoulder as the camera recorded the interrogation of the Gomez twins. It started innocently enough with Alvin asking for Anita's jacket. She reluctantly took it off and gave it to him. Alvin handed it to Deputy Waters. He pretended to search the jacket.

"Look at him. He's planting some drugs in her jacket," Betty exclaimed as she watched over Jim's shoulder.

"Do you think I should intervene?" Jim asked.

"No. Those two are strong women. I think they can take his abuse. We have to be able to document his actions. You can take a statement afterwards, and you'll have this recording to back it up. If the girls find out their suffering was recorded only to reveal the illegal stuff the sheriff gets away with, they will not protest."

I would seek an interview with them tomorrow and take our

friend Ron with you," Jim suggested.

"I suppose you are right, but if he starts beating them or hurting them, I'm going down regardless of my job. This man and his cronies have to be stopped."

Betty and Jim dimmed the lights and focused on the proceedings going on downstairs.

"Looky what I found," said Deputy Keith. "Someone has some drugs in her jacket pocket."

Anita glared at him and screamed, "You just planted that crap in my pocket. We don't do drugs and never have. Those drugs must have come from your stash, Deputy Waters."

The deputy glared back at her, and said, "Gee, Sheriff, I think we need to have a strip search of this pair."

"Sounds like it to me," the sheriff chimed in.

Anita could not believe what she had just heard.

"You've got to be joking. You're certainly not going to do that," screamed Anita.

"Nope, I'm not joking. Yep! A strip search, now! Right here," the sheriff announced.

His face broke into a smile showing his ugly stained teeth. The sheriff chewed tobacco for several years before his wife made him give it up.

"I'm entitled to a search by a female officer and not one of you perverts. Where's Betty Winters?"

"She is at a domestic disturbance in Montpelier and not available."

Anita stood her ground and refused to move. She was

surrounded by four men who had her twin sister handcuffed to a chair on the opposite side of the room. She viewed her situation. One man, the sheriff was in his sixties and quite overweight. His belly hung over his belt, and he had jowls that would make a pig envious. Next to him was Sergeant Keith Waters, the sheriff's enforcer. He was a huge man about six-foot-four and 290 pounds. He had huge hands and arms. He claimed he could bench press 300 pounds. Standing next to him was Alvin Hahn. He had been on the force for forty years and was about ready to retire. He did anything the sheriff desired just to keep his job. Lastly, was Don Greely, the youngest of the four men. He was a good cop, only tonight he was going to get caught in a situation he didn't create.

The stare-down continued. Anita spoke first.

"According to law, I may have one phone call. Are you going to deny me that also?"

"Of course, I don't want to be accused of breaking the law," said the sheriff answering her request. "Don. Get her a phone."

Don went to the office and brought back a phone.

"You must dial nine before the number you're calling. It gets the calls out of the building."

Anita nervously punched in her father's phone number. She knew he was working overtime at West Liberty Foods where he was on the maintenance crew. The phone rang several times.

"Come on, Papa, answer your phone," she said knowing the good sheriff would only give her one call.

"Hello, Anita. What do you need? You know you are not supposed to call me at work," said the voice at the other end.

"I know, Papa, but Juanita and I are in the Muscatine jail, and we need you to come quickly."

"In jail! What happened?"

"I didn't completely stop at the stop sign outside Nichols, and when they pulled us over, they claim they found some drugs in Juanita's purse. Papa, you know we don't do drugs. I only had one beer and that was early. I passed the breath test easily. Even Juanita passed the test, and she wasn't driving. I think it is a setup. Please, can you hurry? Who knows what the sheriff is thinking?" Anita pleaded, almost in tears.

"I'll be done here in half an hour. I'll leave before my shift is over. It will take me another thirty minutes to drive to Muscatine. I can be there in an hour. Be careful, my precious daughter. Don't irritate the sheriff. I'll be there as soon as I can."

Her dad had hung up. She and Juanita would have to stall the sheriff as long as they could. Maybe Betty would show up.

"What did your father say?" asked the sheriff.

Anita lied and said, "He would come right down, and we should wait until he gets here."

"What do we do now, Sheriff?" asked Don.

"You take the quiet one and handcuff her to the bench in the tank. Keith, Alvin, and I will interrogate this one."

Don left with Juanita.

"Now what?" asked Anita.

Deputy Keith answered with a smile beneath his bushy mustache, "Little girl, we found some white stuff in your jacket pocket. It is safe to assume you have more somewhere on your body. In the name of justice, we have to search your clothes to see if you are clean."

"But can't we wait until Betty gets back? Surely, she won't be that long. Please, let's wait, I beg of you," Anita pleaded, because she could see the men had every intention of strip searching her.

It wasn't fair, but she was at quite a disadvantage, three men against one woman.

"Let me put it this way, little girl," Keith continued, "you may take your clothes off peacefully by yourself, or we will remove them by force. It is your choice. Your shoes will be the first."

Sheriff Joe smiled as he eyed Anita's trim figure. She was a beautiful young woman, just like the one's he had seen on the internet. She and her twin almost had him recalled. They lost by just a few votes. Now it was payback time.

"My choice is we wait until my papa gets here or Betty gets back." Anita tried to stall, "How about you let me undress in a private room? You check my clothes and give them back afterwards."

"Obviously, you don't hear well. I said strip now, right here where we can see if you're hiding any drugs, or we will remove your clothes for you. When we are finished, you will wish you had followed my orders."

"No!"

Deputy Waters jumped into action, grabbed Anita's wrists, and held them with one of his huge hands. She screamed in pain as he squeezed her wrists together. He held her arms high over her head. Sheriff Joe moved around behind her and pulled her top out of her jeans and over her head. Keith pulled the top up to her wrists. Anita struggled against the pair. Sheriff Joe pulled out a pair of scissors from his back pocket. He moved around in front of Anita and cut the fabric between her breasts. Her bra fell to each side of her chest. Quickly, before she could react, Keith let go of Anita's arms, pulled her top off, and ripped her damaged bra in two again. He tossed the garments at Alvin, who stuffed the items into a plastic bag. Anita tried to cover herself as she stood before the three men.

"I've heard some of these Mexican women stuff their drugs in their pussy. I think we should check."

"Right, Sheriff, I'll hold her. You and Alvin take off her jeans."

Again, Anita struggled against the huge man as he grabbed both of her hands and held them tight.

She screamed, "No! No!"

By this time, Don returned. Sheriff Joe ordered Alvin and him to pull off her jeans. Alvin unbuckled her belt and unzipped her fly. Don began to pull at her cuffs on her legs. Anita saw an opportunity to rebel. She kicked with her free foot. She caught poor old Alvin in the crotch. He doubled over in pain. The sheriff cussed and slapped Anita across her face. She screamed in pain.

"That'll teach you, you spic bitch," the sheriff growled.

Don finished tearing off the jeans.

"Take off those bikini panties. I've got to check her twat," Joe hollered as he pulled on a medical examiner's glove.

Don followed orders and gingerly slid the underpants down her legs and off. He was careful not to be standing astride her legs.

"Spread your legs," Joe ordered.

Anita refused. He jammed his knee between her thighs and forced his finger into her vagina. She moaned in pain. She threw her hips up in an effort to repel the invading finger.

"That's better, bitch," said the sheriff as he continued to invade her private parts.

When he was satisfied, he stood up and said, "Let her go, Keith. She's clean."

Keith released the exhausted Anita. She fell to the floor. Keith took his big foot and kicked her toward the corner of the room. She crawled to the corner and tried to cover her naked body as best she could. The sheriff and Keith laughed. They commented that a spic woman looked just like any other woman when naked.

The group left Anita alone and proceeded to the room where they had sequestered Juanita. Alvin limped behind the others.

Keith started out by saying, "All right, twin. You have two choices. Either you take off your clothes by yourself, or we will do it like we did for your sister. What's your answer?"

Juanita was scared. She had heard the violence in the next room. What did they do to her sister?

"May I see my sister first?" she stammered with tears already flowing down her cheeks.

Don led her into the room where Anita was curled up naked in the corner. She ran to her and hugged her.

Anita raised her head and said, "Do what they want. Maybe they won't hurt you. Papa will be here soon."

"Okay, sister," Don demanded trying to act tough. "What is your answer, you or us?"

Juanita turned and faced the four men. They were standing like a small pack of wolves waiting to attack a cornered deer. Although she tried not to show it, she was shaking inside. Juanita felt like one of the Jews in a Nazi concentration camp. First, she kicked off her red high heeled shoes. Then she slowly pulled her top out of her jeans and slipped it over her head. She stopped. Alvin collected the top and stuffed it in a bag.

"Go on. What about those jeans next?" ordered Joe.

She unbuckled her belt and waistband, and then she unzipped the zipper. She slowly slid the jeans to the floor and stepped out of them. She kicked the pants over to Alvin. She stopped again. Her captors smiled at the well-toned body filling out the black lacey underwear.

"Stripping in this jail means all the way. Maybe you have something in your underclothes we can't see. Do you need help finishing or will you continue?"

Juanita at first almost started to cry, but then she became defiant and glared at the leering men. She set her jaw tight and reached behind her back to unhook her bra. The lacey garment slid forward and off her arms. Her olive toned breasts tipped with dark brown nipples spilled out. The men whistled and hooted because Juanita was better endowed than Anita. It was the only real difference between the twins. She proceeded to slide her bikini underwear down her legs. After bending over and picking them up, she handed them to Alvin, whose eyes were as big as saucers.

"There, is this naked enough for you, Sheriff, or do you have to fondle me also? I'm sure you have all this on videotape, so you can watch it later. It probably will go with the other porno films you have," Juanita snapped.

"Aren't you going to check out her twat, Joe?" asked Keith.

"No. It isn't necessary. She's clean," he said as he turned to Juanita and continued. "To answer your question, I had the jailer turn off the recorder for this room. See, there is no light on the camera."

Little did he know, the jailer and Betty had been listening and watching all the proceedings. Just before the sheriff looked up at the camera, Jim switched it off. He waited a few seconds before turning it on again. The pair had missed some of the action.

Juanita had asked the sheriff if she could use the bathroom. He laughed and told her she could pee on the floor.

"That's not the problem. I think I'm going to throw up," she replied and promptly knelt down and vomited.

"Shit!" exclaimed Alvin. "Now I have to wash the room down after she's gone."

"No, you don't, Alvin. Get me the hose," Keith growled.

Alvin dragged the hose around the corner.

"Give me that! Turn it on full blast," Keith ordered.

Deputy Waters twisted the nozzle to a solid stream. He blasted Juanita with the cold stinging water. She screamed and then gasped as she tried to catch her breath. He kept the stream pounding her skin until he knocked her over. He laughed and whistled as she tried to protect herself from the blast of cold water.

She tried to crawl over to her sister, but she slipped and fell on her side on the wet floor. Keith kept up the pressure on her legs and back. When she turned to face him, he blasted her breasts and stomach. Anita crawled to her rescue and shielded her from the stream of water.

"Shut it off! You're going to drown her," Anita screamed.

Keith just changed his shot and pounded Anita with the water blaster. She pulled Juanita to the corner and tried to stand. She made it to her feet and pulled her sister up. They stood in the corner as tight as they could, turning their backs toward the pounding stream. Keith continued to pound their naked bodies with the high pressure hose. He laughed as he made them dance when he directed the stream at their feet. Finally, Anita fell on the slippery floor. She pulled her sister down with her. They tucked themselves into the smallest balls of flesh they could. Keith roared with laughter.

"All right, Keith, shut it off," roared the sheriff. "You've had your fun. I don't want a homicide here in the jail. Don, get the ladies some towels. Have them dry off and get dressed. The rest of you come to my office. Their old man will be here soon, and we'll have to explain why we did this."

Upstairs in the monitor room, Jim Smith quickly shut the camera off again.

"I've got to get out of here and fast," Betty exclaimed. "How fast can you copy that?"

"Instantly, but you'll have the previous seven days on it, also. The disc will tell you the different times and days. Just go to Wednesday, 10:30."

"What if the sheriff wants this erased?"

"Oh, he already told me not to record this interrogation. I'll just put in another blank tape and give that to him. He'll never know until later."

"Oh, Jim, you're a peach," Betty said as she kissed him on the top of his bald head. "Good thing I'm off tomorrow."

She slipped the precious disc inside her blouse and escaped out the back door.

She heard Jim sigh and say, "I'm glad I'm off, too."

After the twins had dried off their bodies with the towels, they asked for their clothes. Don, who had been watching them dry themselves, came out of a trance. He shook his head, yes, and handed them their clothes.

"Could you have a little decency and turn around, Don?" Anita growled.

"Oh, I guess so," he commented as he turned his back.

"Don, may we use the restroom?"

"Yes, I can just stand outside the door."

"Good, I was hoping you didn't have to watch us pee," Anita said with a smile.

She figured deep down Don was a decent guy, and he was just following the orders of a crooked sheriff.

When the pair emerged from the restroom, Don led them to the sheriff's office. He offered them a chair on the side of the room. The door buzzer sounded. It was Ernesto Gomez, the girls' father. He glanced at his daughters as he entered. For some reason, the twin's younger sister, Benita, was with him. He approached the sheriff's desk. Benita stared at the three men standing by her sisters. Her siblings' hair was a mess. Their clothes had damp spots on the sleeves and back. Anita held her arms across her chest. Because the sergeant had torn her bra in two pieces when he forcibly removed it, she had none to wear. It was the big man with the bushy mustache and toothy grin, who Benita had seen before. She continued to stare at him while her father spoke to the sheriff.

"Isn't arresting someone for not stopping at a stop sign a little over the top, Sheriff? I know there is some mistake. My girls don't do drugs. Now, please release them in my custody, and I'll take care of them."

Benita butted in, "That man with the big mustache, I've…"

"Hush, child, you can tell me later."

"Now, Sheriff, is it possible someone planted those drugs?"

"Well, really it was a big misunderstanding. The drug we found in your daughter's jacket was actually just a packet of sugar. Wasn't it, Keith?" the sheriff replied.

"Yes, Sheriff, I believe that is the case. Sorry for what happened. I apologize to your daughters if we caused them any discomfort. I'll see that my boys don't do it again," he replied as he looked over at the twins sitting there with their clothes rumpled and their hair a mess.

"Tell you what, Mr. Gomez, if you and your daughters won't press charges, I'll wipe this incident from the books. No questions asked. Is that a deal?" asked the sheriff.

Ernesto Gomez with his dark eyes and graying hair thought a moment, then reached out his hand and said, "Deal!"

Anita's eye was becoming black and blue. Her ribs hurt where the sheriff had kicked her. It was embarrassing sitting braless in front of strange men. She wanted out of there.

The girls glared back at their captor, but didn't say a word. They would talk after they got out of the jail. Mr. Gomez led his three daughters out of the station. As soon as they were in the car, everyone talked at once.

Papa spoke to his daughters, "Now, one at a time. Benita, you go first."

"But, Papa, we were strip searched by those idiots," protested Anita.

Papa put his finger to his lips and pointed to Benita.

"Papa, I tried to tell you. That man with the bushy mustache. I've seen him at high school. He sells drugs to Howie Langben. He doesn't have his uniform on, but I know it is him. He comes around every Wednesday after school. He meets Howie on the corner just across from the school."

Anita butted in, "Are you sure, Benita? Are you sure it was Deputy Waters?"

"I'm positive, and I've seen the fat guy there once in a while, too" she continued.

"This is great! Maybe we can nail that crooked sheriff."

"Now, let's not get excited," Papa warned. "Benita is only sixteen, and they are not going to listen to her. You know the county

attorney will side with the sheriff. We have to have more proof. Now, what is your story, Nita?"

"I was tuning the radio and didn't come to a complete stop at the junction of 22 and 70. I got pulled over. I know they were after us, because they made us get out of the car for a minor offense. I know one of them planted the dope in Juanita's purse. Next thing, we were arrested and in jail. The old man asked for our jackets, and that's when they found some white stuff in my pocket. That's when I called you, because they threatened to strip search us. I was okay with it until I found out there were no women officers in the building. It was then I knew they were serious and only wanted to play with us. They had no real case against us. The sheriff let it slip that he was angry with us because we had the recall petition. It was all trumped up. First, they stripped me and then Juanita. She got sick and vomited. Deputy Waters sprayed cold water on us."

"Is your story the same, Juanita?"

"Yes, but Anita refused to take off her clothes, so the men ripped them off. I mean, they ripped her bra in two pieces. The sheriff hit her when she kicked the old guy. The old fart even searched between her legs. It had to be awful. They let me talk to her and Nita told me to follow their orders. I did. Everything was okay until I threw up. I tell you that water hurt."

Ernesto was quiet for a few miles. The girls knew he was thinking. They knew their papa.

He started to speak, "My dearest daughters, we must be very careful about what we say and who we talk to. I think we should talk to our friend, Ron Puck."

Chapter 8

Walcott

Thursday morning, Phil was sipping his third cup of coffee. He was in the middle of a story for the North Scott Press. He tilted back in his chair and rested his stocking covered feet on the chair next to him. Sherry had left for the library. The doorbell rang.

"Just a minute," Phil called.

He slipped on some slippers and pulled up his lounge pants. He straightened his desk a bit before he went to the door. He opened it and before him stood a fairly young woman.

"Mr. Phil Robbins?" she asked.

"Yes, may I help you?"

"I'm Betty Winters, Deputy Sheriff of Muscatine County. Well, maybe after last night, I'm not. You're a newspaper reporter, aren't you?"

"Yes."

"Do you have a lot of computers?"

"Some. Why do you ask?"

"I have a DVD I'd like you to view and copy. It is a recording of what went on at the Muscatine jail last night. When you put it in your computer, go to Wednesday, 10:30 p.m."

Phil invited the woman into his home and escorted her to his office. He inserted the disc and dialed up the date. He couldn't believe his eyes. The sight of police brutality was played out on the recording. This was serious stuff.

"Could you make me some copies? I want to send one to the attorney general in Des Moines, one to the DCI, and I want to give one to Ron Puck," Betty asked.

"I can do that for you. No problem. Why don't I make five copies, just in case you need more, and I will save one copy on my hard drive as a backup measure."

"By the way," Betty stated, "I'm meeting with Ron and the Gomez twins at the Pizza Hut in Tipton. We decided to meet outside county lines, so the sheriff wouldn't interfere. They are the two women in the recording. If you look closely, you can see one of the deputies planting something in one of the twin's jacket pocket. This strip search was planned and illegal."

"How did you get this disc?" asked Phil.

"It's sort of a long story."

"I've got the time and although this looks authentic, I have to make sure of the complete facts before I write anything."

"I understand.

"Our loyal sheriff sent me on a bogus domestic call to get me out of the building. I knew it was bogus, because there is no Elm Street in Montpelier. He also made the mistake of sending me to a trustee's house, and I knew they were on vacation. He has pulled the same trick a couple of other times. You see, Sheriff Ward and I are not the best of friends. Yes, he is my boss, but he would like to get rid of me if he could find a legit reason. I was hired because the state told the old sheriff he had to hire a woman. I was the first woman deputy in the department. The only women before me worked in the office or as a jailer. A year ago, two young black women were visiting some friends from Chicago. They made the mistake of going to a bar and grill in the little village of Fairport. The sheriff's department provides the law enforcement for the villages. The pair was quite lovely to look at. The sheriff's deputy stopped them for DWOI. I don't know if they tested drunk or not, but they were hauled into town. Sheriff Joe decided I should check out a shooting in Atalissa when the pair entered the station. I protested, but I was young and new. I followed orders and left. Sergeant Waters took one look and decided the pair of good-looking black women might be carrying drugs because they were from Chicago. Therefore, they should be strip searched. I was gone about an hour to a non-shooting. The only shooting were some legal firecrackers. The two women were relieved to see me. They told me after they undressed to their underwear and handed their clothes through the doorway, they asked for some robes. Instead, big Sergeant Waters opened the door and dragged the almost naked women to the interrogation room. There they were forcibly stripped by the deputies. I immediately protested and said I would go to the county attorney and file charges. The sheriff laughed at me. He said the county attorney was at the strip show. The women were released and quickly headed back to Chicago never to return to Muscatine again. I was reprimanded by getting a salary cut.

This happened a couple of other times. Once, I did intervene because the women were Asian and could not speak or understand English. I found out later they were workers at the Acme plant and were found by a deputy in a barn. They were scantily dressed and scared. They said something about being slaves. Thank goodness, Sergeant Waters was on leave or I believe another party would have happened and I would have been sent to some far part of the county.

After three episodes, I learned to stick around until I made sure the ordered destination was valid. This really irritated the sheriff and the sergeant. I've been on their shit list ever since.

This time I contacted the dispatcher. He claimed he knew nothing of any shooting in Atalissa. I suspected I was on another wild goose chase, so the sheriff and the boys could have some fun. I made sure the sheriff saw me leave. Then I circled back and went upstairs to the jailer's control room. I talked him into recording the interrogation and the strip search. I actually sacrificed the girl's dignity to see if we could pin something on the sheriff. The man is as crooked as a dog's hind leg. I'm sure if it works, they won't care.

"Just how many times do you think you were told to leave under false pretenses?"

"I would say four or five times. Who knows how many times it happened before I came on the scene."

I'll bet Ron would like you to come with us this afternoon. Is that possible?"

"Sure," Phil said, "Name the time. I'll bring the copies. Say, not to butt in, but why don't you bring Ron and the twins to my home? We're in a different county and it would be more private, and I could make as many copies as you think you might need. Sherry won't be home until late."

* * *

Walcott, The Same Day

Betty called Ron to see if he thought the change would work. He agreed. It was two o'clock when everyone arrived and I do mean everyone. It was Ron and Betty, plus Mr. and Mrs. Gomez, plus their twin daughters, Anita and Juanita, but also the twin's younger sister, Benita. It was a house full.

Ron spoke first, "Thanks to Betty, we have some very incriminating evidence against the sheriff and three of his deputies.

Our problem now is not to move too fast. We have to have a foolproof case against them. The strip search was illegal, we know. Is there anything else on the tape we can use? Do you, Anita and Juanita, want the rest of us to view the tape? This may be upsetting to your mother and Benita."

Phil chimed in, "I'll leave the room if you would like. I can set it up and you can view the recording with more privacy."

"Have you seen the recording before now?" asked Anita.

"I had to in order to find the right spot to stop the computer. There is no reason to record more than necessary," Phil answered.

"Then we see no reason for you to leave. We think Mama should see it so she realizes the gravity of our situation and Benita is old enough also. Papa will be the only one really upset. Not about all of us seeing his daughters naked, but because the sheriff thinks he can get away with this as he probably has many times before. The only difference with this incident is the other women he stripped haven't come forward or reported him."

Phil started the recording.

Ron hollered about three minutes into the viewing, "Stop it right there. Back it up a bit."

Phil backed up the scene and punched the forward indicator to make the video display in slow motion.

"See, there's Alvin planting a packet in one of the jackets, that dirty little rat. I'll bet the crack was planted in Juanita's purse the same way. Can you mark this spot somehow, Phil?"

Phil marked the time and continued on. The stripping began.

"I'm sorry I didn't step in at this moment, Anita," Betty interrupted. "I wanted to, but Jim told me not to because this could be a way to rid the county of a crooked sheriff and his cronies. He told me he felt you two and the Hispanic community would understand. I hope you're not mad at me. You must realize I was not supposed to be there, and Jim was not supposed to be recording any of the proceedings. Those were Sheriff Ward's orders."

The part where Anita had kicked Alvin in the groin made everyone snicker.

"I wish it had been the sheriff or Sergeant Waters," Anita snorted. "I probably would not do any damage to the sheriff though. His balls are protected by the fat belly which hangs over his belt."

Everyone laughed, even Papa.

Poor Mama was crying after the showing. Her little baby girls were being seen naked by everyone.

Juanita hugged her mom and said, "Don't fret, Mama. People see worse things at the movies."

Anita asked Phil, "Can you do on your computer like they do on television and blot out our breasts and private areas?"

"No, I don't have that program. I don't need it, but some TV station person might or maybe some communications student at the University of Iowa might be able to."

Ron butted in, "Now, girls. Don't get any bright ideas about putting this on YouTube, at least, not just yet. I want to know more about Benita's accusation of seeing Sergeant Waters selling drugs at West Liberty High. Benita, are you sure Sergeant Waters was the man you saw?"

Benita replied, "I'm positive, Mr. Puck. Not only me, but Sue Windus and Janet Gould were with me. We've seen him several times with Howie Langben. He never is in his squad car though. He drives a gray Buick with 'Sarge 1' on the license plate. Usually, Howie gets into his car and they drive away. In a few minutes, they come back. Howie gets out, they shake hands through the window, and the guy drives off. I know it is Mr. Waters, because of his big mustache and his voice. You just ask some other kids. They will tell you the same."

"Has anyone else delivered drugs besides Mr. Waters?"

"I don't know for sure, but a couple of times the sheriff's big cruiser has been sitting there. He just makes deals through the side window."

"This is all so very interesting."

There was silence for a couple of minutes. Everyone watched Ron.

He said, "Here is what we are going to do. Phil, make one copy for the DCI, one for the state's attorney, because we know the county attorney is in cahoots with the sheriff, one for me, one for the Gomez family, one for Betty, and one for yourself. Let me see, that's six copies. Mr. Gomez. Why don't you keep the original? Do you have a safe or know someone with a safe?"

"Yes, my brother has a big safe in his store."

"Now, Anita and Juanita, I would like you to keep this away from the media until the DCI can interview this Howie Langben. I'm sure they will jump right on it and be here Monday. Captain Stender has been wanting to nail Sheriff Ward for a long time. He already has him for delaying a criminal investigation and trying to destroy evidence for the Karen Hellzer case. If he can pin him with illegal interrogation practices along with maybe some drug charges, we may have a new sheriff in a couple of months."

"May I break this to the news media next week?" asked Juanita.

"Yes, by all means, if you promise to wait until after next Wednesday or if I find out it is okay before. Deal?"

"It's a deal," chimed the twins simultaneously. "We'll work on finding someone to blot out our private parts."

"Okay, Phil, how are you coming with the copies?"

"Two to go."

"Betty, I hope you don't get fired over this," Ron said.

"If I get fired, it will be worth it, especially if we can free this county of a crooked sheriff," Betty replied.

Phil finished creating the DVD copies and handed everyone their copy.

Ron said, "I have a meeting with Captain Stender tomorrow. I will personally hand him his copy. Mr. Gomez, will you send the copy to the state's attorney? I have his address. I think a recording like this coming from a concerned father will carry more weight than coming from me."

"What if I take a day off and deliver the disc tomorrow in person?" asked Ernesto.

"All the better. Now let's get together again in about a week. We can plan from there. Okay?"

Everyone agreed and smiled at each other. This was going to be a great day they would all remember.

Chapter 9

Fruitland

Bobbi and Dan slept in Thursday morning. The last three days had been taxing on the pair. Bobbi was parading around in her cotton flannel pajamas and fuzzy slippers. She thought even though it was April, it was still too cold for summer PJs.

"What do you want for breakfast?" she asked. "I've got eggs, Cheerios, and toast. That's all."

"How about we go out for breakfast? Afterwards, we can check out the area. I think we should go down to Wapello and see this slaughtering plant and maybe try and trace the probable route wrecker drivers took back to Walcott."

"Sounds good to me. I'll put things back in the fridge."

Dan got up to go to the bathroom, and when he came back, Bobbi was sitting cross-legged in bed. She motioned for Dan to sit beside her.

"Did I tell you that Captain Stender offered me a desk job in Des Moines?"

"No, it's news to me. What did you tell him?"

"Nothing. I wanted to talk to you first."

"Well, talk," Dan said with a smile.

"I've been thinking maybe it's time we consider planning for a family. You always said you wanted a couple of kids, and we can't have children while we're traveling all over Iowa. You could still work for the department with another person. I'm sure they could team you up with someone."

"Yeah, I suppose, but what if that person is another woman?"

"I'd make sure she was old and ugly. I'd put ankle bracelets on each of you. When I checked to see what you were doing, if I found out those bracelets were too close together, I'd come over and shoot both of you."

"Wow! No jealousy on your part."

"I'm just protecting my investment in lovemaking, dearie," Bobbi shot back.

With that being said, she pulled Dan over and planted a big juicy kiss on his lips. She continued to kiss him and ran her hand down his chest and into his shorts.

"And this is my investment," she laughed.

Dan took the cue from her playfulness. He unbuttoned her top and began to nuzzle her breasts. She countered by pulling his T-shirt over his head and ran her hand through his chest hairs. Dan climbed on the bed and straightened her legs, then began to pull off her bottoms. She teased by resisting some; therefore, she made him stand to keep pulling.

After the bottoms slid off, and he was tossing them away, she reached up and pulled his shorts down around his ankles. She caught a glimpse of her six foot naked man for only a second standing over her, because he was instantly on his knees and lifted her up to remove the unbuttoned top. He rolled over and threw the top over the end of the bed.

Bobbi was on him like a flash. She hovered over him, her hair falling down on both sides of her face. Instead of flopping down on his chest, she slowly lowered her body down, just lightly touching his chest. She weaved back and forth across his chest to let his chest hairs tickle her nipples, then slowly moved her breasts to his lips.

Dan followed her motion and kissed each nipple tenderly. He was going wild with passion. Bobbi smiled and slowly sank into position. They rocked together and had a passionate lovemaking session. When they were finished, Dan needed a larger breakfast. They lay side by side and gazed into each other's eyes. Dan kept petting Bobbi's back side. He loved to run his hand slowly from her neck all the way down to her hips.

He broke the spell by saying, "I could change my career and apply for the Des Moines Police job. They might need a good detective someday, or maybe I could be a private investigator like Ron Puck."

"That is a possibility, but right now, my back needs a good scrub. Do you suppose we could both fit in the tiny shower?"

"It'll be a tight fit. We may have to rub against each other all the time."

"Oh, shoot! I don't know if I can stand that."

The two lovebirds squeezed into the tiny shower. They soaped each other's backs. The fronts took care of themselves. Soon it was evident, Dan was ready for another round. He smiled down at his shorter partner.

Bobbi whispered, "Honey, we can't do it again. We're on company time, remember? We're supposed to be investigating our case, but I'll give you a rain check for tonight."

"Yeah, I suppose you're right." Dan replied grumpily and turned off the shower.

Within thirty minutes, they were both ready to find some breakfast or maybe now it could be called an early lunch.

Bobbi suggested, "Let's drive to Wapello and see if there is a café or restaurant open. I'm sure there is great home cooked food there somewhere. Afterwards, let's investigate this Acme plant where Karen Hellzer was last seen alive. Never can tell what you might find laying around."

"Sounds like a plan," her partner answered.

* * *

They arrived in Wapello around eleven. They had heard about a café downtown called, "Gramma's Cupboard." The pair sat at a table next to the window. A waitress approached them.

"It's too late for breakfast. We just switched to lunch. Would you like to see a menu?" she asked, then she answered her own question. "Of course, you do, you're new in town. Only the regulars know the Thursday Specials."

She left the pair, retrieved some menus, and returned, placing the menus on the table.

"I'll give you a couple of minutes. Would you like coffee?"

"Sure, it would hit the spot," Dan answered.

Bobbi studied the waitress. She was in her late thirties or early forties. She had some gray roots coming out from an otherwise dark brown hair color. She wasn't fat, but she was stocky with no hips. Bobbi noticed her name tag read, "Melanie."

Melanie set the coffee mugs on the table and asked, "Are you ready to order?"

"Yes, I believe I'll have the grilled chicken sandwich with fruit salad," Bobbi told her.

"I'll have the special chicken fried steak," replied Dan.

"Got it! It'll be a few minutes, since we just switched to the lunch menu."

Melanie gave the ticket to the gray headed lady in the kitchen and came back to their table. She pulled up a chair.

"What are you guys doing in town or is it a secret?"

"No, we're here to check on the Acme Plant."

"You ain't one of those animal lovers like PETA are you?"

"Heavens, no! We wouldn't be eating chicken and steak if we were now, would we?"

"Yeah, I guess not. Then what are you here for? Who are you? The cops?"

Bobbi almost choked on her coffee.

"Cops! Why would you think that? No, we are not cops. I'm Roberta Petit and this is my husband, Dan. We are professors at Central College in Pella. I'm working on my doctorate in social studies. I'm studying the effects of the Mexican-American and the Hung population in eastern Iowa. Acme is one of three plants in eastern Iowa who employ a large number of non-whites in an area that once was basically all white. I'm looking at the impact on the community both socially and economically. Maybe I could ask you your opinion?"

"Sure. I work at the plant on weekends, managing the cleanup crew. Sometimes I feed the employees who work overtime.

It's a nice place to work. Mr. Johnson is really considerate of his employees."

"Mr. Johnson?"

"Yeah! You know, JJ Johnson's son. He's the boss. He plays around and spends a lot of money. He drives hot cars and has a lot of women chasing him. They say his home is like Hugh Hefner's Playboy mansion. It has heated pools, hot tubs, and mirrored bedrooms."

"You don't say," commented Dan. "I'd like to see that."

Bobbi gave him a dirty look and then said to Melanie, "How close can we get to the plant? We don't have to go in, but we would like to talk to some of the workers."

Melanie answered, "I'd check on the lagoon. I hear they have a real efficient lagoon, and the man who manages the area knows everyone. His name is Willie."

"Order up!" came the call from the kitchen.

"Okay, Emma," Melanie hollered. "I'll be right there."

She rose from her chair and retrieved the two lunches. As she set the plates down, two new customers walked in.

"Great talking to you two. Have a nice day."

Bobbi and Dan discovered the food was delicious. They would mark Gramma's as a good place to eat. When finished, they left a generous tip, paid their bill, and left.

Melanie watched from the restaurant window as the old pickup pulled away. She thought to herself, "I'd bet a day's pay, those two are cops. I'll wait until they mess with Willie. He'll flush then out."

Bobbi and Dan headed for the plant, which was located a

mile southeast of Wapello. They slowly drove past the main gate and waved at the guard in the guardhouse. He was watching a ballgame and didn't stop them. Bobbi noticed an addition located on the side of the Cold Storage building. It had no doors or windows and it recently added to the building. She wondered what it was used for. The road beyond the plant turned to gravel, and about one block further, a sand-covered side road appeared. The gate across the road was open and there was a 'No Trespassing' sign, but it was partially obscured by some brush.

Dan turned down the private road. Three blocks later, they arrived at a large lagoon and pump house. The lagoon was maybe two acres in size. There were four aeration pumps floating on the surface. Dan pulled his pickup next to the little building. He got out and walked to the edge of the lagoon.

Bobbi went behind the building toward a high tensile barbed wire fence which surrounded the small lagoon. She spied a faded rag hanging on the bottom wire. It looked like a motorcyclist's doo-rag, which is a handkerchief sewn to cover a biker's head. It keeps their hairdo in place and doesn't become windblown. She picked it from the fence. It was faded and torn. Bobbi noticed some initials written on the side in light black lettering, "MAH." On the opposite side was written "Mike." She had started back to the truck when she heard a vehicle coming. It sounded like an ATV or UTV.

"I think we have company," she said, smiling at Dan.

An ATV roared up the road and slid to a stop in front of the pickup.

The rider hopped off and shouted at Dan, "Don't you know you are on private property?"

Dan answered, "Well, yes, sort of, but we didn't see any 'Keep Out' sign, and I'd heard about your company's waste management. I'm Dan Smalley and this is my wife, Bobbi. I am an engineer with Vander Grif Manufacturing over in Pella. The company is thinking of getting into waste lagoon equipment. I thought I'd like to pick your brain on problems and advantages of your system."

"Do you expect me to believe that crock of bull?" the rider growled.

Dan didn't back off and continued talking.

"I see you have four aerators. Why only four? Do they do a good enough job? I also see you have a heavy plastic liner. How long have you had it? Does it need replacing often? How thick is the vinyl? How deep is the deepest part of the lagoon?"

The man softened a bit.

"I'm Will Hamilton. Everyone calls me "Willie." I manage this lagoon and all the waste which is produced by the plant. All human waste is processed by the town. The only waste water which comes here is from the plant and the stockyards. We use such a high volume of water, which is why the town's system cannot handle it."

Dan and Will continued to compare notes. Bobbi listened. She seemed impressed by Dan's knowledge of waste lagoons. She was about to stuff the doo-rag in her pocket when Willie noticed the rag.

"What do you have in your hand, Mrs. Smalley?" Willie asked.

Bobbi hesitated, and then answered, "It is a rag I found over by the fence."

"Could I have a look at it?"

"Okay, but may I have it back?"

"We'll see."

Bobbi reluctantly handed the headpiece to Willie, because she didn't want to upset the man.

Willie scanned the doo-rag and said, "This belonged to my friend, Mike. He was killed in a motorcycle accident about a year ago. It happened over on the dirt road about 100 yards west of here. I'll bet the wind blew it over here. It was a tragic accident, and he left a wife and little boy."

"I heard of such an accident. Is he buried close by?" asked Bobbi, meaning in a local cemetery.

"I don't know. You know these Mexies. I'm actually from Mediapolis. You do know where Mediapolis is?"

"Yes, I'm from eastern Iowa. I know it's about 15 miles south of here," Bobbi answered. "Maybe he was cremated?"

"Could be, but I doubt it. Cremation is expensive and requires records. The nearest crematorium is in either Burlington or Muscatine. There's none in my little town of Mediapolis. I know they don't bury in our little cemetery. They are very quiet about their dead. I suspect he was an illegal alien. I know his wife, and I'll bet she'd love to have this memory of Mike's.

Bobbi wrote on her notepad, "Check crematoriums." She didn't want to seem too interested since she was just an engineer's wife.

Will politely asked, "Now I'm going to ask you nicely. Will you leave quietly or do I have to call security?"

"No, don't do that. We'll leave. Thanks for your info on the lagoon. May I call you again sometime?" Dan asked.

"We'll see, but it may have to be somewhere in town."

"It's a deal."

Dan and Bobbi climbed into the truck and drove back to the highway.

Once they were safely on the road, Bobbi asked, "Did Ron

say big Mike rode a motorcycle and what was his last name?"

"I don't know, but we'll see Ron tomorrow."

Chapter 10

Friday in Fruitland

Captain Stender, Ron, and Phil met in Dan and Bobbi's apartment. Bobbi brewed some coffee, but Ron surprised everyone by bringing donuts from Casey's, the local quick stop.

Captain Stender started the conversation.

"We have identified two positive fingerprints. One belongs to Freddy Rodriguez, a pimp from Dallas. He has a record as long as my arm. The other is Ricardo Sanchez. We have his prints from when he entered the U.S. legally. I have contacted all the states directly south of Iowa, plus Illinois, and I issued a pick-up and detain order. We feel Freddy is probably in the Dallas area, since he has friends and family there. Ricardo might be with him, but his family, especially his grandmother, lives in Paris, Texas. It may take a few days to find them, but we will find them for questioning."

Phil began writing down the information in his reporter's notebook.

"There were two more sets of fingerprints, both women's. One probably belonged to the victim, but because the skin on her fingers was so badly damaged by the glue, we could not get a positive print. Therefore, we are going to her home to see if we can lift some from a jewelry case or makeup case. Once we determine which set of prints are hers, we can concentrate on the remaining prints. They probably belong to someone who knows either Freddy or Ricardo. The lab people also found some skin under the victim's fingernails. She must have gotten a few swipes in before the assailant stopped her. We'll compare the DNA from the skin to both men. I'm sure one of them will be guilty."

Captain Stender glanced around at each person, and then he looked back at his notes.

"Now, that's the good news. What we haven't found is the truck which hauled the victim's car to the recycling yard, nor have we found the victim's laptop or cell phone. We thought someone might have used the phone by now, but maybe it is with the wrecker and the suspects are waiting for the heat to cool off before they use them.

"We know the truck belonged to J & R Recycling. We checked their registration records and they have four trucks. One of them is brand new. We contacted the yard to verify the others, and they reported one of their trucks had been stolen. Their records show the truck disappeared the day of the accident. The remaining wrecker's logs show they were in Des Moines and Cedar Rapids. Perhaps the computer and the phone are still in the truck. I have a hunch the missing truck is in a garage, storage shed, or old barn somewhere. It is too big of a vehicle to dump into a lake or river. I'm going to ask the local sheriffs to search old abandoned farmsteads and empty buildings as they find time. I'm sure everyone will cooperate except Muscatine. Sheriff Ward, I'm sure, will tell me to mind my own business. Now what have the rest of you discovered or have planned for next week?"

Bobbi spoke first.

"Dan and I decided yesterday to check out the area around the Acme Plant. We first ate at a neat café in downtown Wapello. The waitress was quite talkative and told us about the people working there, which included herself on weekends and evenings. She claimed the workers were treated very well ever since the Johnson's bought the plant. There were still long shift hours, but it counted as over time. They employed some locals as office assistants and maintenance workers, but mostly the floor workers were either Asian or Hispanic. Most of them only lasted five or six years because of the stressful work. She also sent us to the waste lagoon area, because the man who ran that area was quite knowledgeable of the plant's workings and personnel. Dan posed as an engineer from a company in Pella who was interested in building lagoon treatment and cleaning equipment. We drove down the road marked 'Private Property, Keep Out.' It wasn't long before the manager named Will Hamilton showed up on his ATV. He was angry at first, but engineer Dan calmed him and had a friendly conversation with him. In fact, I was quite proud of Dan of the way he handled the situation. Everything went well until I found a motorcyclist's doo-rag hanging on a barbwire fence. Willie asked to see it. He claimed it belonged to his friend who was killed in an accident just a mile away. The interesting thing was even though it was faded, the initials MAH were on one side of the rag, and MIKE was written on the other side."

"Ron, could the rag possibly be that of your girlfriend's husband? Did he ride a motorcycle? Would his initials be MAH?"

Ron quickly replied, "Yes, yes, yes! He was a big Harley man. He and Julia rode all over. They even went to Sturgis one year. He had tattoos on his arms and chest. He wore a rag to keep his balding head warm. His full name was Michael Antonio Herera, hence MAH. Do you suppose this Willie knows more than he let on? All I know is Mike went to work and never returned. The sheriff tried to find out some info from the plant, but everyone was mum. Maybe there was some foul play involved."

The Captain butted in, "That is an interesting piece of information. It makes me believe there is definitely something going on inside the plant more than killing old cows. Phil, how are you and Dan coming along with your article on slaughter plants in eastern Iowa?"

"We are set up for Monday. At 9:30, we tour the Tyson plant at Columbus Junction, and then we go to Wapello. The manager wanted us there before twelve, because that is when the kill line starts. He would like us to follow the whole process through to the freezer," Phil told him.

"Good, it's the refrigerated unit we want to check out. I hope there is some product still there from March 26. The victim's text said, 'check the boxes.' If that day's production is still there, we have to find out how we can acquire it without becoming suspicious. Ron, we haven't heard from you yet. What have you discovered?"

Ron started while Phil quietly sat. He was just a reporter and not a detective.

"Last Wednesday evening after Lola's party, the Gomez twins were stopped by the sheriff's deputies for not coming to a complete stop at a stop sign outside Nichols. The two women, Anita and Juanita, are in their twenties and very good looking. According to Anita, someone planted some drugs in Juanita's purse. Sheriff Ward arrived and decided to book them and he took them to the Muscatine Jail. To make a long story short, he ordered a strip search."

"He did what?" exclaimed Cal. "A strip search on what grounds?"

"It gets worse. He had sent the only female officer on duty on a bogus domestic abuse call in the eastern part of the county. The twins protested, but he insisted. The pair of young women was ordered by the sheriff to strip while three male deputies looked on. One of the women resisted. The men forcibly removed her clothes and also searched her female parts," Ron went on.

"This is terrible and he'll get away with it, because no one will challenge him with the county attorney in his pocket. What about the female officer?"

"This is the good part. The officer, Betty Winters, disobeyed orders and returned to the jail instead of checking out the call. She knew the jailer on duty and had him record the interrogation. He did it reluctantly, because he had been told by the sheriff not to record anything. Betty risked her life and job to expose the sheriff and his cronies."

"Do you have the recordings or did the sheriff delete them?"

Ron smiled and said, "Not only do we have the recording, but we have several copies, thanks to Phil."

"How did you acquire them?" asked Bobbi.

"Betty brought them to Phil's home in Walcott. She wanted him to get them to the proper authorities. He made several copies and kept one on his computer in something called 'the cloud.' We asked the Gomez twins to review the recordings. They verified the proceedings. I have a copy with me. The original video clip is in the possession of the twin's father, Ernesto Gomez. I think, if you would like to see the recording, you will discover the evidence the sheriff used to demand the strip search."

"By all means, can we play it on our TV?" asked Dan.

Phil replied, "I think I can make it work. This looks like a fairly new TV."

Phil slipped the disc in a slot on the TV and started the viewing. About five minutes into the video, the scene showing Alvin planting the drugs into Anita's jacket pocket, appeared.

"Stop the recording! Is that what I thought it was? Can you rewind it? It looked like someone planted a white package in the girl's jacket," Bobbi blurted out.

Phil reversed the video recording, and they viewed the scene again.

"See, that guy planted the drugs."

Captain Stender remarked, "This is illegal as sin. I finally have proof to nail Joe Ward. I couldn't prove the wrecker situation, but this is different. And you say the county attorney won't prosecute the sheriff. I'll take this to the head of the department and report the attorney to the Board of Ethics. Is there more?"

"Most definitely, there is abuse of power, unlawful search, and violation of the suspect's rights," Ron answered.

They watched the entire video. The scenes were not doctored in any way and were quite graphic.

"You say the victims have a copy of this?"

"Yes."

"Do you know what they intend to do with it?"

"I think they are going to have their copy sent to a computer specialist and have him blot out their breast and pubic areas. Then they might send it to a news station or put it on YouTube. I told them to be sure and check with me before they proceeded, because there is more evidence I have yet to tell you, and you might want them to delay."

"There's more?" exclaimed Cal.

"Yes, Cal, when the twin's father bailed them out of jail, he brought along his youngest daughter, Benita. She recognized one of the deputies as the man who sells drugs to a student at West Liberty High School."

"Really, I'm getting so I can't believe all this, but I'll try. Which deputy was it?"

"It was Deputy Keith Waters. She claimed she knew him

because of his big mustache. She said he came after school every Wednesday. He drove a big gray Buick with the license plate SARG 1."

"Does she know who he sells it to?"

"Yes, Howie Langben. He's a popular kid in school. No record."

"I'd like to talk to him before the recording goes viral. Could you talk the young women into delaying their releasing the recording until after Wednesday? I'll send a couple of agents from the narcotics division to speak to him and his parents. Wow! This has been quite a session," Captain Stender said with a smile. "Could I get a copy of this recording? For evidence to show to the courts, of course."

"I figured you would want one. I have an extra untouched copy for you," Phil answered.

Bobbi teased her boss by saying, "Don't wear your eyes out by too much viewing."

By this time, it was almost noon, and the captain wanted to return to Des Moines. Ron and Phil left also.

Chapter 11

As they rode home, Phil asked Ron, "Would you like to go to a custom-classic car show in Rock Island tomorrow? I heard it is quite a show. Drivers come from miles away. I have to report on the show for the North Scott Press."

"Gee, I'd like to, Phil, but tomorrow is the first meeting for little league, and I've got to be there. Thanks for asking," he answered. "I'll be anxious to hear about the plant tour though. Call me Monday evening."

"Sure."

* * *

Saturday, Rock Island

Phil wished Sherry would have come with him. He didn't like wandering around alone in a big show like this one. He took a few camera shots of some of the classic cars. Over by the east wall were the classic sport cars—Mustangs, Corvettes, Thunderbirds, some Shelbys, and Chrysler Prowlers. Phil wandered over to the area and admired the beauties.

"May I help you?" a male voice questioned.

Phil turned and there was Gary Dawson, a sports and classic car enthusiast from Muscatine. Gary had retired from a large company in town and was bored. He always had a couple of Corvettes in his garage. When the biggest auto dealer in Muscatine moved from downtown to the shopping malls on the northeast end of town, Gary bought the old garage for his hobby. Soon, his hobby became a business in classic cars. He bought and sold his own and provided that service for others. He maintained them in his huge garage.

"Well, hi, Gary," said Phil. "How's business?"

"Just fine, I'm busier now than when I was working."

"You've got a fine line of cars here."

"Yeah, they all aren't mine. Take this Porsche. It belongs to Jacob Johnson, the guy who manages the Acme plant in Wapello. In fact, here he comes now. Hello, Jake. I'd like you to meet my friend, Phil Robbins."

Phil and Jake shook hands.

Phil commented, "I think I'm scheduled to visit your plant on Monday. Your manager told us to be there around noon. It has something to do with starting the kill line early enough to run the rest of the lines. He wanted us to see the entire process."

"Great! I'll be glad to be with you personally. I'll have Frank tell me when you start. I'm proud of our record and our plant. I feel we have improved the working conditions immensely."

"Good! I'm anxious to tour the plant."

"You said 'us.' Is someone coming with you?"

"Yes, I'm bringing a photographer with me. It gives me more time to interview."

"Will I have the right to view the pictures before he leaves?"

"By all means, we are not trying to cause anyone any trouble. I just want to report the facts."

The three talked cars for a while before Phil decided to move to another area. He'd definitely remind Dan to be careful.

* * *

Sunday was a day off for all of them. Ron spent the day with Julia and little Mike. Phil and Sherry went to church. Bobbi and Dan attended the Island Methodist Church just to meet their neighbors.

On Sunday evening, Dan called Phil.

"I don't think I should go with you on your tour. I might be seen by the man who manages the lagoon. I told him I was an engineer. If I show up as a photographer, he might get suspicious."

"I see your point. We don't want to blow your cover. I think I can handle it."

* * *

Monday morning

Phil kept his appointment with Tyson at nine and arrived at Wapello before twelve. Jake Johnson met him at the office door.

"I'll call Frank, the plant manager. Meanwhile, I'll get you a lab coat, hard hat, glasses, and plastic boots to use. Where's your photographer? Is he sick?"

"No, he was with me at Tyson, but he received a call from his wife and their little boy was sick at school, and he had to pick him up. His wife is a surgical nurse and couldn't leave her job. I

122 • Iowa Exposed

brought my own camera. I think I can take good enough photos."

Frank arrived and led both Jake and Phil on the plant tour. They started at the beginning at the killing floor. Frank described the humane way the livestock were killed. He assured Phil the animals felt no pain. In the cutting room, he showed Phil the safety equipment provided for the employees. He also had Phil exam the cleanliness and the power washing equipment. Phil observed that Jake was as fascinated by the plant's working environment as he was. Obviously, Jake was just the owner's son and knew little about plant management.

Frank introduced Phil to the three inspectors.

"We have two state inspectors and one Federal inspector. We need the federal inspector in order to ship our product across state lines. They have the say over all the meat products here. If an animal is suspect, which means it might be diseased or tainted with antibiotics, it is pulled from the line. It depends on the severity of the fault to whether it can be used for pet food or if it has to be tanked. Tanking means the carcass is shipped to a rendering company and made into animal protein products. We allow no suspect animal to enter the human food line."

They continued through the plant and stopped by the grinders.

Frank pointed out, "All meat which has made it to this point is ground into hamburger. Since a majority of the animals are dairy animals, they are very lean. We seldom have any beef leaving here under 90 percent lean. We sell to major food chains, so they can adjust their beef product to any fat level. We also sell to major fast food restaurants and government food banks. There is nothing wrong with our meat except it is very lean."

They moved around the grinders to the packaging side. There, the meat was being squeezed into long tubes and placed into black tubs. Frank pointed to the tubs with a smile of pride.

"These are our pride and joy. One of the employees suggested the design, and it works. If you look at the design, there is a pedestal in the middle filled with holes. There is room to place three, fifty-pound tubes of meat on each side of the pedestal, 300 pounds to a layer. The second layer is laid crosswise to the first. After the two layers are filled, a plastic tray is snapped in over the pedestal and eight tubes are placed in it. Then, another layer is laid crosswise. When the process is completed, there are two layers of 300 pounds and the two top layers of 400 pounds equals 1,000 total pounds. The meat is quickly moved to the freezer to be frozen. The pedestal in the middle shortens the cooling time immensely. We feel we can have the meat below freezing in less than ten minutes. Would you like to see our refrigeration unit, Phil?"

"Sure," answered Phil.

He was becoming warm anyway.

"You'll have to put on some extra clothing, because it is twenty below zero in there. I'll get some coats for you. Are you coming in also, Mr. Johnson?"

"No, I'd better get back to the office, but thanks anyway."

Frank went to a room and found some appropriate coats and gloves. They entered the big freezer. Inside, there were rows and rows of the black plastic tubs. At the end of each row, there was a sign designating the day of production. All the rows were quite recent, but one. It had March 26 on the sign. A yellow plastic ribbon was strung around the entire column.

Phil asked, "Why is the one row different?"

Frank replied, "On that particular day, the inspector chose to spot check our inventory, as they are required by law. The inspector made the mistake of doing it at the end of the shift. She asked the forklift driver to randomly pick a tub. She lifted some of the tubs, and he said her face turned white. Right at that time, the quitting time bell rang. She told the operator to replace the tub, but she would be back tomorrow to finish. She slapped a hold on the sign and hurried out. We could not move the product until she released it. The interesting thing is she was the inspector who was killed by the train near Walcott. The woman never filed a report of what she found with the Department of Agriculture, as far as we know. The inventory sat for ten days before I started to ask questions. Finally, the state sent new inspectors to check this batch. There is 36,000 pounds of meat in this row. The state selected several tubs and found nothing out of place, so they released the meat. The sales department had a difficult time finding a buyer, since it was almost two weeks old. There is nothing wrong with the product except age. We had to discount this batch, plus throw it in with two other day's production. It took a large retailer like Hi-Val Foods to buy it. Tomorrow, they are scheduled to pick it up. From there, they will deliver it to their warehouse where it is then sent to one of their stores somewhere in the Midwest. Once the meat from the March 26 batch is thawed, it will blended with fresher meat and sold as a sale item. Again, I say, there is nothing wrong with the meat except it has been frozen longer than most of our products. Any questions?"

"Not that I can think of, Frank. This is quite a comprehensive tour. Before I send the article to the paper, I'll send your office a copy for your approval. Is that fair?"

"Quite! I've enjoyed showing you around. Have a good day. Oh, by the way, you may leave your heavy coat and gloves in my office. I'll have someone take care of them."

Phil exited the freezer and wove his way through the plant to Frank's office. By the time he reached Frank's office, he was sweating from wearing the heavy coat. A young woman opened the door for him and welcomed him in.

"Frank radioed me to be ready for you," she said. "I'm Connie, his assistant. Here, let me help you with the zipper."

She unzipped the coat and helped Phil slide it off. The cool air in the office felt refreshing.

"Would you like a glass of water before you go?" Connie asked.

"Yes, that would be great, but then I have to hurry. I have a city council meeting in Eldridge tonight. Thank you."

Phil gulped his drink and headed home. He was supposed to report to Ron about what he had seen or heard. The only thing interesting was the batch of meat going to Hi-Val Foods. Everything else was pretty much normal packing plant stuff. Phil stopped at the gas station north of Muscatine. He dialed Ron's number. If he reached him, they could talk on his new Bluetooth phone while he drove home.

Ron answered, "Ron Puck, private investigator. How may I help you?"

"Ron, this is Phil. I'm just getting back from the plant tour."

"Did you find anything out?"

"Not really, it was a typical tour. The only unusual discovery is the meat which Karen Hellzer inspected is still there, but it will be shipped out tomorrow. Hi-Val Foods bought it after it was finally released. So, we don't know why she sent a text message to look into the tubs."

"Well, if there is anything fishy, one of the stores will find it. Say, I'm going to change the subject. Would you want to go with me to visit Mr. Johnson's home? Maybe we can snoop around a bit. How about I pick you up about ten?"

Chapter 12

Ron and Phil turned off of Highway 61 just before they crossed the Iowa River. The road was blacktopped for a mile, and then it turned into gravel. At the end of the blacktop, a surfaced lane turned to the left. It had a heavy wrought iron gate closing it. Ron stopped at the entrance and located the intercom box. He punched the send button.

A woman's voice spoke, "Who is it?"

"Ron Puck, a friend of Mr. Johnson. Is he home today?"

"No, he is at work. Please go away."

Ron continued, "Could we talk to you and leave him a message?"

There was a pause. The gate buzzed and opened. Ron eased his old Jeep through the gate. He stopped outside the front door.

"I'll go to the door. You watch for dogs or other people. If the lady gets ornery and turns on me, I'll hurry back."

"Be careful," Phil warned. "You've only got one good leg."

Ron smiled at Phil and grabbed his can of pepper spray, just in case. He rang the doorbell. The door opened a bit and a weathered faced woman appeared.

"I'm Ron Puck. May I talk to you?"

The voice shouted from behind the door, "I know who you are, and you are not Mr. Johnson's friend. Mr. Johnson's list says you're a cop, and you're not to be here. Get out before I release the dogs."

Ron continued to plead, "I just want to see if there is any information you or Mr. Johnson might have on the case of the woman who was killed in the train-car accident."

"I'm not telling you nothing, now git!"

Ron stood there for a minute and waited for the woman to reappear. All of a sudden, he heard a bell ring. He looked to his right. Two big German shepherd dogs were bounding toward him.

Phil screamed, "Ron, look out. Here come the dogs."

Ron ran as fast as his crippled leg would carry him. Phil slid behind the steering wheel and started the Jeep. He charged at the dogs with the truck as they crossed the lawn. He cramped the wheels and spun around on the grass, putting the vehicle between Ron and the dogs. Ron made a lunge for the door and jumped in just as the second dog hit the closing door. The dog's vicious teeth grabbed the handle and tried to pull it open. Phil floored the old Jeep. First, it spun in the wet grass, but as soon as it hit the blacktop, the tires squealed and smoked. He looked up the driveway and saw the gate closing. The motor howled as it climbed the incline. Phil almost made it cleanly, but the passenger's side hit the iron gate and the side mirror went flying into the air. Once out of the gate, Phil turned left onto the gravel instead of right toward the highway. He slowed down about a block from the gate.

Ron hollered at him, "Why did you go this way? Now we have to go back."

Phil smiled at the frazzled Ron and said, "While you were being so brave back there, I realized my dad and I used to hunt this ground. This road ends in about a half mile. It then becomes a trail and enters a pasture. It follows the river to a farmstead. It used to be a through road. I know the farmer. Maybe we can come onto this place from another direction."

"Why you sneaky devil! I didn't know you ever hunted."

"I did when I was a kid. I just didn't like to clean what I killed, so I quit."

"Phil, I need to stop for a bit. That dog chase really got to me. I need to take a leak."

Phil pulled over. They both got out and relieved themselves. The road was a dead end so no one would be coming. The trees had not leafed out yet and down through the woods, Ron spotted a building. The roof was shiny, and it reflected the afternoon sun.

Ron paused, and asked, "Say, Phil, what do you suppose is in that shed? You don't suppose it could be housing the missing wrecker, do you?"

"It could," replied Phil, "but how are you going to get to it?"

"You said you hunted around here. Is there anything we can hunt right now?"

"Spring turkey season is about now. I'd have to find out the dates."

Ron smiled at his friend.

"Phil, we are about to get two turkey licenses and become

hunters. Do you suppose the old farmer still knows you?"

"I don't know, but we can soon find out. His name is Cliff Hanson. I don't think we should drive in from the pasture though. Let's turn around and take the county road on the other side."

This time, Ron resumed driving and they headed back to the highway. As they passed the Johnson farm, the dogs were still roaming the grounds. Ron flipped them the bird as they drove by. He chuckled as both dogs slammed against the iron rails.

"I hope they break some teeth."

It took twenty minutes to drive around the wooded area to get to the Hanson farm. Mr. Hanson was just coming out the back door when they pulled in. Phil got out first.

"Mr. Hanson, remember me? It's Phil Robbins. My dad, Ralph, and I used to hunt here."

The older gentleman squinted his eyes. Then he reached out his hand to Phil.

"Sure, I remember your dad. But you've grown up a bit. It has been a long time. I suppose you want to do some turkey hunting. There are a lot of them around here. They are becoming pests."

Phil continued, "This is my friend, Ron Puck. He is the one who encouraged me to get back into hunting. He claims turkey hunting is the most fun. I've known Ron for years. He spent ten years in the Marines as an MP, and then he worked as a cop until he got his legs shot out from under him."

Ron stepped forward and shook the old farmer's hand.

"Nice to meet you, sir."

"I found out turkey season doesn't start until Thursday, but we'd like to scout out the area a bit tomorrow, if it is all right with you," Phil asked.

"Sure, go right ahead. Park your Jeep behind the shed and don't wake me up when you drive in. I've retired and I don't get up as early as I used to," Cliff said with a smile.

Then he warned us about his weird neighbors.

"I think his name is Jake something. I've never met him. The boys at the café said he was the owner or manager of the Acme plant. He has a chain link fence around his land. Evidently, he doesn't want visitors. I know he has guard dogs, also. There are nights when my wife and I can hear a party going on. The sound travels up the river valley pretty easily. One night about a year ago, two young women came stumbling into our yard. They knocked on the door at three in the morning. I answered the door and found the pair huddled under the deck. They were naked and afraid. I called Wilma, and she found them some robes. I asked them how they got here. The one who could speak English told me they were at a party at Mr. Johnson's. A group of them decided to go swimming in the river. She claimed Mr. Johnson made all the girls take off their clothes and swim naked. She continued to tell me the men at the party didn't have to strip, but they could swim or just watch the girls in the moonlight. It became cloudy, so Mr. Johnson rigged some powerful lights to show off the young women. I asked how they escaped. They said they swam out to a sandbar and walked upstream. Finally, they swam ashore and came to our house. They pleaded with us to give them a safe place to stay. I told them we would try in the morning, but an hour later, a van drove into our yard and the driver asked if we knew anything about two young women. I said, 'No.' He asked me if I didn't know about the women, then why was I awake at this hour? I didn't have a good answer. The next thing I knew, he hit me in the face and knocked me to the ground. Wilma screamed and came running. He grabbed her and began to twist her arm behind her back. Just as I was about to tell him I knew about the women, one of them ran out and saved us. She and her partner calmly followed the man into the bus. He hollered at them to do something. As they drove away, he threw the robes out his window. I'm guessing the girls rode back to Mr. Johnson's naked. I reported the incident to the sheriff and he said he would check in with my neighbor on the condition of the girls. Of course, by the time he got there, everything was cleared away. I don't have any idea what might have happened to those poor young women."

"You were pretty brave protecting those women. I'm going to see if there is a report filed at the sheriff's office. About what time did this happen?"

"Let me see. It was warm. The river was low. I'm thinking it was about mid-July. Check last year's calendar and find out when there was a full moon, because it was a couple of days either side of a full moon," Cliff recalled.

Ron wrote down the time on a pad and thanked Cliff for his information. Then he and Phil headed for Muscatine.

"Well, ol' hunting buddy, I guess we have to buy some hunting clothes. There's a farm supply store on the north end of Muscatine where we can get outfitted. I'll call Captain Stender and see if he can get us some hunting licenses."

The pair spent a couple hundred bucks on camouflage jackets and pants. They purchased a turkey caller and some shells. Ron had some old shotguns, but they really didn't intend to actually hunt. Ron laughed at Phil as he pulled the face mask over his head.

He said, "Maybe we could rob a bank on the way home?"

* * *

Wednesday Morning

Ron picked Phil up at 5:00 a.m. They quietly parked the Jeep behind the machine shed. They noticed the house was still dark. It was easy this morning, because they weren't carrying weapons in order to look official as they scouted. They walked toward the river and the Johnson property. At the edge of the river, the chain link fence stopped about twenty feet shy of the river bank. From there, the fence consisted of three strands of barbed wire strung on creosote posts. Ron reached into his backpack and pulled out a pair of fence pliers. He pulled the staples holding the bottom two wires. He put the pliers back and removed two zip ties. He tied the second wire to the top in two places and placed a nearby log on the bottom wire.

"After you, hunting buddy," he said and motioned for Phil to crawl through.

The terrain changed on the Johnson side of the fence. There were a few old oak trees and a couple of shagbark hickories scattered among the young box elders, cottonwoods, and black cherry. At one time, it had been a woodland pasture like what the pair had just walked through, but now it was full of undergrowth, multi-floral rose, honeysuckle, and gooseberries. It made their walk much more difficult.

They stumbled and grumbled through the brush. It wasn't until the last fifty feet before they came to landscaped ground. The shed was now only thirty feet away. Ron motioned for Phil to stay put while he circled around to the other side. Phil stood quietly. Those pesky dogs started to bark. They must have spotted Ron. Ron returned to where Phil was standing. The dogs quieted. He slowly approached the rear window of the shed. He was too short to look inside. He waved to Phil.

"Get down on your hands and knees. I'll stand on your back and see what's inside," he whispered.

He stood on poor Phil's back and looked inside. Bingo! There was a wrecker and a black bus. Phil moaned as Ron searched the edge of the window frame.

"Just a minute, ol' buddy," he told him.

He jumped off of Phil's back and crouched low to the ground. Then he helped Phil stand upright.

"We've got to find the power box. It should be near the ground or next to the gutter. It should be gray or black. You go to the right. I'll go left. Do not go in front of the garage door. The dogs might see or hear you. They are in their kennels right now, but I don't want the old lady to let them loose."

They split and started the search. It didn't take long before Phil spotted a box near the ground. He started to go after Ron, but found him coming back already. He pointed to the box. Ron squatted down. He pushed the side of the box and the cover slipped off. He reached into his pocket and pulled out a small LED flashlight. He grunted and groaned a bit, then he replaced the cover. He stood up and motioned for Phil to head back to the fence. He was quiet until they reached the fence.

"Tomorrow we'll come back and go inside," Ron said.

"How do we do that?" Phil asked.

"I work part-time for a security company when I'm not doing investigations. It was my third job. I have installed many of these systems. I can neutralize the one on this garage with ease. We always neutralized the systems when we worked on them. That way we didn't alarm the business or homeowner accidently."

"What about the dogs?"

"A little hamburger laced with some tranquilizers will quiet them. I have a veterinarian friend who can supply me. It is amazing what a little quiet talk and some delicious raw meat can do to a guard dog."

Ron and Phil walked quietly back to the farmstead. Phil could tell Ron was running ideas over and over in his mind. He himself was wondering if he should get involved with this covert stuff, because it was sort of exciting.

Ron dropped Phil off in Walcott and said, "I'll pick you up at 4:30 tomorrow morning. I want the dogs to be sleeping and hungry when we arrive. If everything goes as planned, we'll be out of there by 6:00. If you could bring some sandwiches for breakfast, it will look like we're real hunters to our farmer friend. I'll bring some old shotguns from my brother-in-law. He has a couple of guns to shoot varmints. I'm sure he will let us use them. "

Chapter 13

West Liberty

A policeman from West Liberty, two DCI agents, and his mother were waiting for Howie Langben in the principal's office. He sat down next to his mother. She looked like she didn't know whether to be angry or sad.

"What's this all about Mom?" Howie asked.

Howie's mother took a deep breath and said, "These gentlemen say you have been selling drugs. They have witnesses. They also have one of your friends telling them you sold him drugs. I want you to be honest with me and everyone else. Did you sell drugs to other students?"

Before Howie could answer, Mr. Petersen, the principal, said, "These are serious charges, Mr. Langben. I would like you to cooperate with the police and the DCI so we can catch your supplier. It is my understanding he delivers the drugs every Wednesday afternoon after school. Is this correct?"

Howie could tell he was in deep trouble. Why should he protect El Lobo? He probably wouldn't protect him.

"Yes, he comes every Wednesday. He drives a gray Buick and all I know him as is El Lobo."

The DCI agent, who introduced himself as Sam, said, "We would like you to purchase drugs from this man today, because it will help us catch him in the act. If you are willing to help us, it will help you in court. You already have upset your mother, so why not help us to rid the city of this crook?"

Howie looked at his mother who was crying. Then he looked at the others.

"Okay, I'll do it, but keep my mother out of this. She had nothing to do with it. I did it all by myself. It was so easy to do. El Lobo delivers. I buy drugs from him, and I sell at a slight profit. I was cheaper than anyone else, but volume makes more money. It's economics."

The adults all had to smile a bit after his last statement. This kid wasn't dumb. He knew how to market.

While the interrogation of Howie was going on, Sarg was approaching West Liberty in his private car. He had gone home, changed his clothes, put on a heavy sweatshirt, and parked his squad car in his garage. He circled the high school. He noticed the police car parked in front. This wasn't unusual, but then he noticed a car with official Iowa government plates on it. The DCI had made a mistake by parking where he could see the car. He circled around one more time from the opposite direction. He wanted to make sure. He drove away, headed south, and then stopped in a field driveway.

Howie was being instructed on how he was to act when making a drug deal when his cell phone buzzed. Instinctively, he looked at it. It was a text message. He blinked and then showed the message to the DCI agent, Sam. Sam groaned, because the text read, "I see you have some friends with you. I'll see you next week, maybe. El Lobo."

The sting was not going to happen. They would have to try some other way. Howie was suspended from school and put in custody of his mother for the time being. He and his mother were told a court date would be set at a later date. Her attorney would be notified.

Chapter 14

Phil was ready at 4:00 a.m. He waited for Ron and thought, "Why am I doing this? Am I nuts? I could get killed or arrested."

Ron arrived and the pair headed for Wapello. As they traveled along Highway 61, Ron spotted fog hanging in the Mississippi River valley. A warm front had arrived early in the morning and had capped off the cool air above the river, forming a dense fog, but only over the water.

"Good!" exclaimed Ron. "If the same fog is in the Iowa River valley, it will make the leaves damp and not crunchy. The dogs won't hear us quite as soon. I hear we are in for some good weather. It's supposed to be in the low 70s today and tomorrow, then maybe the 80s by Easter Sunday. The weatherman said no rain for six days. The farmers will be going full blast by then."

Phil replied, "I'm glad, too. After today, I may need a vacation. I'm not much for this covert stuff."

"Covert stuff? Say, ol' buddy, remember we're going turkey

hunting not spying. Heck, hunting turkeys is easy. You just got to outsmart them. It's sort of like breaking into a garage and not getting caught," Ron said with a smile.

They parked Ron's Jeep behind the Hanson barn. Ron had two backpacks of equipment plus the shotguns. It took twenty minutes to get ready. Ron didn't think it was necessary to unpack the guns from their cases until after they returned from the shed. He told Phil they would have to play like they were hunting until about 9:00. Otherwise, Mr. Hanson might wonder if they were legit or not.

They approached the line fence through a dense fog. They left the guns and breakfast food by an oak tree on the Hanson side of the fence. Ron led the way. At the edge of the trees surrounding the garage, he stopped.

"You stay here. I'm going to try and reach the dog kennel before they wake up."

Ron opened up one of the backpacks. Inside, he had two plastic containers of raw hamburger. He dumped a container in one hand and had Phil dump the other in his other hand. He winked at Phil and took off running and loping toward the kennel. His bad leg wouldn't let him outright run. Just as he reached the pens, the dogs awoke and came charging out. One jumped high on the fence, but could not clear it. Ron slammed the hamburger into each dog's feeding dish and pushed them under the gate. The dogs quieted immediately and began to gulp the fresh meat. Ron talked to them quietly. The pair seemed to begin to trust him, and they quit growling while they were eating. Ron stood by the pen for a few minutes. The big guard dogs finished their meal and retired to their respective kennels. Ron gave Phil a thumbs-up. The dogs would be asleep for three or four hours.

Ron motioned for Phil to meet him at the garage. He knelt down next to the control box and slipped the cover off. He removed a tool kit from his backpack and began to adjust wires and fuses.

"Oh, rats!" he exclaimed. "I forgot my black tape and this

unit has a door override. How am I going to fix that?"

"Is this bad?" Phil asked.

"Well, if I can't disarm the door, I'll have to go through a window, which is time consuming and difficult."

"What if I hold my finger on the button while you go in the garage?"

"It might work if your finger doesn't get tired. I'd suggest a thumb and also lie down so your legs and feet don't cramp up."

Phil lay on his side and Ron showed him the red button.

"Now push it in and hold it solidly until I return and shut the door, or we'll be in big trouble," he ordered.

Phil licked his thumb and pushed the button in. Ron put on some plastic gloves and gingerly turned the door knob. He gently shoved the door open and stepped in. He gave the high sign to Phil. Inside, he found two vehicles, the wrecker, and a black luxury mini bus with pink letters on the side saying, "Ping's Pleasure Trips." The windows were covered with a black-out material blocking the view inside. The only window without a dark tint was the windshield. Ron walked around to the front of the bus and looked through the windshield. Inside were overstuffed benches which could seat two people. They were covered with a velour-like material instead of leather. Ron surmised the leather would stick to bare skin if the riders were ladies.

He hurried, because he didn't want Phil's thumb to become weak. On the other side of the bus was a tilt bed wrecker for hauling automobiles. It was blue and yellow with J & R Recycling, Washington, Iowa on the door plus a phone number. Ron took photos of the truck with his cell phone. He climbed on the running board and shot a photo of the VIN of the truck. From this vantage point, he spotted a cell phone and a laptop computer on the seat. The cell phone was yellow-green with some initials on the back.

"Could this be Mrs. Hellzer's phone?" he thought.

He took a chance and pushed the door button. The door opened slightly, which indicated it was unlocked. Quickly, he pulled two plastic bags out of his pack. He slipped the phone in one and put it in his pack. He noticed the initials on the phone were K. H. The computer was too large to fit in his pack, so he opened his jacket and stuffed it inside. There was a small tag on the laptop stating it was property of the Dept. of Agriculture of Iowa.

He stepped out of the truck cab and slowly closed the door until he heard a click. He snapped a couple more pictures and hurried to the door. He stepped outside and closed the door slowly, making sure the contacts matched again. When he reached Phil, Phil was holding his right hand with his left. Ron reached down and pulled Phil's thumb away. No alarm sounded, and Phil breathed a sigh of relief.

Ron helped Phil get up and motioned to him to head for the fence. Ron knew it was still possible to trip the alarm if he didn't arm it correctly. He gently pulled the overriding wires. There was a slight spark, but no alarm rang. He slipped the cover back in place. Then he went back to the dog kennels and retrieved the empty dishes. He did not want anyone to suspect any tampering.

Picking up his backpack, he headed for the fence line. Phil had already crossed and was loading up the guns and breakfast backpack, when Ron reached the crossing. He gave Phil the thumbs-up sign and turned to re-staple the barbed wire to the post. He was wringing wet with sweat. If they ever got caught, he didn't want Mr. Hanson to be at fault. Ron pointed to a grove of oaks on the hill about one hundred yards away. He didn't speak until they sat down.

"I think we hit the jackpot, ol' buddy. We found the wrecker, which hauled Mrs. Hellzer's car, plus I took her cell phone and laptop from inside the truck. They should give us a clue why they had to kill her."

"Let's hurry and get out of here!" Phil exclaimed.

"Not so fast. We still have to hunt some turkey. If we go back now, Mr. Hanson might become suspicious. Not that he'd tell anyone, but let's be on the safe side. Besides, I'm getting hungry, so let's see what Sherry packed for us. "

Phil reluctantly sat down and rested against the tree trunk. Sherry had packed a good breakfast—ham sandwiches, a couple of sweet rolls, water, a thermos of coffee, and orange juice. It tasted good. They sat and ate, then rested their eyes a bit. Before shutting his eyes, Ron wrapped the laptop in a towel Sherry had put in the lunch bag. He then put the laptop inside the now almost empty food bag.

Ron awoke first and said, "I wonder if I can call any turkeys with this device."

"You brought the turkey caller?"

"Well, I'm hunting turkey, aren't I?"

"Let me get my gun ready. I might as well be official."

Phil unpacked his shotgun and loaded it. Ron started his call. They sat quietly. All of a sudden, a turkey answered Ron's call. Ron and Phil looked at each other with amazement. Ron called again. The turkey gobbled back. On the third try, a big tom turkey strutted out from behind a bush with his feathers all splayed out. He was a beauty. The old hunting prowess took over in Phil. He leveled his gun and "Balooie!" The turkey took one step forward and dropped over dead. Again, both men stared at each other in amazement. They had shot a turkey.

Ron began to laugh. If this wasn't a good cover for what they had just done, there never would be one. If Jake Johnson heard the shot, they could prove it was them shooting turkeys.

Phil asked, "What do we do with the bird? I've only dressed out pheasants."

Ron admitted, "I've never cleaned any kind of a bird, but I

can take pictures."

Pulling out his little point-and-shoot camera, Ron took pictures of Phil's kill, and they jubilantly headed for the farmstead with the dead turkey in tow.

They were packing away their gear when Cliff Hanson appeared from the back door.

"Did ya git one?" he hollered at them. "I heard a shot."

Phil reached inside the Jeep's trunk and pulled out the prized bird.

"Well, lo and behold, that's a big one. Who did the shooting?"

"Phil did," Ron told him. "Now we don't know what to do with him."

"Phil or the bird?" Cliff said with a smirk.

"The bird. Phil has dressed pheasants before, but never a turkey."

"They can be tricky. I'll tell you what. Go to Columbus Junction. You go over the bypass, and as soon as you come to the road back to downtown, you turn. There's a butcher shop called "Ronnie's" about three blocks down the street run by a Mexican. He'll butcher anything—goats, sheep, ducks, chickens, whatever, and he is good and also cheap. He's done a lot for me. Tell him Cliff sent you over. He'll understand. I'd have him smoke it, too. Wild smoked turkey is delicious."

"Thank you, Cliff. We'll do that and thanks for letting us hunt. Maybe we'll come back next year," Phil told him.

"You won't be so lucky next year," Cliff warned with a smile.

They chatted a little longer and packed up for Columbus Junction. It was only a few miles out of their way, and they might as well enjoy their turkey.

Ron had Phil drive home so he could contact Captain Stender. He explained to the captain what they had found and wondered what he wanted them to do with the evidence.

Captain Stender replied, "Have Bobbi or Dan bring everything to Des Moines. Maybe we can find out what the victim was texting about before they snatched her phone away. There are probably some fingerprints on both items, so be careful handling them."

"We'll drive right by Fruitland on our way home. If one of them could be there, we'll give them the items."

"Sounds good. Did you have any luck hunting turkey?"

"Yup, Phil bagged a big one. We're having it processed in Columbus Junction. We're planning on a big picnic once this case is solved."

"Great! I'll be there."

Ron pulled up to Bobbi and Dan's apartment. Before he got to the door, Bobbi met him.

"What brings you here to our little abode?" she asked.

"Phil and I were turkey hunting next to the Johnson place and just happened to discover a shed containing the wrecker used in hauling Karen Hellzer's car. Inside was her computer and cell phone. Captain Stender wants you to take it to Des Moines, pronto!"

"That will suit us just fine. We were going back to our apartment there to pick up some things, because we're going to my folks in Maquoketa for Easter. We'll have it there in three hours. What are you doing for Easter, Ron?"

"I'm going over to Julia's. There is some kind of all-night vigil going on at her church. Little Mike has some part in it. I guess they will let me in."

"Sure, they will. Julia will get you through the mass. See you Monday."

Chapter 15

Muscatine

  Deputy Betty Winters pulled into the sheriff's parking lot. She was scheduled to go on duty in half an hour. She sat in her car contemplating what she should do with her Gomez CD. She didn't want it to fall out of her duffle bag while inside, so maybe she should leave it in her car. She pulled it out of her bag and slipped it under the driver's seat. It should be safe there.

  She got out and headed for the women's locker room. She liked to dress at the office instead of at home, because she felt conspicuous driving her Toyota in uniform. It was time for a fresh uniform anyway. She went to the supply room and picked up a clean uniform. The women's locker room was small, since there were only three women on the force. They each had a locker to store items. The restroom consisted of a small shower, one stall, and lavatory with a mirror. Betty never showered before going home, because it was always cold in the bathroom especially in the winter. It seemed easier for her to go home and shower. The only one she knew who showered there was Trudy. Trudy was a single woman and very attractive. Many times right after work, she had plans or she went to the 'Y' to work out, which is why she said she liked to shower at the office. Betty figured the only reason she was hired was so the men could ogle her. She evidently didn't mind, because instead of wearing crewneck T-shirts under her uniform, she opted for V-necks, which disclosed more of her chest.

As Betty changed, she glanced around the small room and wondered if there were any cameras hidden in there. After last Wednesday night, she wouldn't put it past Sheriff Joe to do something like that."

She saw nothing as she quickly glanced around in the dressing area, but she didn't have time to check the shower stall. She combed her hair and applied some lipstick before heading to the ready room. She passed Alvin at the reception desk.

"Good morning, Al," she said cheerfully.

Al scowled and answered back, "The sheriff wants to see you before you leave."

Betty entered the sheriff's office. He had all the blinds shut, and he was standing by the window peeking out.

"Is someone going to shoot at us?" she joked.

"No! Sit down Betty," he shot back.

Sheriff Joe opened the blinds and returned to his desk. He was smiling.

"Betty, I hear you didn't go to Montpelier and check out the domestic violence report last Wednesday."

"No, sir, I didn't."

"Could you tell me why?"

"I felt the report was bogus, because there was nothing from the dispatcher. Alvin was the only one who seemed to know about it."

"What made you return to the jail?"

"Before I was out of the drive, I saw that two women were in custody. I thought you might want me to help interrogate them. You know, woman to woman."

"How come you went to the jailer instead of coming to me?"

"I forgot my keys and Jim let me in."

"Did you know he was recording the interrogation of the women?"

"Not until I was in his office."

"Why didn't you intervene?"

Betty paused for a moment and sighed, "Because I figured you and the others were going to do something illegal. Jim told me to wait and see what actually happened. Sir, you strip searched two women without justifiable cause. They should have been searched by a female officer, and you know it. I know you planted the drugs in one of their jacket pockets, then proceeded to accuse them falsely. The strip search was not warranted. It was just for your pleasure. If you want me to resign, I will. I don't want to be a part of this crooked department."

Sheriff Joe squirmed in his chair and replied, "If you want to resign, fine, but first you must turn over all evidence from last Wednesday. Do you have it with you?"

"No! Where could I carry a CD disc on my body?"

The sheriff was quiet and eyed the trim deputy.

"Do you want to strip search me like you did the Gomez

twins?" Betty asked him as she began to unbutton her blouse.

Again, the sheriff was quiet and eyed Betty as she unbuttoned the third button.

"No, Betty, I don't think it will be necessary. I can tell you don't have it on you."

Betty took her badge off and threw it on his desk. She watched the old man finger the badge while he stared at her chest. All he was seeing was a T-shirt. What was so intriguing about that? Then it hit her. He had seen her dressing and undressing somewhere else, and it had to be in the ladies locker room.

She blurted out, "You and your buddies have been watching the women deputies dress in their locker room, haven't you?"

The sheriff was silent.

"That's the reason you hired Trudy, the blonde bombshell, so you and your buddies could watch her shower. There must be a camera in the bathroom somewhere."

"I didn't do it."

"Yes, but someone did. Let's see, if it wasn't you, it could be Sergeant Waters. No, he isn't that smart. It's not Alvin, because he doesn't know much about electronics, and he's old. So, that leaves Don."

The sheriff's face darkened. She had hit a button.

"Okay, it was Don. He records everything that goes on in the ladies room and probably puts it on YouTube or someplace like that."

"You men are sick!" Betty said, sounding insulted.

The sheriff replied, "I'm sorry to see you go, Betty, but under the circumstances, I can't keep you on staff here. You can turn in your uniform and leave. You know everything we have talked about is confidential. If you do say anything to the press, I'll deny it and so will all the others. It's four against one."

Just as Betty was about to rise, Alvin burst into the office.

"Here's the CD I think you might want, Sheriff."

Betty was shocked and she screamed, "How'd you find that? You searched my car while I was in here, didn't you?"

"No, he didn't, I did," said Sergeant Waters walking into the room. "May I ask if there are more copies?"

"None of your business, Sarg. I don't have to tell you now. I resigned."

"Oh, you resigned, did you? Now I can treat you as a suspect. Let's go to the back room and see if I can change your mind."

"That won't be necessary, Keith," Sheriff Joe butted in.

"Betty, who has the other copies of this CD?"

Betty remained quiet. She knew she was at a disadvantage.

The sheriff flipped the CD case around and said with a smile. "It says on the side of the CD case, 'Property of Phil Robbins.' I'd imagine he is the one we need to contact. Isn't that so, Betty?"

Betty remained silent.

"I guess I proved my point, didn't I, Betty! You may go now. Remember, we'll be watching you and it is four against one."

Sergeant Waters held the CD in front of Betty's face and bent it, double, cracking the disc in two pieces. He broke it again into four littler sections.

"Here, stuff this inside your shirt and see if it fits better.

Better yet, put it inside your bra for safe keeping or would you like me to do it?" growled Waters as he threw the crushed disc on Betty's lap.

Betty rose, threw the shiny plastic remains in the waste basket, and snapped, "You'll all pay for this, I swear. If you think I'm dumb enough to have the only copy, you are mistaken. Good-bye!" she hollered and stomped out of the office.

Betty re-entered the women's locker room. She looked all around, trying to find the hidden camera, but she didn't see one.

"Don did a good job, but this is one time they won't be watching Betty undress," she thought to herself.

She turned the lights off, grabbed a towel from the bathroom, and covered the window. It darkened the room considerably. There it was, inside the fourth locker shooting through the locker's vent. The little red light gave the camera away. She ran to the sink and got a paper towel. She wet it and shoved it into the vent to cover the intruding camera. She changed into her jeans and sweatshirt, and then she threw her uniform out into the hall. As she crossed the parking lot, she could see the three men watching her. She flipped them the bird.

"She'll go right for Robbin's place, I'll bet you ten dollars," said Sheriff Joe to Sarg.

"She may try to go there, but she'll never make it. Alvin and me we took care of that," Sergeant Waters replied.

"What did you do?"

"We cut the brake line and the emergency brake cable, plus I slit the power steering hose. She'll have problems very shortly."

Betty drove out of the parking lot and turned onto Mulberry Avenue. She headed toward the river. There was a stop light at Second and Mulberry, and the street sloped down just before the light. At the stop sign on Third, she noticed her brakes were sluggish, because she had to pump them twice before they stopped the car. She approached Second Street and the light changed to red. Betty pushed the brake pedal. Nothing happened. She tried the emergency brake, and it just flopped forward. She tried to steer away from the oncoming traffic, but the steering wheel was slow. She looked to her left and could see a large van truck bearing down on her. He was honking his horn and trying to stop. The van hit her car midway on the front door. It pushed her car across the intersection into a light pole on the other side of the street. The impact of the lamp post exploded her airbag. The big truck actually rolled up over the back of her car and came to rest on the trunk. Its huge fuel tank was right over Betty. The fuel cap was loosened and diesel fuel began to drip on Betty. A semi-trailer truck was following the van. He jackknifed but didn't hit either vehicle. The driver hurried out to Betty's aid. The driver of the van got out on the passenger side of his truck. He was shaken, but unhurt. More people arrived.

"The car is smoking. There must be a fire! Someone get an extinguisher! The driver is covered with diesel fuel!"

The semi driver retrieved a fire extinguisher from his cab and sprayed the smoking engine. Others were trying to extricate Betty, but she was pinned inside. Within minutes, the firemen arrived and began to use the Jaws of Life to extricate her. The police directed traffic around the accident.

"Do you suppose we should help?" asked Sheriff Joe, "We're only two blocks away."

He had heard the report on the police scanner.

"Yeah, we should go over there. Maybe it's not Betty."

"Or if it is, maybe I'll be interviewed by the media. That would be good."

The sheriff and the deputy drove down the street. They could see by the color of the wrecked car, it was Betty's Toyota. They helped direct traffic. The firemen were using the Jaws of Life to extract Betty from her car. She was alive but badly injured. The EMTs were inserting fluid lines in her arms. They carefully laid her on the gurney and put her in the back of the ambulance. Sheriff Joe watched them go, and in his heart, he hoped she would survive.

A reporter from the *Journal* cornered the Sheriff.

"Did you know the victim was a deputy, Sheriff?"

"Not until I got here. I had just talked to her. She was coming off her shift and was heading home."

"Do you have any idea what caused the accident?"

"Not really, and this is Captain Hendrick's jurisdiction. He will do the investigation, but I suspect it was a vehicle malfunction. You know these foreign cars are not as safe as American made."

The pair of officers hung around for a few minutes more. Sergeant Waters tapped the sheriff on the shoulder.

"I guess that takes care of one problem, two to go, the jailer, and Phil Robbins. Phil has the rest of the recordings. I'll take care of him first. Can I have the rest of the afternoon off, Joe? I feel the need to talk to a reporter in Walcott."

"Sure, don't hurt him too much. Just destroy the discs and his computer. Be sure he doesn't know who you are."

"Don't worry, Joe. He'll never know what hit him."

* * *

Walcott

Sherry had gone back to the library, and Phil decided to take a nap. It had been a long time since four o'clock. He settled down in his lounger and pushed it back. Soon, he was sound asleep.

He was awakened by a pounding on the front door. He pushed his feet down and tried to get up. The pounding started again.

"All right! All right, I'm coming. Hold your pants on," he shouted.

He reached the door still half asleep. He looked out and saw no one. He cautiously opened the door and then the storm door. He didn't see anyone.

"Hello, is somebody out there?"

"Are you Phil Robbins?" a voice asked.

"Yes, may I..."

The next thing Phil knew, the door had been jerked from his hand. A huge man dressed in camouflage with a ski mask over his face pushed Phil back into the room. He hit Phil along the side of his head, then pushed a baseball bat into his stomach. Phil doubled over. A knee met his chin. He collapsed on the floor. A big boot kicked him several times in the ribs.

Phil opened his eyes and tried to get a look at his assailant. He caught a glimpse of a bushy mustache poking out from under the ski mask and that was all. A bat hit him in the face and he lost consciousness. He lay on the floor drifting in and out. He could hear the man destroying his equipment. Glass and plastic were flying all over.

He heard the man say, "Here they are."

Then he heard more smashing plastic. It didn't take long and the man left.

As he went out the door, he shouted, "Remember, Mr. Reporter, I know where your wife works, and I don't want to have to hurt her. So, you don't know nothing, right?"

Phil lay there on the floor. He was afraid to move. He had no phone or cell phone. The thug had destroyed them. He'd have to stay there until Sherry came home.

About 3:30, Sherry pulled into the drive. She noticed the front storm door hanging open.

She went in the side door and called, "Phil, are you here?"

She heard a moan. When she reached the dining room, she found her husband on the floor. He was covered with blood.

She screamed, "Phil, what happened?"

Phil just moaned. Sherry looked at the destroyed office. She called 911. In a few minutes, the fire department was there. The Walcott police chief followed quickly. Phil had been the fire chief of the Walcott Fire Department for several years. He was well respected in the little town. As soon as they got him stabilized, the EMTs loaded him into the ambulance and headed for Genesis West Hospital in Davenport.

Chapter 16

Good Friday

Bobbi and Dan returned from Des Moines around noon. She turned on the TV to catch the latest news report and immediately was drawn into the reporter's story. Apparently, a small town news reporter named Phil Robbins had been beaten up and his office had been ransacked. His condition was serious, but not life threatening. Dan immediately put a call into Ron.

Ron answered, "Hello, Dan. Yes, I'm aware of Phil's problem. I visited with him this morning. He is afraid to say much. The thug who beat him up said he would get Sherry if he talked. I'm at his home right now with the Scott County sheriff and the Walcott police. We are searching for clues, but the guy really smashed Phil's computers and other equipment. It will be days to piece this together."

"Should we come?"

"You can, but I think you might do better going to visit Phil in the hospital."

"We'll do that on our way to Bobbi's parent's farm. I'll talk to you Monday, if not before. Have a good Easter."

It was four o'clock when Dan and Bobbi arrived in Phil's room. They found him sitting in a chair dressed in sweatpants and an old flannel shirt. His nose was bandaged, one eye was swollen shut and the other blackened, his right ear was scabbed with several stitches, and his hand was bandaged. He smiled as they entered. He pointed to Sherry.

"How's he doing, Sherry?" Bobbi asked.

"The doctors say he will be fine in a couple of months. Outside of what you can see, he has two broken ribs and his jaw is broken. He'll have to eat his supper through a straw. I guess he'll lose some weight," she answered with a slight smile, "and he'll have to be quiet for a while. We're waiting for our son, Kyle, to get here from Mason City. The doctor said Phil could go home, but I'd have to have help for a couple of days. The hardest part will be getting him into the house. Once inside, I think, he will be able to shuffle around. He can sleep in his chair, or we'll get a bed for him downstairs for a while."

Phil gave Dan and Bobbi, a thumbs-up. Despite his ordeal, he was in good spirits.

"Do you have a clue who did this?" Dan asked.

Phil just shrugged his shoulders. He motioned for a piece of paper. With his bandaged hand, he wrote a message in big letters, 'HE HAD A MUSTACHE STICKING OUT OF HIS SKI MASK AND A DEEP VOICE. I'VE HEARD IT BEFORE BUT DON'T KNOW WHERE.'

"Hmm. Where did we hear someone say something about a thick mustache? Maybe Ron knows. I'll call him Monday."

Dan and Bobbi stayed a little while longer before heading out to Maquoketa. As they were leaving, Kyle was entering his dad's room.

* * *

Bobbi and Dan arrived at her parent's farm around 5:30. Bobbi's dad saw them as he was walking out the machine shed's big center door.

As they got out of the car, her dad greeted them, saying, "Glad to see you two. How are things in the detective business?"

"Oh, you know, busy for a while and then calm. Right now, we are working in Muscatine and Louisa Counties. We hope to get the case cleared up in a couple of weeks."

They went inside to a hungry man's smelling kitchen. Millie, Bobbi's mother, had a feast prepared for Dan and Bobbi. They were still eating dessert when her dad asked if he could watch the news. Millie reluctantly nodded, yes.

The news anchor started with a breaking news bulletin.

"We are taking you live to the Muscatine Court House. The head of the Department of Criminal Investigation of Iowa is about to speak."

The next scene was a picture of Captain Cal Stender.

He stepped to a microphone and said, "As of four o'clock this afternoon, three men have been arrested, but are out on bail at the present time. Muscatine Sheriff Joe Ward, Deputy Alvin White, and Deputy Don Larson have been charged with sexual harassment, false arrest, racial profiling, and tampering with state's evidence of a crime scene. Deputy Keith Waters has also been charged with possession and selling of controlled substances, but he has not been apprehended. An arrest warrant is now out for him."

The focus of the broadcast reverted to the news team inside the studio. The news anchor began relaying more information.

"We have exclusive video of the strip search provided by the family of the young women. Their names are being withheld to protect their privacy. I must warn you, the video we are about to display is quite graphic and shows some nudity."

Dan's mouth dropped. He looked at Bobbi. She returned the stunned look.

Bobbi's Dad spoke first, "I guess by looking at your faces, this was not expected."

"Yes, it is a surprise. We are working in Muscatine County and met the sheriff at a crime scene. He reminded me of a southern redneck sheriff like you see in the movies. I knew our chief was after him, but didn't think he'd actually charge him and his buddies," replied Bobbi. "This information must be new and incriminating. Our boss doesn't go before the media unless he is positively sure he has a solid case."

Dan continued, "We aren't involved in this case, but it is interesting they haven't found Mr. Waters."

"Wasn't Mr. Waters one of the men in the news video? There was a man with a big mustache who was holding the water hose," Bobbi remarked.

Dad said, "I'm sure he was one of the men."

"Didn't Phil say his assailant had a bushy mustache?"

"I'll bet Deputy Sergeant Keith Waters was the man who beat up Phil."

They talked about the surprising news for a short while and then the conversations changed to family and weather.

"Hey, Buttons, (Dad called Roberta, Buttons, and her sister, Carol, he called, Bows, so the pair of girls were Buttons and Bows.) Would you like to drive the tractor tomorrow? I need someone to harrow before I can seed the oats and alfalfa. After that, you can roll it in."

"I'd love to, Dad. I haven't driven a tractor since high school."

The evening was filled with laugher and stories. Because of the six o'clock news, they stayed up for the ten o'clock news. The ten o'clock news was about the same. It showed the DCI Captain Stender and the shortened video. After the segment, the news anchor revealed that during the questioning of Deputy Alvin White, he admitted to planting the drug package in one of the women's jackets and that he had done this several times before. He claimed he was sorry for what he had done, but he was only following the orders of Sergeant Waters, his superior. He also admitted to tampering with Deputy Betty Winter's car just before her accident. He and Sergeant Waters had compromised her brakes and steering mechanisms. He claimed he was sorry for what happened to Deputy Winters and hoped she would survive.

The reporter continued, "Mrs. Winters is recovering at Muscatine Memorial Hospital at this time. Her condition has been upgraded from critical to serious. The doctors feel she'll recover with many months of therapy ahead of her."

"Well, the news keeps getting better and better," commented Bobbi. "Now I'm sure Mr. Waters had something to do with the beating of Phil Robbins. I wonder where he is hiding out."

"I'm sure they have an APB out on him, so he won't get far," Dan added.

The weather was the next concern. Tomorrow was to be dry and breezy. The high temperature would be in the 70s. The five-day forecast revealed the weather for Easter Sunday would be close to 80, and then Monday and Tuesday the temps would continue in the 80s. A cold front would arrive sometime Wednesday, which promised to bring temperatures back to normal.

"Boy, this is great," said Bill, Bobbi's dad. "We'll get an early start tomorrow, Buttons. Can you be up and ready by seven? You'll need an extra jacket to start with, because you'll be driving the old 190 Allis, and it doesn't have a cab."

"I'll be ready, Dad. I brought along some extra jeans and sweatshirts just in case. Mom, have you got anything you want Dan to do?"

Millie thought a moment and said, "It's time to plant potatoes, peas, and radishes. If Dan doesn't mind, he can run the rototiller and dig the holes."

"Sounds great to me, Mrs. Stroud," Dan replied.

Millie eyed Dan and said, "Dan, when are you ever going to quit calling me Mrs. Stroud? I would much rather you call me, Millie or Mom."

Dan smiled and answered, "I'll try, Millie."

Everyone had a chuckle over the conversation.

Bill announced he was going to bed, because he had a big day planned for tomorrow. They shut the TV off and all headed down the hall to the bedrooms. Bobbi headed for her community bathroom as she called it. She had to share it with her sister when they were younger. The bathroom had two doors, each opening to each girl's room. It had worked fine until the girls married. Then some embarrassing moments had occurred with the husbands. Bobbi was dressed only in her underwear when she returned and began searching through the luggage for her pajamas. Dan stripped to his shorts before entering the bathroom. He knocked before he entered.

"Why did you do that?" Bobbi asked. "Carol and Tim aren't here."

"Habit, I guess. After walking in on your sister while she was sitting on the toilet, I just wanted to be sure it's safe to enter."

"Yeah, and remember the time Tim thought it was Carol taking a shower, and he found out it was me? Boy, his eyes were as big as saucers and did he get embarrassed. Carol has kidded him and me many times over that moment."

When Dan finished brushing his teeth and getting ready for bed, the bedroom was dark when he opened the bathroom door. Bobbi was dressed in her pajamas and looking out the window. She had opened the window just a bit to let in the spring breeze. He walked up behind her and wrapped his arms around her waist.

"A penny for your thoughts, hon," he whispered.

"I wish I would have been born a boy instead of a girl," she answered.

"Why?"

"Because then I could come home and farm with my dad. Boys get to do that. Just look at my boy cousins. They both are farming with Uncle Harry. They farm a huge amount of land. Their wives live on the farm. One works in town as a CPA, and the other is a stay-at-home mom and is pregnant all the time. A farm is a good place to raise a family. Just look outside right now. The moon is full, the trees are just starting to leaf-out, the tulips are up, and it just smells new. I'd love to raise a family out here."

"Why can't girls farm?" he asked.

"Because they are not supposed to; farming used to be hard physical work. But now, it's mostly just long hours along with timely planting and harvesting. There are a few women running farms today, but they are definitely in the minority."

Dan didn't say a word and instead, he gave her a little squeeze. She turned toward him and pulled his head down for a kiss.

"We'd better get some sleep instead of dreaming out loud. My dad will be hollering down the hall if I'm not ready at seven o'clock tomorrow morning."

Chapter 17

Sioux City, Iowa

Hal arrived at the Hi-Val store for his late shift. He and his partner, Kurt, were the night butchers. They cut and packaged meat for the next day. One of their main tasks was to receive the hamburger and make sure it was mixed to the specifications of the store. The hamburger was divided into three different categories— 80%, 85%, and 90% lean. Hal rolled his pallet mover into the cooler and brought out a tub of meat from Acme Pack. It contained 90% lean meat. He and Kurt would have to unwrap the fifty-pound tubs of meat and re-package it into smaller units or mix the very lean meat with the higher fat content meat to meet the advertised standards. He removed the top layer and grabbed a small pry bar to lift the plastic tray. He didn't look inside until he had put the tray on the table.

"Holy geez! Kurt, come look at this. Better yet, get Mr. Bowsman back here," he blurted out when he returned to the tub.

Kurt ran over to the tub, looked in, and then he ran out to the main room.

"Mr. Bowsman, Mr. Bowsman, we need you in the back butcher room right now," he called out.

Mr. Bowsman came running. He figured one of the men had cut himself badly or worse. He entered the back room and found Hal and Kurt standing over the tub. Hal was as white as a sheet.

"What's up?" he asked when he could see both men were okay.

"T...h...e...r...e...'s a body in here. A woman's body," cried Hal.

Mr. Bowsman looked into the tub. There was a body of a young Mexican or Latino woman wearing only underwear. She had a tattoo of a serpent running up her leg. She was wrapped around the pedestal in the middle of the tub.

"Holy cow! We'd better get the cops over here, and pronto. Don't touch anything else."

Mr. Bowsman called the Sioux City police and locked the front door. He went to the intercom and said, "Ladies and gentlemen, due to some circumstances beyond our control, we are closing in ten minutes. Please finish your shopping and leave. All employees, please meet in the break room right after we close."

The police arrived in three minutes. Mr. Bowsman guided them to the butcher room. The officer took one look and called the station for the homicide squad. They arrived twenty minutes later. They questioned Hal and Kurt about the find, and asked each of them if they knew anything about the girl. They said they had no idea except the tub came from the main warehouse in Clarion. The detectives noticed the sticker on the tub. It read, "No. 23, March 26, Light weight, Acme Packing Co., Wapello, Iowa."

"This is more than a Sioux City crime. Wapello is on the other side of the state. We'd better call in the DCI. Maybe they have more information on this case. We'll put a call in early tomorrow morning. Hopefully, someone is still around, considering this is Easter weekend. Can you put this tub back into the cooler?" asked the officer in charge.

The DCI sent a couple of agents to Hi-Val by ten on Saturday morning. They interviewed the employees and policemen. They said they would file a report, but it was unlikely anything would be done before Monday.

They advised the Sioux City police to call the coroner and get the body to a safer place in a morgue. The news about the lady in the meat tub was on the local news channel, but it did not reach eastern Iowa until late Sunday.

Chapter 18

Stroud Farm

Bobbi was up and eating breakfast when her dad poked his head in the back door.

"Are you ready to go, Buttons?" he hollered.

"In five minutes. I just have to go to the bathroom one more time," she answered.

Dan arrived just as Bobbi was leaving the table.

She gave him a quick hug and a kiss and said, "I've got to go to work. Hope you and Mom have a great day. Mom, don't work him too hard."

Dan watched as his petite wife hurried to the bathroom and then left through the back door to meet her dad. She was running across the drive and trying to zip up her jacket while she ran. He had never seen her so excited and happy.

"Have a chair, Dan. Would you like one egg or two?"

"Two."

"Bacon?"

"Sure."

"Coffee and a sweet roll?'

"Yes, definitely."

She fixed the eggs and bacon and poured two cups of coffee. She placed a plate with two big sweet rolls on the table and sat across from Dan.

"How are you doing, Dan?" she asked.

"Just fine, Mrs. Stroud."

"Millie, remember?" she corrected him. "I'd like to know more about your family. I really don't mean to pry, but the only time I met any of them was at your wedding. I know your dad was a cop and your mother's a teacher. I know you have a couple of sisters, but beyond that I know nothing about your family."

Dan had his mouth full of eggs and bacon, so she had to wait a moment for an answer.

"Yes, my dad was a policeman for the Des Moines Police Force. He retired last year after forty years on the job. His health was an issue. His knees needed to be replaced. He was one of the old-time cops who had a walking beat in East Des Moines. He claimed he liked to walk rather than ride in a squad car. It was more personal, he claimed. People knew him and loved him. When he retired from the beat to take a desk job, the neighborhood threw him a going away party. He's waiting for my mom to retire before he has his knees replaced. We kids wish he would go ahead and have it done earlier. My mom has so many vacation days she hasn't used, she could easily stay home and nurse him for a couple of months, but she loves her students and claims it would upset her system if she took off. She can retire next year."

"And what about your sisters? Tell me about them."

My two sisters are as different as night and day. One lives in Ankeny and is married to her high school sweetheart. They have three children. She is a stay-at-home mom until her children get into high school, so she says. She has a degree in interior design and would like to start her own business. My other sister is and will always be a flight attendant. She married an airline pilot and they live in Miami, Florida. They have no children and probably won't have any. They like to travel and be free."

"And what about you and Bobbi? Do you plan to have any children?"

Dan studied his mother-in-law's face and said, "Funny you should ask. Bobbi and I were just talking about that very same thing the other day. She's been offered a desk job at the head office. It would mean she wouldn't be traveling all over the state. I don't know what I would do. We're such a good team."

"Well, it wouldn't be as dangerous as your job is now, right?"

"Yes, but really there are very few times we are in a dangerous situation. We spend a lot of our time investigating other cases and not just serious crimes. We do it because it crosses county lines and jurisdictions."

Dan finished his coffee and sweet roll, and then he helped Millie with the dishes. She suggested they get to doing the garden work before it got too hot outside. She showed Dan the old rototiller in the machine shed. He pushed it out and filled the tank with gas. He gave it several pulls, but it wouldn't start.

"That darn thing seems to get more stubborn every year. Bill just hates it. We should get a new one," Millie said sadly.

"Just let me work on it a few minutes. You can get your garden tools out. I'll go over to the shop and find some tools to work on the tiller."

Dan worked on the stubborn tiller for ten minutes. He shot some ether into the air intake and gave the rope a pull. It coughed and sputtered. He choked the carburetor, the motor popped and smoked, and then it began to smooth out. He throttled it down to an idle. Now the tiller purred.

Once in the garden, he shoved the throttle forward and threw the tines in gear. The machine took off. Dan had to hang on tight to keep it from getting out of control. He ran the tiller back and forth across the ground. Millie had a very big garden. It took Dan thirty minutes to till the whole area, and he was wringing wet with sweat by the time he finished.

Millie looked at her overheated son-in-law and said, "Why don't you sit on the deck for a while and cool off? I've got some iced tea in the fridge. I'll plant the radishes before we do the potatoes."

It was close to noon when they finished. Dan was very dirty, but satisfied with his work.

"Is it all right if I shower before we eat lunch?" he asked.

"Sure, go right ahead. I'll start lunch. Bill and Bobbi will be in from the field shortly."

Dan showered and changed his clothes. He just made it into the kitchen when the pair of tractor drivers arrived. Bobbi's face was dirty with dust and her hair was wind-blown, but she didn't care. She hurried to the bathroom to clean up.

"You and Mom having a good time?" she asked when she returned.

"Yup! We're having a great time. The radishes, peas, and potatoes are all planted. This afternoon we're going to clean up the flower beds and maybe mow the lawn," Dan told her.

Millie said, "He got that old tiller going, and I told him maybe he should work on the lawnmower, too. You two keep working in the field. Dan and I will be fine."

They finished lunch and Bill took a quick nap. A power nap, he called it. The other three just sat and talked. At one o'clock, they returned to the field. Dan and Millie started to clean up the flower beds. They stopped for a rest before Dan tackled the lawn mower.

Dan said to Millie, "Millie, don't tell Bobbi I said this, but last night before we went to bed, I caught her standing by the window. She told me she wished she was a boy, because boys can come home and farm. She told me about her cousins. She loves this farm and would like to raise her children on a farm. Do you think that's possible? Do you think maybe I could learn how to farm? I know I don't have any experience, but Bobbi does. You don't have to say anything right now, but would you think about it?"

Millie looked at Dan as if she didn't know what to say.

Finally, she said, "I'll ask Bill. I know he would love to pass the farm on. He was really disappointed when Bobbi wasn't a Bob."

"I'd better get to work on that mower. Maybe I can have the front lawn done before the workers return."

Millie smiled at him and said, "Why don't you fire up the gas grill first? I can get some hamburgers out and we could have a cookout tonight. I could make some potato salad and baked beans. You can grill, can't you?"

"Yes, ma'am, and Bobbi says I make a fine pot of beans. I'll bet the grill needs a fresh tank of LP gas. I'll run into town and exchange it. When I return, I'll start the beans, then if there is time, I'll work on the lawn mower."

Dan ran into Maquoketa to the hardware store and exchanged gas tanks. He was back by 2:00 p.m. The grill needed some cleaning, but with a little steel wool brushing and scraping, he fired it up. Step one was complete. He decided to switch to the riding lawn mower next. He took off the mower blades and sharpened them. He changed the oil and filled the gas tank with fresh gas. He put the charger on the battery and headed for the house.

"I'll get the beans cooking while the battery is being charged," he told Millie. "I like to slow cook the beans with plenty of bacon in the mix."

Millie just smiled and let her son-in-law work. He had much more energy than she. She continued to peel her potatoes and got them ready to boil. Dan asked her to stir the beans once in a while, while he attended to the mower. The mower cranked a couple of times, back fired and roared to life. Dan was excited. He hopped on and threw the blades in gear. He crossed the yard with fresh cut green grass spewing out the side. He mowed for about an hour, and then he remembered the beans. He drove to the back of the house and ran inside. Millie was stirring the beans.

"I forgot about tending to the beans. Are they okay?"

"Yes, they're fine. Do you add some molasses and brown sugar?"

"Yes, and I add some ketchup for flavor."

"I thought so. You and I cook alike, Dan. We're going to get along fine. Now you go finish the lawn. I'll tend to the supper."

It was five o'clock when Dan finished. He found Millie on the deck.

"I think I'll shower again. Maybe I should wash a load of clothes."

Millie couldn't believe a man would do so much woman's work.

She suggested, "Why don't you just put your clothes in the laundry room? Bobbi will have some dirty clothes, too."

Dan cleaned up for the second time. He helped Millie set up the picnic table on the deck. His timing was right, because here came the tractor drivers. First, it was Bill and the seeder. He backed it into the shed and walked over to the deck.

"I'm going to check the cows. Bobbi will be here in a few minutes," he said.

Ten minutes later, Bobbi drove her rig in. The packer was a noisy machine, because it consisted of heavy cast iron rings mounted on a strong axle. She drove part way into the corncrib, leaving the packer outside. She dropped the packer with a loud clang. She idled down the engine, and pulled the stop knob. Everything went quiet. Bobbi climbed down and stretched her cramped legs. She shook the dust from her hair and headed for the deck.

Dan started to fire up the gas grill.

"Hi, sweetie, how's the tractor driver?" Dan asked.

"Tired and dirty, but happy," she said with a big toothy grin on her dirty face.

She was wind-blown, and her hair was sticking out all over. Her flannel shirt was unbuttoned revealing a grease-stained T-shirt. Her jeans were dusty and had grease and oil streaks on their legs. Her shoes were muddy and speckled with oil spots.

She stepped onto the deck and was about to sit on one of the chairs when her mother scolded her, "Don't sit on the clean furniture with those dirty jeans." In a second breath, she asked, "How did you get so dirty?"

Bobbi answered, "A hydraulic hose popped loose, and I had to push it back in the coupler. I had to wipe my hands in the dirt first, then on my jeans or I wouldn't have been able to drive the tractor. I really got dirty, didn't I?"

Bobbi looked around and asked, "Where's Dad? He came in before me."

"He said he was going to check the cows for the last time. There are two cows which are late calving. Until they calve, he has to see what's going on," her mother told her.

"Good, then I'll strip right here and Dan can take my clothes to the laundry."

She quickly sat down on the step and took off her shoes and socks. She flipped her flannel shirt on the railing and pulled her T-shirt over her head. She undid her jeans and pushed them down. Soon, she was standing on the deck wearing only her underwear.

"There!" she said with some satisfaction. "Now I'm down to clean clothes. May I go inside now?"

"Not until you pick up your dirty clothes," Millie answered.

"Dan can do that."

"Your husband, Dan, is busy and has been busy all day. You pick your own clothes, my little girl."

Bobbi stared at her mother, and then grumpily picked up her clothes. She held them close to her chest and had her shoes in her other hand. She pulled the deck door open, just as she spotted her Dad coming across the farmyard.

She waved and shouted, "Hi! Daddy!"

He waved back and smiled, because he had not seen his grown daughter in just her underwear for a long time. Dan watched his wife as she exited. He noticed even though she acted like it didn't bother her that her Dad had seen. Her face was a bright red.

Bill reached the deck and was about to sit when Millie tore into him with, "Oh, no, you don't. You get yourself inside for a shower. You can use the mud room shower. I'll bring you some towels and shorts."

Bill didn't say a word, but headed for the back door. His

many years living with Millie had taught him to obey her orders around HER house. Dan put the burgers on the grill. He wanted them ready when Bobbi and Bill returned.

Bill showed up first and said, "Boy, those burgers smell good!"

Bobbi appeared barefoot and wearing a pink T-shirt and some short shorts. Her hair was still damp. She looked like a teenager.

Millie looked at her and said, "I hope you don't wear those shorts in public. They are not much more than a wide belt."

Dan had to laugh at that statement. He was enjoying the scolding Bobbi was getting from her mother. They said a prayer and began to eat. Everyone praised Dan for his cooking. After supper, they discussed what they'd be doing on Easter Sunday.

"Why don't we all go to the sunrise service and stay for church breakfast? The service starts at 7:30 and breakfast is at 8:30. We could just hang around and go to regular services at 10:00. We have enough leftovers tonight, and we can eat lunch before you two go home. I could put an Easter ham in the oven so it will be ready to eat when we get back," suggested Millie.

"Sounds good to me. Do you want me to help with the ham?" asked Dan.

"Heavens, no! I can do that. You just get ready for church."

Easter morning was lovely. The temperature was in the sixties by seven o'clock. The youth of the church held the sunrise service. Bobbi reminisced when she and her sister took part in the service. A farmer's breakfast followed—eggs, sausage, pancakes, and rolls; everything was homemade. Dan claimed he had never eaten such a good breakfast. There was a slight break before the regular services. Dan and Bill sat across from Hal Chapman.

Bill asked Hal, "Suppose the fish are biting, Hal?"

"Don't know, but they should be hungry this time of the year."

"Could Dan and I try out your pond sometime?"

"Sure, why not today?"

Bill turned to Dan, "You got your fishing gear with you?"

"Yup! Never leave home without it. Never can tell when an opportunity might arrive to go fishing."

"Well, Hal, we'll be over right after lunch."

The church was packed for the Easter service. Bobbi met many old friends. Bill and Millie had to cut off her visiting to get her home. Bill was also anxious to go fishing. They hurried through lunch. Bill asked Buttons if she'd like to go with Dan and him. She turned him down saying she needed to spend some time with Mom.

Dan and Bill arrived at the pond a little after one. The weather was almost hot. They baited up and threw in their lines.

After a few minutes, Bill spoke, "I hear you might want to try farming?"

A surprised Dan answered, "Yes, but I admit I'm quite a city boy."

"Let me give you this proposal. Millie's parents want to retire. Grandpa Henry is seventy-one. The only reason he hasn't retired before now is because he doesn't want my brother, Harry Stroud Farms, Inc., to gobble up his farm. He likes Harry, but doesn't want him to farm his place. He thinks it will be difficult to turn him down. I'm only fifty-eight and have six or seven years to work yet. I've been helping Henry plant and harvest for several years. I'm wondering if he would allow you and Buttons to farm their place. You could use my equipment and help me. He has 200 acres. You would probably have to have a part-time job, but there are plenty of small towns around here looking for law officers.

Buttons could get a job in Maquoketa. It might work. I know Buttons would really like to live out here."

Dan looked at Bill. He could not believe his ears, a kid from Des Moines, becoming an Iowa farmer.

"It couldn't happen until next year, could it?" Dan asked.

"No, but we should know by September. Let me talk to Henry and Edna first and feel them out. Then you and Buttons could inquire."

Dan's bobber jumped. He set his hook and reeled in his catch. He caught a nice sunfish. Bill's line jumped. He caught a crappie keeper. The fish were hungry, and by 4:00 p.m., they had a nice mess of fish.

"Let's hurry home and clean these. We can have an old fashioned fish fry before we head home."

"Right on, partner. I'll call Millie and tell her to mix up some batter. Millie can save the ham for a later date. I wouldn't say anything about what we talked about to Buttons, I don't want to get her hopes up."

"I understand. Maybe we can come out on Memorial Day."

It was after seven when Bobbi and Dan left for home. They promised they would be back for Memorial Day weekend. It was 9:00 when they walked in the door of their little apartment in Fruitland. Bobbi was tired and so was Dan. They were in bed by ten.

Chapter 19

Paris, Texas

Rick and Freddy rode the bus to Paris, Texas. They went directly to Rick's grandmother's home. Grandma Sanchez was a small woman but a spitfire. She lived in a small two-bedroom, one bathroom house, but it was big enough for her. The neighbors all called her *abeula izzy,* (gramma Izzy), because her given name was Isabella. She was very popular in the neighborhood, and the neighbors took care of her needs. She knew she had respect and played her power to the hilt. She had a room for Rick, so Freddy slept on the sofa. Sometimes, her bossiness was a little overwhelming, because Freddy lasted only two days with Grandma before he split for Dallas. Poor Rick had nowhere else to go. He loved his *abeula e*ven though she treated him as if he was still only five years old.

For the two weeks he lived there, he had mowed the lawn, carried out the garbage, and started to paint the house. It was not just warm today, it was hot. The southwest wind was blowing in from the

Mexican desert. The temperature in Paris was close to ninety. The same wind would blow all the way to Iowa. It was today after painting all day when the dam broke. He was tired and sweaty. All the while he was painting alone, the look of Karen Hellzer as he left her trapped in her car haunted him. The others he had helped dispose of, he could justify in his mind that they deserved it, with one exception, Mike Herera. He wasn't really the cause of his death, his speeding motorcycle was. If Mike had been going slower, he might have seen the cable stretched across the road. The taunt cable nearly severed Mike's head completely off. His motorcycle kept going and ended up in the company's lagoon. He helped bury Mike next to the fence behind the pump house. Now he was running from another of Mrs. Boss's schemes. She provided good money, but she couldn't buy his conscience.

He walked into the kitchen.

"Gramma Izzy, I'm going to quit and take a shower. It's too hot to paint."

Gramma Izzy had a memory problem, and she said, "Okay, I'll be right in to wash your back, Rick."

Rick quickly answered, "No, Gramma, I'm a big boy now. I can take care of myself."

He retired to the bathroom and stepped into the shower. The spraying water felt good until he heard the door open.

"Gramma, get out of here. I'm showering, and I don't need your help," Rick shouted at her as he turned toward the corner and pulled the shower curtain around his body trying to cover himself.

She left some clean towels on the stool, turned, and left the room.

Before she shut the door she ordered, "Wipe down the shower with your towel before you leave. I'll stay in the kitchen until you reach your bedroom, because I threw all your dirty clothes in the washer. I couldn't find any clean shorts for you."

Rick, although somewhat embarrassed, had to smile at his old granny. She was doing what she had done for years with all her children and grandchildren—take care of them and boss them. After all, she had some twenty-two grandchildren and several great-grandchildren. He could tell she wasn't a bit embarrassed. He had heard from more than one of his girl cousins about how Gramma had invaded their privacy and thought nothing of it.

He dried and opened the bathroom door. Granny was cooking something on the stove, and she couldn't see him. So, he hurried to his bedroom. He pulled on some jeans and a clean T-shirt and went to the kitchen. Gramma was now sitting in her favorite chair across from the table. On the table was a large glass of milk and some freshly baked cookies. He guessed he had survived the bathroom intrusion.

Gramma started the conversation, "Rick, when are you going to get married? Do you have a girlfriend?"

"I don't know, Gramma. I do have a girlfriend named Rosa, but we're just friends."

"Where does she come from?"

"San Antonio."

"Where is her family from?"

"I guess somewhere south of Nogales."

"Nogales, is she legal or illegal?"

"Legal, I think."

"You don't know? Illegals are trouble, you know. What happened to that friend of yours, Freddy?"

"He decided to go over to Dallas, where his friends live."

"You really mean he went back to his old job of pimping for

whores."

Rick about spilled his milk from her response. How did she know about Freddy?

"You didn't think I knew about your friend, did you? I didn't like the looks of him from the start. I knew he was trouble, so I asked around. He's got a police record as long as this table. You'd better stay away from him."

"All right, Gramma, I will."

"I think you should trim that bushy mustache, too. It looks like you're wearing a dog's tail. Your dad had a nice trimmed mustache. It gave him class. Do you want me to trim it?"

"No, Gramma, I'll do it myself."

The phone rang. Gramma answered.

"Yes, he's here. He should leave, because there is what out on him? What's an APB? An all-points bulletin? Does that mean he'll get arrested? Yes, I'll tell him."

Rick was fidgeting in his chair while listening to the one-sided phone conversation.

She hung up the phone, turned toward Rick, and said, "That was your cousin, Lanny. He's a cop. He was warning you. He didn't want to be the one to arrest you. He wishes you would turn yourself in."

Rick got up from the table and began pacing, while running his hands through his hair and mustache.

Gramma kept on questioning, "Rick, are you in trouble? I bet you are, because why would you show up at my door when I haven't seen you for two years? Now I receive a phone call from someone telling me he wants to arrest you. What'd you and that Freddy do, rob a bank?"

Rick looked down at the table and said, "No! Nothing like that."

"Great Holy Mother Mary of Jesus, you did do something. You didn't shoot someone, did you?"

Rick set his glass down and looked at his wonderful grandmother. Big tears rolled down his cheeks.

His voice shook as he spoke, "Gramma Izzy, I have done something awful. I put an innocent lady, who was a grandmother like you, in her car and glued her hands to the steering wheel and her feet to the floor. She couldn't move. We placed her car on a railroad track just before the train came. She was killed by the train."

Gramma was speechless for a moment, and then she said, "Rick, why did you do this awful thing?"

"Because my boss said so. My boss said the lady had viewed her girls and no one lives to tell anyone afterwards. I also know she saw a dead body of one of the girls while doing her job."

"What boss? What girls?"

"Mrs. Boss, we call her. I don't know her real name. She has these young women she recruits from Central America and Southeast Asia. They work for her. They go to men's parties and serve them. That is all I know. I just guard them and make sure they don't leave. Freddy works with me. He knows how to handle girls. The money is real good."

Gramma shook her head and started to cry.

"Oh, my little Rick, you are in big trouble. Have you killed anyone else?"

"Not really. I've caused a few accidents to happen and helped bury some girls which Mrs. Boss had cleansed. She told me the spirits killed the girl. Sometimes, when we knew the girl was an illegal alien, we'd just drive a hundred miles away and dump the body. I don't know what happens to them."

"Rick, you must tell the police about what you have done. First, you must go to Father Juan and confess. He can't save you from prison, but maybe he can save your soul from hell. I'm going to call him right now."

"Gramma, no!"

"I'm not taking no for an answer. You're coming with me. Then we will go to the police. I want you to tell them everything. Maybe they won't kill you," she said, hollering at him. "My little Rick, a murderer, a convict, and a dummy. Oh Mother Mary, why me? Why me? What a terrible Easter!"

Rick could have fled, but his conscience and his respect for his grandmother wouldn't let him. He knew there had to be an end to Mrs. Boss's schemes.

Chapter 20

Fruitland, Monday

It was 7:00 a.m. when her phone rang.

Bobbi mumbled, "Good morning, Bobbi here."

"Bobbi, this Captain Stender. Are you wide awake?"

The sound of the captain's voice jolted Bobbi to immediately become wide awake.

"I wasn't, Captain, but now I am. What's up?"

"Great news! First, I got a call from the Sioux City police that an employee at a Hi-Val store found a woman's body packed into one of the hamburger tubs they received from Acme Packing. She was wearing only underwear and her head was shaved. The date on the tub was March 26. It is the same date of Mrs. Hellzer's death. She had texted to have someone check the tubs. We did, but evidently not thoroughly enough. Second, one of the men who placed Mrs. Hellzer on the railroad tracks has turned himself in at the Paris, Texas police station. The Paris police said he and his grandmother arrived last night after midnight. He has given a complete statement and wants to return to Iowa and face charges. He claims there is a prostitution house or call girl business running out of the Acme Packing Plant. He stated the manager of the plant and several others are in charge. The packing plant is just a front, and it houses the young women. I feel this has turned into more than a suspected homicide; it's a case of human trafficking. I've sent McCoy and Graham down to Texas to verify his statement and bring him back. The news about Sioux City will be statewide at noon. The news of the man turning himself in will travel fast in the underground. I need you and Dan to go to the plant and delay the manager before he tries to move the girls. I already have Ron Puck staked out in Wapello. He is watching for all unusual activity around the plant. I don't care what kind of delay tactics you use, but be careful. I'm contacting the state police and the immigration bureau to assist us. Unfortunately, they can't be there for three hours. We won't do anything until they arrive. We're meeting at the police station in Wapello before the raid. Do you think you can be there in less than an hour?"

Bobbi had put the captain on speaker phone so Dan could hear his orders, also. She dressed while he was talking.

Dan answered, "We'll be there, sir. We'll leave in ten minutes."

"Great! I must warn you these people are dangerous. Anyone who murders innocent people is risky. Please don't do anything foolish. If the situation becomes more than you two can handle, bail out! We will subdue them another day. I treasure your lives more than catching a criminal."

Dan hurried out to the squad car. Bobbi quickly combed her hair. She could apply make-up on the way. She hopped in the passenger door. Dan turned the key. The engine groaned. He tried again. Nothing! The battery was dead. He jumped out of the car and ran to get his pickup. Bobbi flipped the trunk open and got out the jumper cables. They flipped up the hoods and attached cables to both vehicles. Dan had Bobbi try to start the car. Smoke rose from below the engine. It just happened the neighbor car mechanic, Jim, was passing by in his truck. He stopped to offer his help. He had Bobbi try again. More smoke! He crawled under the right front wheel and stuck his hand under the engine. He cursed and slid back out.

"The starter is shot. It is so hot, I almost burnt my hand. You'll need a new starter."

Dan looked at Bobbi and after seeing the mechanic's name on his shirt, said, "Look, Jim, we have an emergency. A call just came in from headquarters. We can't wait. Can you get this to your shop and fix it today? This is a DCI vehicle and is owned by the state. I'm sure they will pay the bill."

Jim stared at the frantic pair, "You two are state detectives?"

"Yes, can you do it?"

"Well, I'll be jiggered. I never met a real detective before. Yes, I'll be glad to replace the starter. It should be done by noon."

Dan thanked him. Bobbi and he drove his old pickup with Dan's fishing gear rattling around in the back. They made Wapello in twenty minutes and checked in with Ron.

"Why are you driving your pickup, Dan?" he asked.

"It's a long story. I'll tell you later. Has there been any activity?"

"The only thing I noticed was the black bus drove past me and was headed toward the plant. It hasn't come back. I suppose they are going to try to move the young women."

"That's what Captain Stender told us. We are supposed to delay the process until he and the immigration authorities get there. We're going to check in at the head office and talk to the manager, whoever he is."

"I can solve that riddle for you. It's JJ Johnson's son. JJ made him CEO of the plant. He doesn't know diddly about the meat business. He just spends the profits on women and expensive vacations. I'll follow you down to the last drive. If you run into trouble, call me."

"Thanks, it's good to have a backup."

"I'm going to call Phil Robbins. I promised him I'd give him the first scoop."

"He's all banged up and in the hospital. He can't come," Dan replied.

"That's right, but I'll still call him. Maybe Sherry can call his editor, and he can do something. I'd hate to see Phil miss out.'

The Acme plant was surrounded by a high chain link fence. The company was not concerned with people or animals getting in, but they were concerned with cattle escaping if a gate broke or if someone left a gate unlatched. The fence had four gates. The front gate was the one where most employees entered and parked. It was located on the old highway strip and was the entrance to the office area. Gate two led to the lagoon and the outside storage area. Gate three was the largest and the busiest. That was where the many trucks delivered cattle to the plant's stockyards. Plus, it was where the dock was located, which meant it was the place where refrigerator trucks picked up the processed meat. That particular gate had its own highway spur directly to Highway 61, so the truck traffic would not drive through Wapello. Gate four was a service gate. It accepted deliveries of supplies which were needed inside the plant. It had a small loading dock and was uniquely located in a spot between two buildings. Very few workers knew it was there. One of the lanes leading away from the dock connected drivers with an old highway road, which made it easy for them to leave the plant unnoticed. Today, however, a large black luxury bus was parked at the side of the building. It looked like the same bus Ron and Phil had found in the shed.

Dan stopped at the guard house and showed his credentials. The guard waved the pair through. Some of the regular workers were arriving when Bobbi and Dan parked their pickup. It caused no alarm. They opened the front door to find the office was a large room holding only six desks and some filing cabinets. The staff was already booting up their computers. Dan could see someone in the next room. They figured it was the manager's office. Bobbi asked one of the ladies behind a desk if she could speak to Mr. Johnson.

"Whom shall I say is wanting to see him?" she asked.

"Detectives Stroud and Dorman of the Department of Criminal Investigation of Iowa. We would like to talk to him."

The lady went to the private office door and returned a few moments later.

"Mr. Johnson said he is busy right now. Could you come back later?"

"Sorry, this can't wait."

Bobbi flashed her badge as she brushed past the startled office assistant and knocked on the door. She could see the person quickly rise and walk to the back of the room. He opened a door and disappeared through it. Dan turned the door knob. The door opened.

He called, "Mr. Johnson, Mr. Johnson! May we speak with you for a moment?"

The man continued to hasten his steps and closed the door. Bobbi and Dan followed. The door opened to a long hallway. It had several doors on each side of the hall. At the end of the hallway was a door marked, "DO NOT ENTER." The door was just closing shut as the pair entered the hallway and soon reached the forbidden door. Bobbi motioned to Dan. They drew their weapons. Captain Stender said to be prepared. Bobbi knocked on the door.

A woman's voice spoke from the other side, "Come in, my

friends."

Bobbi slowly pushed the door open. The room was very dark except for a light over a Chinese looking woman sitting in a big throne-like chair. The chair was trimmed in red with gold leaf accents. The floor was carpeted with plush red carpet. They could tell there were others in the room by the sounds of motion and quiet conversations.

"Welcome to the home *shi loa fu dao* (the temple of truth). Here, we always tell the truth and those we find untruthful, we cleanse."

Bobbi and Dan let down their guard just for a moment. Then, the lights went out, and a bright spotlight blinded both agents. A strong arm or heavy bat hit their weapons. Bobbi's fired. The bullet hit the floor and ricocheted into the wall. A woman screamed.

Dan was wrestled to the floor. Bobbi's arm was twisted behind her back. The spotlight dimmed and the room lights came on. After their eyes adjusted to the dimmer light, they saw several young women standing against the wall on the opposite side of the room. They had two mature women guarding them. Standing at one side of the room were two men, and another two men were restraining Dan and Bobbi. The Chinese lady sat in the middle of the room in her throne-like chair.

The seated lady said, "Rosa, take their weapons and throw them away. I hate violence. Melanie, check for any identification."

Rosa and Melanie advanced. Bobbi recognized both of them. Rosa picked up the guns. Melanie frisked Bobbi first and took her ID. She motioned for the man holding Dan down to have him stand. She ran her hands all over Dan's body. She seemed to enjoy her job. She retrieved Dan's wallet from his back pocket and gave them to the Chinese lady.

"Here you go, Mrs. Ping," she said.

Bobbi took notice. Now she had a name for the person who

seemed to be the boss.

"Secure them!" the boss lady told her helpers.

Two men, one who was a very large man with a big mustache, handcuffed both agents with plastic cuffs behind their backs.

"Remove their shoes. No one enters the temple with street shoes."

A lady and one of the smaller men stepped forward and removed Dan's and Bobbi's shoes. Dan was now in his socks and Bobbi was barefooted. In her hurry to leave, she opted not to wear any stockings. They stood silently. The lady whispered into the ear of the Chinese lady.

"It says here, you work for the Department of Criminal Investigation of Iowa. Is that true?"

"Yes."

"Your names are Roberta Stroud Dorman and Daniel Dorman. Does this mean you are married?"

"Yes."

"Mrs. Dorman, Rosa tells me she has met you before, and you told her you were an insurance investigator. Do you remember that meeting?"

"No!"

"It was at a birthday party in Conesville. Rosa has a beautiful voice. Does that jog your memory?"

Bobbi thought for a minute. Should she say yes or no? Maybe stick with the truth, after all, since this is the "Truth Temple."

"Yes, I remember Rosa. She and I met in the women's

restroom."

"Roberta, why did you lie to Rosa?"

"Sometimes it's best not to reveal your true identity when you're working for the DCI."

"Roberta, why are you here this morning?"

"Please call me Bobbi. We are here to seek answers to a homicide case we are working on."

"Okay, Bobbi, now please tell me which case that might be."

"I'm afraid I can't answer that question, because it's confidential information?"

"I see. I suppose your husband will be quiet, also."

"Yes, ma'am," Dan answered.

"Mr. Dorman, my sources tell me you posed as an engineer from a bogus company to seek information from one of my workers at our lagoon. Is this true?"

"Yes."

"And you were seeking information about a homicide, also?"

"Yes."

"One more question. I understand Ron Puck is now employed by the DCI. Is this true?"

"Yes."

"That little rat. I thought he was an okay guy, but you never know. Willie, you go outside and keep an eye for Ron, the Rat. I feel he might be watching us."

"Okay, Mrs. Boss."

Bobbi noted another name. Mrs. Boss. She wondered how many aliases this woman had and who was she really.

"Now, my two untruthful guests, I will introduce my staff. You've met Rosa. She takes care of my girls. Next is Melanie. I'm sure you remember her from the restaurant downtown. She and her employer feed the girls, but her boss is so dumb, she doesn't realize who she is feeding. She just likes the money. The men by the wall are my enforcers. There's Freddy, my scheduler, Willie, the one who just left, is my informer, El Lobo, he is new but effective. He just quit the Muscatine Sheriff's Department. There seems to be a scandal going on in Muscatine. The last of my enforcers is Jake, who manages the plant and the transportation. Finally, we have my girls who serve my clients in many ways. The girls come from poor families in Central America and Mexico. Some come just to get away from home. Some are here, because Mrs. Ping has loaned money to their parents, and they're helping to pay off the debt. Some were street people and needed help. Everyone works for me until they have paid their debt. Several girls have been here four years, others less. After they are debt free, I help them become citizens of the U.S."

There was knock on the door. It was Willie.

"I checked with the gateman. The red Jeep sedan with the white fender has been sitting at the Number Two drive for an hour."

"A red Jeep with a white fender, that's Ronnie's all right," Rosa blurted out.

"Can you get rid of him, Willie?" asked the now Mrs. Boss.

"I think I can."

"Do you need help?"

"Nope, I'll crush him with the end loader. He'll think I'm just driving down the road, but then I'll run him into the brush. It'll be quick."

"Okay, but be careful. We don't want the other employees to sense trouble," Mrs. Boss told him.

Willie left. Mrs. Boss, or Ping, or whatever her real name was, turned back toward her captives, and said, "In my temple, I am chief priestess. What I say goes. All my subjects answer and do what I want. The girls are no exception. If they do resist, they are cleansed. Let me show you. Gena, will you come forward?"

One of the young women came alongside Mrs. Ping's chair and stood in obedience, as if waiting for a command.

"Sit in front of me."

Gena sat down by her feet. Mrs. Ping gently pulled her head toward her lap. She began to caress the young woman's long black hair. The girl endured the petting and smiled sheepishly. Mrs. Ping seemed to be, for a moment, dreaming. Quickly, she snapped out of her trance.

"You may go now," she said.

Gena rose and attempted to return to the others. Mrs. Ping touched her hand.

"You didn't kiss me."

"Sorry, Mrs. Ping," replied Gena as she bent down to give the older lady a kiss on the cheek.

"Gena, that's not correct."

Gena stopped a moment and bent down again. This time she kissed her boss on the lips.

"That's better. Now don't forget to do that next time," Mrs. Ping reminded her.

Bobbi thought to herself, "What kind of lady is this Mrs. Ping? Does she crave attention or affection? Is she actually gay? She surely controls the group of young women. They jump when she asks. What will she do next?"

It didn't take long for Bobbi to find out.

Kara, will you come forward?"

Bobbi and Dan watched as a young woman walked forward. Kara was a slim woman, maybe only eighteen, or nineteen. She wore ballet slippers, which were permitted in the temple. She had on a pink top and a short, tight, light blue skirt. The only difference from the other women was her hair was very short. It was only an inch or two inches long. She forced a smile as she stood beside the priestess' chair.

Mrs. Ping said to the girl, "Kara, you like living here, don't you?"

"Yes, Mrs. Ping."

"I feed you and clothe you, don't I?"

"Yes, Mrs. Ping."

"You'll do anything I ask, correct?"

"Yes, Mrs. Ping."

"Did you learn from your cleansing not to disobey?"

"Yes, Mrs. Ping."

"Are you sure?"

"Yes, Mrs. Ping. I will always do what you ask."

"Kara, I want you to take all your clothes off and hand them to me."

A shocked look instantly appeared on Kara's face, and the girls along the wall began to whisper.

"Right now? Here?"

"Of course! You don't want another cleansing, do you?"

Poor Kara shut her eyes. A big tear rolled down her cheek. She slipped off her slippers and put them at the foot of her boss's chair. Next, she pulled her pink top over her head and gave it to Mrs. Ping. The older lady nodded approvingly and motioned for her to continue. Kara unsnapped her skirt and slipped it off. She had only her undergarments left. She hesitated.

Mrs. Ping said in a stern voice, "Everything, Kara."

Poor Kara reached behind her back and unhooked her bra. There were hoots and whistles from the men as she let it slide down her arms. She sighed after she handed her bra to Mrs. Ping. She turned away from the men's prying eyes as she slid her panties to the floor.

"Thank you, dear," said Mrs. Ping. "Now, you may return to the others. I'll give your clothes to Rosa to keep for a bit, because you hesitated. Next time, when I ask you to strip, I don't want any hesitation. Do you understand?"

"Yes, Mrs. Ping, replied Kara, sounding as if she was trying to hold back tears of embarrassment.

Mrs. Ping gently slapped Kara on her bare behind.

"I think next week at our party, you will be the '*anything goes*' girl."

Kara turned to face the lady in the chair and pleaded, "Please, Mrs. Ping. Don't make me do that! Please, please?"

"But I think your hair will be just right, and you need to go through the experience."

Kara quickly returned to the group in tears. They parted and let her hide toward the back. Many of them had had the same experience once or twice and being announced as, the *anything goes* girl, was traumatic.

Mrs. Ping returned her attention to Bobbi and Dan.

"You see, my girls do whatever I command. If they do what I command, they are treated very well and are paid. I believe after your cleansing, you will agree with them that in my temple, I rule!"

Bobbi and Dan exchanged a quick glance.

"Lobo and Jake, take the mister and get him ready for his cleansing. I want to talk to the wife for a minute."

Lobo took Dan's arm and led him across the room and through a double door.

Mrs. Ping focused her attention on Bobbi and asked, "Bobbi, I want to ask you again, why are you and your husband so interested in this plant?"

"I must reply again, Mrs. Ping. It is confidential information. We are not allowed to discuss cases until after they are resolved. Only then can we offer information as long as it will not jeopardize the department or those working there."

"I see, Bobbi. You are a good agent for the department, but I will find out the truth before you are released. Rosa, will you check to see if the others have the husband ready for his cleansing? Freddy, escort Mrs. Dorman to the cleansing room when she comes back. Melanie, take the girls to their rooms and have them pack for a couple of nights' stay. We are leaving as soon as I finish with *Miss Super-Agent*."

Freddy grabbed Bobbi by the shoulder and led her toward the door. In typical Freddy fashion, he pretended to stumble. He just accidently grabbed Bobbi's blouse and put his hands on her breasts. She quickly pulled back.

"Pervert!" she hollered at him.

He smiled and opened the door. He asked if those on the other side were finished with getting their captives prepared. They waited a couple of minutes before the door opened. Inside, Bobbi saw Dan sitting on a stool under a powerlift winch which was attached to rail on the ceiling. His head had been shaved, and his hands were cuffed behind his back. They had apparently removed his shirt, because all he was wearing was his T-shirt. Over the T-shirt was a harness made of webbing. It was strapped around his waist and chest, and two straps went over his shoulders. At the top of his harness on the shoulders were two metal eye hooks. He was gagged with a rag tied around his head. He looked worried.

Freddy led Bobbi to a stool positioned in the middle of the room. It had a back and arm rests. He motioned for her to sit. She tried to jump up onto the seat, but with her hands cuffed behind her, she couldn't reach the seat. Freddy removed her cuffs, grabbed her at the waist, and helped lift her up. He tied each of her arms to the arms of the stool. He continued to wrap a rope around her chest, making sure he touched her as he went across her breasts.

Bobbi scowled at him, then looked around the room. It was much different from the one she had just left. It was a sterile, stainless steel room. The walls were painted white. The floor was concrete with a large drain in the middle. There were metal tables and cabinets lining the opposite wall. Several tables were fitted with casters. In the corner, there were hoses and vats for cleaning. The most unusual item was a toilet stool on one wall. It was all by itself, no stall, no partitions, no doors, just bare.

Mrs. Ping appeared at the door with Rosa at her side. She slowly walked over to Bobbi. It appeared she was thinking of her strategy.

She circled Bobbi's chair and said, "Miss Bobbi is a very good agent for the DCI. She is doing as she is told and not revealing any information. In the next few minutes, we will see if she will tell me the truth. You have one last chance before we cleanse your husband."

Bobbi remained silent.

It was apparent Mrs. Ping was becoming angry. She put her face right up to Bobbi's. Her breath almost made Bobbi gag. She pointed to Dan.

"Thrip the bathard," she ordered with a lisp.

Bobbi took one more look at her captor. She noticed a mole on Mrs. Ping's face—a mole heavily covered by makeup. Then all of a sudden, the lights went on in Bobbi's brain—bad breath, a lisp, short stature, and a mole on the face right above her lip.

Bobbi blurted out, "You are not Mrs. Ping! You are not Mrs. Boss! You are Rita Johnson, the wife of JJ Johnson who is running for Congress. Jake is your son. You two run this prostitution business from this plant. We're in the little addition to the cold storage unit. It is built away from the rest of the plant, isn't it? Somehow, Mrs. Hellzer discovered your racket, and you had to kill her. Isn't that the truth, Mrs. Johnson? You and your truth temple are a farce, because it is headed by the biggest liar in the place. That is really the truth, isn't it, Rita?"

There were murmurs and oh's of astonishment from those standing at the edge of the room. Bobbi had blown Mrs. Johnson's cover. She now would have to operate as Mrs. Johnson and not Mrs. Ping, priestess of the Temple of Truth.

"You little thexy cop. You'll wisth you never said that," Mrs. Johnson screamed at her.

She was so angry that when she turned around, her fake pigtail caught in the armrest of Bobbi's stool. Her wig twisted sideways. She quickly straightened the askew hairpiece.

Trudging forward with a mean scowl on her face, she stomped over to Dan and hooked the cable from the winch herself.

She grabbed the controls from Jake and pushed the *up* button. She raised Dan to a standing position.

"Rosa, take his jeans and socks off. Leave his underwear on. I hate seeing naked men."

Rosa quickly undid Dan's jeans and stripped them off. She removed his socks. Dan couldn't move. He looked at Bobbi. She could tell he was now very afraid of the next event.

Rita raised Dan off the floor. His shorts hung on his hips. Bobbi had to watch in horror as Dan was raised to the top of the hoist. While this was going on, Lobo and Jake rolled a huge vat under the hoist. Rita punched a button and the hoist rolled Dan over the vat. Poor Dan could see the vat was full of some type of liquid. He felt the heat from the liquid below his feet.

"Now, Mrs. Dorman, you are going to witness the cleansing of your husband. This vat contains extremely hot water plus a touch of acid. It's the same temperature we use to clean the equipment in the plant. I want you to know there is no stopping me at this point. I am in control."

With that being said, she hit the *down* button. Immediately, Dan was dipped into the scalding mixture. His scream sounded guttural, because of being gagged. His eyes closed from the pain. Because of his height, he only went chest deep. To him, the time must have seemed like minutes, but it was only several seconds before Rita hoisted him out. He writhed in pain.

She turned to Bobbi who looked to be in shock, and asked, "Now, will you tell me the truth, or do I dunk him again?"

One of the men shouted, "Dunk him again. I think his shorts will come off."

Another shouted, "No, they won't. It'll take two more dunks. I'll bet you."

"Hold up, gentlemen. Let's see if pretty Bobbi wants to tell us more," Rita scolded them.

"Ms. Bobbi, do you want to say more, or do I dunk Dan again?"

"All right, all right! We know you ordered Mrs. Hellzer killed. One of your men came to the Paris, Texas police station and turned himself in. He confessed everything. We know he and a man named Freddy glued her hands to the steering wheel and her feet to the floor of her car before they put it on the railroad tracks."

"How did you know that? The car was destroyed," Rita asked.

"The chipping machine was being repaired and her car was delayed being destroyed. We discovered this and switched cars. Her car was sent to Des Moines and examined. We found glue on the steering wheel and floor plus many fingerprints. One set was a woman's, which I now believe we will find belong to Rosa. We also found Mrs. Hellzer's laptop and cell phone in the garage of your son's place. They gave us a clue as to why you had her killed. Finally, a man at a grocery store in Sioux City found a body of a young woman stuffed in a meat tub coming from this plant. Dan and I were sent to talk to your son. We knew nothing about your call girl business."

"Are the cops going to raid us?"

"Yes."

"When?"

"I don't know. They didn't tell me."

"You lie. You know when!"

"No! I don't."

"Does your husband, Danny boy?"

"No!"

"We'll see. Okay, boys, one dip or two?"

"You said you'd let him go if I told you everything," Bobbi shouted.

"But, my little sexy agent, I don't think you have told me everything. After a couple of dips, maybe Dan will remember."

Despite Bobbi's pleas, Rita hit the *down* button. Dan descended into the vat. He writhed in pain, but his underwear was still on. It was below his hips on the back, but still high in the front.

"One more time, Mrs. Boss," shouted one of the men.

She immersed Dan for the third time. It didn't appear he was in as much pain, maybe because the water had cooled somewhat.

Rita pushed the *up* button. Dan rose up quickly to the top of the hoist. His shorts stayed in the vat. The men in the room laughed at who lost the bet. She rolled the hoist to the side and lowered him to the floor. He collapsed only to his knees, because he was held up by the cable. Jake removed the gag. Dan could do nothing but moan. He was pink up to his nipples and a bright reddish pink from his waist down. Rita hadn't immersed Dan completely the last two times.

Rita turned to Bobbi and said, "Now, my smart sexy agent, it is your turn. We do women a little different. This was the first man I have had the opportunity to cleanse, so I decided to let the men decide how to do it. I believe before we are finished, we will know everything. Is Willie back yet?"

Just as she spoke, Willie walked through the door.

"Have you taken care of Mr. Puck, Willie?"

"Yes, ma'am. I caught him thinking I was just driving down the road with the endloader. I turned quickly and pushed his Jeep into the woods. I smashed it against a tree. I don't know if I killed him or not, but I could see his leg sticking out from underneath the car. He is pinned there for a while. When they find him, it will be too late to save these guys."

"Good job! Now, I need you to cut someone's hair, and after you're done, I want you to load this pair's vehicle onto the wrecker. Park it at the dock and pull the dock curtains across so the others can't see what we are doing."

Willie crossed the room and grabbed the hair clippers.

"Willie was a barber in the Army. He is an expert at giving quick haircuts," Rita told Bobbi with a chuckle in her voice. "But first, you need a cocktail, Mrs. Cop. Rosa, please do the honors."

Rosa quickly brought Bobbi a small glass of some kind of liquid. Bobbi refused to open her mouth. Rosa pinched Bobbi's nose and held it until Bobbi opened her mouth and gasped for air. Rosa tossed the liquid in her mouth. Bobbi gagged.

"Here, take this glass of water and wash it down," Rosa ordered.

Rosa held the glass to Bobbi's lips and helped her sip some water. Bobbi screwed up her face.

"It tastes awful," Bobbi hollered.

Willie stepped forward. He put his hand on Bobbi's head and tipped it forward.

Bobbi didn't fight him. She knew it would only be worse if she resisted. Reluctantly, she let him bend her head down as she closed her eyes and winced.

Willie clipped her neck and continued up over her head. Bobbi's hair went flying. In three minutes, he was finished. Bobbi's head was as smooth as a cue ball. Willie quickly swept up the clippings and deposited them in a garbage can. He didn't say a word.

Rita knew he did not like being present at cleansings.

Rosa and Freddy untied bald-headed Bobbi. Bobbi instinctively rubbed her hand on her shaved head. She had seen people with bald heads after chemo treatments for cancer and always wondered what it felt like. Now she knew.

Rita stepped closer to the chair and said, "Follow me, Ms. Bobbi."

Bobbi slid out of her chair and walked behind the woman. She could see no chance for escape, and decided to follow orders for a while. She also knew Dan was still vulnerable.

"Stand here on this piece of carpet," Rita ordered. "Lights, please."

The lights in the room dimmed, but a spotlight was turned on over Bobbi's head. It was like being on a stage. She could not see well beyond the brilliant eye-piercing light.

Rita approached Bobbi close enough for Bobbi to see her.

Rita said, "Mrs. Dorman, I see you have good taste in clothing. They must pay well at the DCI. You are wearing a denim jacket found only in the better stores and not in Walmart. May I ask how much you paid for it?"

"I think about fifty dollars," Bobbi replied, wondering why Rita was asking such a dumb question.

"You're about a size six, aren't you, Bobbi?"

"Yes."

"Rosa, do we have any girls who can wear a size six?"

Rosa answered, "Yes, several. I'll give you $25.00 for it."

"Fine. Bobbi, please remove your jacket and give it to Rosa. She just bought it."

Bobbi complied. Now, she was beginning to realize what was about to happen to her. Rita, aka Mrs. Ping was going to auction the clothes right off of her body. Evidently, she had no intention to return them to her.

From the darkened room, a voice shouted, "I'll give you $10.00 for her blouse. My girlfriend is a size six."

Rosa butted in, "That's my size. It would be a little tight in the bust, but I'll bid $20.00."

"You'd be tight in a sweatshirt, Rosa," someone called with a snicker.

"Twenty it is! Please remove your blouse and give it to Rosa. Jake, you keep track of what everyone owes."

All of a sudden, Bobbi felt as though she was going to vomit.

She held her stomach and said, "Mrs. Johnson, I'm going to throw up. Can I go to the bathroom?"

"By all means, my lovely kitten. We don't want a mess on the floor. The toilet is over by the wall."

Bobbi hurried to the porcelain, knelt down, and vomited. She heaved until she thought her stomach was coming up. Finally, she rested. Rosa handed her another glass of water to wash her mouth out. Bobbi did and spit the remainder in the toilet bowl. Rosa flushed the toilet.

"Now, come back to the light, lovely kitten, and we will continue," Mrs. Johnson ordered.

"I'll give you fifty for her jeans."

"Sold. Please take off your jeans, Bobbi."

Bobbi had suspected this would happen, since they had stripped Dan. There was nothing she could do. She unsnapped her jeans and slid them down and off. A man's hand appeared to collect the garment. Bobbi took a deep breath and stared straight ahead. She was not going to let the audience know she was trembling inside. She was wearing a camisole, so she wasn't completely naked yet.

"I'll give you twenty for the camisole."

"Thirty."

"Thirty-five."

"Sold."

Bobbi didn't have to be told what to do. She lifted the camisole over her head and handed it away. She looked over at Dan. He was watching now. His pain had either lessened or he was just tolerating it. He said nothing, because what could he say? Their captors had the upper hand at this moment. The only out they had would be if the raid would be moved up in time.

Rita paced around Bobbi standing in the spotlight. She teased Bobbi by running her fingers up and down her sides. She pulled Bobbi's underpants away from Bobbi's body and peered down inside. Rita leered at Bobbi. She stepped behind Bobbi and tugged at her bra. She ran her hand again on the lace side panels of Bobbi's hipster panties. She stepped back to view the almost naked woman standing in front of her. Rita seemingly enjoyed what she saw.

"This lingerie is from Victoria's Secret. Very expensive. The bra and panties will go as a set. What am I bid?"

A husky man's voice came from the back, "I'll give you $100.00, and I get to take them off."

"Sold!!"

Bobbi could hear heavy footsteps approach her. A big face appeared out of the darkened room. It was the man Rita called 'El

Lobo.' He put his index finger on the strip of fabric between her breasts. He tugged enough to cause Bobbi to move forward a bit.

The big man spoke, "You say, Mrs. Ping, this is really good stuff. It would a shame to tear it into pieces. A couple of weeks ago I arrested a couple of Mexican cuties. I planted some drugs on one of them so I could demand a strip search. The kind sheriff sent the only lady cop on duty on a wild goose chase. Therefore, I and my fellow officers had to do the search. One of the gals was a little feisty. I just had to tear her underwear off. It wasn't even good for rags. Rosa, there is a little gal in the back room with a funny looking pinkie finger. She likes my mustache. She is about this lady cop's size. Don't you think?"

Rosa answered, "You mean Lola? Yes, I think she is a size six or smaller."

"Good, I'll give her this stuff from Victoria Secret. Tell her it's from Lobo."

Lobo looked at Bobbi and snarled, "Take it off! But you do it. I want to save your pretty little bra and panties for Lola."

Bobbi closed her eyes and reached behind her back, but shaking fingers couldn't unhook the clasps.

Lobo put his ugly face close to Bobbi's and screamed again, "Take off your pretty underwear, now."

Still Bobbi fumbled. Now her stomach was beginning to act up.

"I can't do it. I need help!" she cried, her voice quivering.

Rosa stepped forward and said, "Here, I'll help the liar."

Rosa easily unhooked Bobbi's bra. Lobo pulled it off with his finger.

"That's better. Now, off with the shorts, uh...panties."

Bobbi complied and slowly slid her panties to the floor. She stepped out of them, then bent down to give her underwear to the huge man. She noticed he was giving her the once over from top to bottom.

"Turn around, Miss," he ordered.

Bobbi turned.

"Now sideways."

She followed orders.

"That's enough, Lobo. We haven't time for this sightseeing," Rita reminded him.

He patted Bobbi on her bare bottom and left. Bobbi stared straight ahead. She felt like a store mannequin with no hair or clothes, but she was alive.

A spasm raked her abdomen again. She didn't ask permission this time, and she ran over to the stool and sat. It was humiliating to be seated naked on a toilet with several people, especially men, watching. Her bowels released their contents. She held her stomach to quiet the spasms. Rosa went to a cabinet, removed a can of air freshener, and sprayed the room. The men laughed.

Rita walked over to the humiliated Bobbi and said, "Are you done crapping? We haven't got much time to finish."

She reached behind Bobbi and flushed the toilet. Bobbi searched for some toilet tissue. There wasn't any.

Rita laughed and said, "You won't need any wipes. I'll take care of that."

Rosa helped Bobbi to a standing position. She could see Bobbi was getting weak. She walked her back to the light. Now, the rug was removed, and Bobbi was standing on a huge floor drain. The steel grate hurt her bare feet. The light moved higher. Rita reached above Bobbi's head with a hook and pulled the handle hanging there. A gush of water cascaded over Bobbi's body. The thrust of the water flow was so violent, it made her gasp for air. There were two blasts of water which came from beneath the grate. They thoroughly washed her bottom areas. It only lasted a few seconds, but it was cold water. As the water dripped off, Bobbi could hear something being rolled across the floor, but she couldn't see what. The bright light limited her vision. She was getting a little chilly, so she folded her arms across her chest.

"No! No!" Rita scolded. "I want your hands and arms at your sides where I can see them. I want you totally exposed and humiliated. It is part of my ritual. You will do exactly as I ask."

Bobbi dropped her arms. The funny thing was there were no whistles or cat calls as she stood there naked. Everyone was silent.

"Lights up, please."

The light in the room returned to normal. Bobbi's eyes adjusted to the light. To her right was a metal table on casters. It was parked over another large floor drain. Lobo was standing at the table with her underwear hanging out of his rear pocket. Rosa was now dressed in a plastic coat and boots.

"Rosa, put the apron on her," Rita ordered.

Rosa wrapped a heavy plastic apron around Bobbi's waist, only she put it on backwards. Bobbi's backside was covered, but not her front. Bobbi tried to pull the plastic together in front.

"That won't be necessary, my little kitten. The apron will be removed soon, and you'll be naked again. I must say you are in great shape. You must work out a lot. Please follow me over to the table." Rita ordered.

Bobbi followed like a puppy. She stood at the table facing Rita.

"Turn around and face Lobo. He likes to see women's boobs.

Now put your arms out straight."

Bobbi followed her instructions. Lobo smiled as he put heavy cloth gauntlets around each wrist and secured them with the commercial grade of Velcro. To the gauntlets were tied nylon ropes, and he threaded the opposite end through a couple rings near the bottom of the legs on the table.

"Bend over," Rita continued.

Bobbi started to bend, but before she was touching the top of the table, Lobo pulled her down tightly against the top. Her arms were stretched up to the top of the table. Her toes barely touched the floor. Her chest was flattened against the cold stainless steel. She cocked her head to one side so she could breathe.

"Clamp her legs," Rita told Rosa.

Rosa grabbed each leg and secured a cuff around each ankle. The cuffs were attached to ratchets. Rosa cranked the ratchets out about six inches. Bobbi's feet were off the floor. Her feet stuck out beyond the table leg. Bobbi's legs were spread wide. She could see Rita downing a plastic coat, gloves, and boots.

"Is she going to pour hot water over me?" Bobbi wondered.

Lobo rolled the table back to the drain and spotlight. Rosa carried a bucket of water over to the table and set it on the floor.

Rita said, "Is everyone ready? We shall begin the cleansing of this untruthful woman. May we cleanse every lie from her body so she can be free. We have cleansed the outside of her body. Now, we must do the inside. May the truth gods be with us."

"Rosa, will you get us started?"

Bobbi could feel Rosa raise the heavy apron over her back. Next, she felt a slimy cream being applied between her butt cheeks.

"Put plenty of veterinary lubricate on her ass. She'll need it," ordered Rita.

"Now, put the fill tube in the hot vat."

"You're going to use the vat water?" Rosa asked with astonishment.

"Sure, this little lady needs a thorough cleansing," Rita chuckled.

Rita turned and lifted a huge enema syringe from a leather case. She pulled the plunger back and filled the syringe. She rammed the syringe into Bobbi's anal opening and squeezed. The hot acidic liquid streamed into Bobbi's bowels. At first, Bobbi was too shocked to scream. Her eyes just bugged out. The pain was ferocious. She felt as if her gut was on fire.

Rita hurried and pulled the plunger back, refilling her syringe automatically. She repeated with a second intrusion into Bobbi's bowels.

This time, Bobbi screamed and cried, "Stop, stop, please stop."

But Rita didn't stop. She drew a short fill and rammed it into Bobbi again. Bobbi thought she was about to explode. Her lower abdomen swelled. The pressure increased. Her body told her to get rid of this hot burning substance. It began to react.

"Quick, pull the apron over her legs. We don't want crap all over the room."

Rosa flipped the apron over Bobbi's spread legs. Bobbi's bowels erupted. A very foul smelling stream of yellowish-brown fluid squirted out. It coated the inside of the apron and gushed to the floor. There were three or four explosions. Bobbi held back her screaming as best she could. The acid ate at her skin between her legs.

"One more time," Rita announced, "but now I'll draw water

from this bucket."

"Oh, please, not another one. Please, I beg you, please," Bobbi cried out.

Bobbi felt ice cold water being injected into her. Then out came clear water as Bobbi's bowels expelled the liquid.

Rita began to reload.

Dan screamed, "Not again. Don't you have any mercy? What is it you think she didn't tell you?"

"When is the raid? What time? Is it today?"

"Yes, yes, it is today. The state police, the DCI, and the immigration people are meeting in Wapello at 10:00. That's all we know. I swear."

"Well, thank you, Danny boy. Now I will finish my job and clear out of here."

"Finish?"

"Oh, yes, I have to see if I did a good job. If the fluid comes out clear, we will be finished."

She shoved the syringe into Bobbi again. The cold water was too much for Bobbi's system. She groaned and passed out. Her body went limp. The cold fluid didn't squirt out; it dribbled out and down her legs, but it was clear. A yellow stream flowed from between Bobbi's legs. Her body was letting every liquid go.

"Wash her down, Rosa. We have to be out of here by 10:00, and it's already 9:15."

Rosa unbuckled the apron and laid it on the floor. She reached for a garden hose and sprayed Bobbi's rear and legs. Lobo released her arms. She moaned. Freddy gingerly released the ratchet cuffs, which held her ankles. He never felt pity for the other cleansing victims, but the diabolical way Mrs. Boss handled this woman was scary.

Bobbi started to slide from the table like a wet dishrag slipping from the edge of a dishpan. Only Lobo's ropes kept her from hitting her head on the floor. He dragged the unconscious woman away from the drain. Jake rolled the vat closer to the drain and opened the petcock. The water gushed out and covered the floor where Bobbi stood. The rush of water washed every trace of the cleansing down the drain. The dripping apron was thrown in a waste container.

"Jake, go and get Melanie. Lock the girls in their room," ordered Rita.

Jake left and soon returned with Melanie. She looked at Bobbi lying motionless on the floor. She stared at Dan kneeling under the hoist. He was wearing only his T-shirt and was turning red.

"What did you do? Kill her? Are you going to kill him, too?" Melanie exclaimed.

"No, she isn't dead, yet. She just had a super cleansing. She was a very bad liar and needed special attention. The truth gods spoke to me to clean her with acid," Rita explained.

"You and your goddamn truth gods. This is the third one you've killed. It's on the morning news. The cops found a dead girl in a meat tub in Sioux City and the tub came from here. You're in big trouble with your truth temple, Mrs. Ping. You'd better get the girls out of here, pronto. Another thing, I quit. I don't want to be part of this murdering bunch."

"You can't quit!" Rita screamed back.

"Yes, I can, and I will."

Melanie started to head for the door. Jake blocked her exit.

Rita changed her tone of voice and said, "Okay, Melanie, you may go, but will you help me load the girls? You can ride the bus into town, and Jake will drop you off at Emma's."

Rita looked at Jake and winked.

"You'll be glad to take Melanie home, won't you, Jake? She lives just past the bridge on the right. You know the one with the concrete abutments."

Without stopping to take a breath, Rita called everyone to the center of the room.

"Willie and Freddy, you drive the wrecker with their pickup and these two inside the back to the end of the levee on Two Mile Creek. Dump them and the truck into the creek. With a little luck, the current will be strong enough in the spring to carry the truck to the river. The cops won't find them for days. Don't lollygag around to see if it floats. Get out of there as fast as you can. Freddy, you take Willie to his home in Mediapolis and then deliver the wrecker to Peoria. Go to 652 South Second Avenue. Big Al will be there to help you hide the truck. You wait there until I text you. Do you understand?"

"Yes, Mrs. Boss."

"Lobo, you carry the lady to the pickup and put her inside. Freddy, you walk the fried one out. Use a cattle prod, if necessary.

Lobos, after you dump the woman, get the bus and bring it around to the loading dock. Jake, Rosa, and Melanie will have the girls ready. You and Jake take the girls to Jake's place for the night. I have to go home and clean up. JJ has a debate in Burlington, and I have to be there. I will text you after we get home. He goes to bed early. I'll stay up and find a place for the girls to stay until the heat is off. Now does everybody understand their job?"

Lobo spoke, "Isn't there something we can wrap the woman up in? Heck, she may take another crap, and I don't want it all over me."

Rosa came to the rescue, and said, "Here's a small plastic tarp some farmer left. You can roll her up in it."

She laid the tarp on the floor next to Bobbi and rolled the unconscious woman onto it. Lobo wrapped it around her and lifted her onto his shoulder like a bag of feed. Bobbi moaned. Freddy unhooked Dan's harness from the hoist. He told Dan to stand. Dan tried, but it was painful. Freddy reached over to a counter and grabbed a cattle prod. He stuck it on Dan's rear and pushed the button. Buzz went the prod. Dan jumped. He moved as fast as his boiled feet could carry him.

Willie opened the door to the outside dock. He had pulled the heavy curtains across the dock to shield any events going on from prying eyes. Dan crawled into the back of his pickup. Lobo followed closely and slid Bobbi alongside him. Willie shut the tailgate and rear door on the topper cover. Freddy had the wrecker running and ready. As soon as they pulled away from the dock, Lobo backed the bus in. Rosa led the girls out with their luggage. Lobo then opened the rear door of the bus and tossed in their luggage, which were mostly duffel bags. The girls entered through the front door. Jake settled into the driver's seat. Rosa took her seat near the rear of the bus and Lobo sat behind the driver. Melanie was the last to step aboard.

Jake ordered, "You stand in the door well, Melanie. I want you getting off in a hurry. I don't want to have to wait for you to come forward."

Melanie didn't question the request. She was getting out of the mess anyway. The bus picked up speed and headed for Wapello. They would take the side streets as much as possible. Just before the city limits sign, the road passed over a small creek called Two Skunk Creek. Most creeks were bridged by culverts, but this one had a concrete bridge, which was left over from the days when this was the main road in and out of Wapello.

Jake looked at Lobo in the rearview mirror and nodded. He held up three fingers indicating on the count of three. One, two, three, he opened the door. Lobo pushed the surprised Melanie out. He watched as she rolled on the pavement and hit the bridge abutment with her hips. Her body flipped around and crashed into a post holding the guard rail. They were over the bridge and roaring away too fast to see if she was still alive. Rosa and the girls said nothing.

Jake continued driving through town. He had to drive on Highway 61 to get across the river. Cautiously, he pulled onto the highway. He met two highway patrol cars coming at him, but they drove past. Evidently, they were not looking for a black luxury bus. Jake turned off the highway toward his home. He hit a button on the dash. It opened the gate. He drove through and closed it behind the bus. He stopped outside the front door.

Before he let his passengers disembark, he warned them, "I want everyone to stay inside. Don't try to escape. After I put the bus in the barn, I will let the dogs loose. They are trained to attack anyone outside the house. Do you understand?"

There was a chorus of yes's.

Everyone hurried inside. Lobo guarded the door.

The last one to leave the plant was Rita. She didn't take time to change out of her Chinese outfit. She would be home before JJ and he'd never know. She got into her BMW and headed toward the lagoon. She planned to take the back roads to avoid the cops, and she figured she could be home in twenty minutes. She was showering when JJ arrived.

"Where have you been, honey?" he asked as he poked his head inside the bathroom door.

"I've been at the gym working out with the ladies. I just hurried home, because they always have juice or coffee afterwards."

It satisfied JJ, so he closed the door and returned to his office.

* * *

Before Jake reached his exotic home, and before Rita reached the county line, two mushroom hunters, Jane and George, were walking along Two Skunk Creek. It was early for mushrooms, but they thought maybe the warm weather might have just awakened a few morels. Jane spotted an overturned car or Jeep-like car resting against a tree just ahead of them. She didn't think much about it, until she saw steam rising from the front of the vehicle. They walked closer but were cautious.

A moan came from inside the vehicle. George spied a leg sticking out from underneath the car. Jane peered into the windshield and saw a man covered with blood. He was trying to grab the steering wheel to free himself. George tried to right the car, but it wouldn't budge.

He stuck his head inside the passenger's side window and said, "Hang on there, sir. We'll get some help as soon as possible. Don't move."

Jane dialed 911.

"Emergency, how may I help you?"

"This is Jane Wood. My husband and I just found a man trapped in his wrecked car. He needs help."

"What's your location?"

"We're somewhere along Two Skunk Creek. We can't be far from the Acme Packing plant, because we can hear it. There's a path where something pushed the car back here. I'll give my husband the cell phone, and he can walk back through the path and tell you more. I'll stay with the car."

George walked back through the brush until he reached the road. He still had the dispatcher on the phone.

"I've come to a paved road. I'm about one block from Gate 2. I can wait here until someone arrives."

"I'll have someone there very soon. The town is crawling with cops right now."

Almost simultaneously, an electrician, Tyler Koen, was returning to Wapello after a call from the plant. He needed some more parts to replace a blown breaker. He spotted what looked like a body next to the bridge over Two Skunk Creek. He pulled to a stop and got out to check. It was a body all right. It was a woman. She was still alive, but barely breathing. It looked like she had fallen or maybe she had been pushed out of a moving vehicle. Her face was scraped and scratched. One leg on her slacks was ripped to the knee and her leg stuck out at a horrible angle. She was bleeding from her mouth and nose. Tyler knelt beside the injured lady.

"I'll get you help as soon as I can, lady. I won't leave you," he said as he dialed 911.

"Emergency."

"This is Tyler Koen of Koen Electric. I'm just returning from the Acme Plant and I found a woman lying alongside the road. She's in pretty bad shape. She needs an ambulance in a hurry."

"Geez!" exclaimed the dispatcher, "I just sent an ambulance out that way. A couple of mushroomers found a man trapped in his car. I better get the sheriff out there, pronto. Stay with her, Tyler. Help is on the way."

"Please get my head uphill," the lady whispered to Tyler.

Although Tyler knew you are not supposed to move an injured person, he slid his arm under her head and gently pulled her up the slope.

The lady opened her eyes and studied Tyler.

"Tyler? Tyler Koen? It's me, Melanie Osgood, from Gramma Emma's Café."

Tyler couldn't believe his eyes or ears. Melanie was so beat up, she was virtually unrecognizable.

"If I don't make it, tell the cops the girls are at Jake Johnson's place."

Melanie passed out in Tyler's arms. He could hear the ambulance's siren wailing in the distance.

The first response truck stopped. One look at Melanie, and they knew it was more than they could handle. They called the ambulance and asked them to stop here first. They would continue on. The EMTs from the ambulance slid to a stop next to Tyler. One of them had his stethoscope on and ready. He checked Melanie's chest. He felt her wrist for a pulse. Sadly, he looked at Tyler.

"She's dead, Tyler. There's nothing we can do. Could you wait for the next ambulance? We have another call just ahead. I hope the results are better."

Tyler shook his head, yes. He had tears in his eyes. He had never seen a person die before. The EMT patted him on the shoulder and returned to his vehicle.

The first response truck stopped when they saw George waving. He led them back through the brush to the car. Immediately, a fireman called for the brush fire truck. It could navigate the rough terrain and brush with its big cattle bumper and four-wheel drive. The EMTs waded through the brush carrying their equipment. With enough men now, the firemen could roll the car back on its wheels. The techs started IV's and checked Ron's vitals. He was alive although in much pain. Being so close to town, the brush truck arrived quickly. It pushed a path to the accident and returned to the ambulance to pick up the cart.

By checking his wallet, one of the EMTs discovered who they were working on. He was a friend of everyone, and they knew the situation was urgent. Luckily, he was not pinned tight. They slowly removed him from his car and tied him to the cart. Then they placed him in the brush truck's bed. The brush vehicle plowed its way back through the undergrowth to the ambulance. Ron was quickly transferred to the ambulance and he was on his way to the hospital. Because all the deputies were committed to the raid, they were slow in getting to the scene. Finally, when one did arrive, she was apologetic for being late. She wanted to interview Jane and George about how they discovered the accident and also, she wanted to thank them for their quick response.

When she had finished, Jane asked the deputy if she would inform them about the condition of the detective once he was treated at a hospital. The deputy assured her, and she told them Ron would probably like to meet them. Jane and George said they would be available when that time came.

It was after ten o'clock. The raid was in full swing. Immigration was entering the front gate with several state police. Once inside the office, they asked the office personnel to stand away from their desks. Nothing was to be touched on their computers. All of the office personnel were told to gather in the lunchroom.

Two agents entered the kill floor with four state police officers. Frank Hughes, the real plant manager met them. They showed Frank their credentials and asked if he'd shut down the plant.

"I can't do that right now. We're in the middle of a shift. Once a shift is started, it cannot be stopped until the last animal is processed."

"We're here to check ID's. We are only concerned with illegal immigrants working here," said an agent, "but I realize the problem. We will secure every exit and check each employee as they leave. You will be able to stop the next shift, won't you?"

"Yes, but with some difficulty. Cattle are already arriving for the next kill. I can hold them for twelve hours and deny any more deliveries for tomorrow. The government will compensate the plant for this inconvenience and loss of time and product, won't they?"

"Yes, if we find there are fewer than 10 percent illegals."

While the immigration agents were dealing with the inside, the sheriff and the Wapello Police secured the gates. Playing on the confession of Rick, four DCI agents led by Captain Stender stormed the dock at Gate 3. They entered the autopsy room and found the floor still wet. The lights were still burning but nothing else. The second room was covered with plush carpeting and was also vacant. In the middle of the room was a throne-like chair. Behind the big chair was a plastic sack. Captain Stender peered inside and saw two handguns. He had one of the agents put on gloves and lift one of the weapons. On the butt of one pistol were the initials R. O. S. He instantly knew those initials stood for Roberta Olive Stroud. Bobbi and Dan were here earlier. They opened what looked like the dorm room and it was also cleared. There were just beds, tables, and clothes strewn around as if they had to leave in a hurry.

Bobbi and Dan were nowhere to be found. They were either still being held captive or worst case scenario, disposed of. Captain Stroud started backtracking. He knew Ron had been found in his car and was gravely injured. He also knew he had passed an accident scene where a woman was being attended to. He reached the second scene just as the man who had discovered the victim was leaving.

"Did she say anything before she died?" asked the captain.

Tyler answered, "Only that the girls were at Jake Johnson's."

"Do you know where that is?"

"Oh, yes, sir, everyone in Louisa County knows about Mr. Johnson's house. I've even been there. I helped wire the place. It's just about a mile north of the river, back in the woods."

The captain thanked Tyler and called for more help. Hopefully, Bobbi and Dan were being held with the girls.

* * *

The wrecker carrying Bobbi and Dan was traveling down Highway 99 heading for Oakville. Dan knew the fate of him and his wife. Despite his burning skin, he had to do something. Nature has a way of pumping adrenaline to make one forget one's pain when preservation of life is more important.

Dan pulled his legs up as close to his chest as he could and brought his cuffed hands around underneath his feet. Once that was painfully accomplished, he had to find a way to cut the cuffs. Bobbi would be no help. All she did was moan. Dan spied his tackle box above his head. He reached for it and slid it back. With his thumb, he flipped open the latch. The lid was an automatically opening type. He tried to reach his filet knife, but it was crammed at the bottom. His first choice was a set of side cutter pliers. With his fingers, he maneuvered the pliers so the jaws were over the plastic cuff connection. He placed the palm of his other hand on the handles and waited for a bump in the road. Bang! There it was. His hand pressed the jaws tight. They cut the thick plastic. His hands were free. He quickly cut the cuffs off.

He touched his semi-conscious wife and called softly, "Bobbi, Bobbi, can you hear me?"

Bobbi opened her eyes and smiled. She tried to move, but the tarp was snuggly wrapped around her.

"What? Where? How?" she asked.

"We're in the back of our pickup. They are going to dump us in the river. We have to be able to escape before we drown. I'll help you loosen this tarp."

She wiggled and squirmed and Dan pulled until Bobbi was free of the fabric. She had just about forgotten the pain in her gut until a spasm hit her.

She curled up in pain and screamed, "I'll never make it, hon."

"Yes, you will. I'll help you."

The wrecker slowed and turned off the highway onto a gravel road. The ride was getting rougher. The metal ribs on the floor rubbed Dan's burning skin. He gritted his teeth. It wasn't long before the truck slowed again. This time, the road was very rough and Bobbi bounced clear off the truck bed. She reached for Dan and hugged him. The wrecker slowed a third time and stopped. Dan threw the tarp over Bobbi again. He put his hands behind his back and acted as if he was still handcuffed. The last thing he wanted his captors to know was that they were free of their bonds. The wrecker bed rose. The angle of the pickup bed steepened. Dan braced his feet against the tailgate. Bobbi slid backward and lay against Dan's chest.

A voice shouted from outside, "How you two doing in there?"

A face appeared in the rear window. It was Freddy's.

He smiled as he said, "Well, have a good time with the fishes. Too bad your hands are tied, or you could swim with them. They tell me the water is cold. Sorry, I didn't pick a warmer day. I opened the windows of the cab to let the water in faster. I don't want to prolong your agony. Good-bye."

With that being said, there was a bang as the coupling snapped open. The pickup rolled down the sloping truck bed, down the levee bank, and into the cold water of Two Mile Creek. The rear of the small truck hit the water first, but the weight of the motor and the quick-filling cab swung the front end of the pickup downstream. The cab submerged, but the rear with its top cover floated above the surface for a second. Willie and Freddy, because they were obeying orders, left without watching to see if anyone surfaced.

The water poured in through the gap between the tailgate and the bed. Dan and Bobbi struggled to turn around inside the bed. Bobbi shed the tarp. There was a significant air bubble still in the topper. They knew they had a chance if they could get the back window open.

Dan said, "We'll take a big breath of air, and then I'll push the window up. Once in the current, it should stay open. We will swim out the window to the surface. We'll go on the count of three. You count."

Bobbi counted, "One, two, three!"

They both took a deep breath. Dan turned the latch and pushed the rear window open. He was right. The current in the creek caught the window and flipped it up over the back of the truck. The water poured in. They waited just a second for the pressure to equalize and swam through the opening. It seemed like forever, but actually, it was only seconds before they broke the surface. Bobbi broke first. She gasped and searched the water for Dan.

She screamed, "Dan, Dan, where are you? Don't leave me."

Dan surfaced just behind her. He grabbed her arm.

"Come on. We have to get out of this water, or we will freeze," Dan warned her.

They splashed to the opposite bank from where they entered. As they came near the shore, they could feel the bottom. It was deep mud, but it saved them from thrashing around. Dan pushed Bobbi onto the grassy levee bank. She turned and planted her feet into the sod and reached for his hand. With her as an anchor, he hoisted himself onto the grass. They lay back on the dry grass and sighed with relief.

It was warm, because this bank faced the sun and the dry grass insulated their cold bodies from the chilly ground. The sun felt good. Bobbi closed her eyes just to rest a minute. The cold water had zapped all the strength from her muscles. Dan lay beside her and watched her breathe. Her pain seemed to be subsiding for a moment. He reached up and touched her bald head. As he patted it, Bobbi awoke. She slid over and kissed her very pink husband.

He said, "We have to get going. We can't stay here very long, or I'll become one big water blister and I don't know what is happening to your insides. There has to be a road or farmhouse not too far away. If I had some matches, I'd set this dry grass on fire. That would bring attention, but I didn't have any pockets to carry any matches, so I guess we are out of luck there," said Dan trying to lighten their dire situation.

"But we are alive, and we have each other," reminded Bobbi.

"Let's crawl to the top of the levee and see what our situation is," Dan replied.

They literally crawled by hanging on to the dry grass clumps to reach the top of the levee. Dan stood and looked to his right. The levee was straight for one hundred yards and then dog-legged to the right following the drainage ditch. The far edge of the field was at least one-half mile away. To his left, the levee continued for a quarter mile and then turned left for a short distance before turning left again. The levee on the other side was a road.

Dan could see a road sign. He followed the levee and there was their salvation. A red pickup truck was sitting on the top of the levee beside a driveway that led down into the field. If they could reach the truck, it might have the keys in it. Farmers have the tendency to leave keys somewhere in their vehicles.

Dan helped Bobbi stand and pointed to the pickup. She shook her head that she understood, but it looked a long way off. It was over a half of a mile if they walked the top of the levee, but straight across the chisel-plowed field was only about 250 yards. The close way was rough with clumps of root balls and cut corn stalks. It did seem to be the right way though. A hike of a short mile through tall grass would be difficult. Bobbi coughed and she grasped her stomach. More bloody fluid trickled down her legs. A large black and red blood clot landed on the ground.

"We've got to get you to a hospital and fast," he exclaimed. "Let's try the direct route. I think my feet will hold out."

They slid down the grassy bank to the field. It was more difficult than they thought. The root balls did not crumble, the surface was uneven, and the splintered corn stalks cut and poked at their bare feet. Bobbi had another spasm. Dan held her up. They stumbled out from the field edge about fifty yards.

Bobbi clutched her stomach again and kneeled on the rough surface.

"You go on and leave me here. I can't go another step," she begged.

"I can't leave you here. What if the truck doesn't start, or even if it does, I can't drive it across this rough field. We'll just wait a bit, and maybe you can go a little further."

Dan pulled his dirty T-shirt over his head and was about to give it to Bobbi, when the roar of an engine with a high-pitched whine of a turbo charger caught his attention. He looked right and around the dog-leg in the levee charged a yellow rubber tracked tractor pulling a huge implement which smoothed out the ground behind it. The dust flowing out behind the implement was blowing high in the air.

Dan could see the driver inside the cab was concentrating on the edge of the field and not looking where they were standing. He waved his T-shirt. He didn't dare let the tractor pass them by. It might be a long time before he returned.

In desperation, he reached down and grabbed a cornstalk and its root ball. He threw the ball underhanded like a softball. It arched high in the air and came down right on the top on the hood of the yellow tractor with a bang. The dirt exploded and showered the cab glass with dirt. The startled driver turned and spotted a pair of naked people, one standing, and one sitting in his field. He stopped the big tractor and idled the engine. Dan could see him studying the pair of humans. Dan started to limp back toward the yellow machine. The door to the cab opened, and the operator climbed out on the opposite side. The cab sat high. There were three steps to the ground level.

As the driver appeared in front of his tractor, Dan called,

"Can you help us? Please, can you help us?"

Dan could tell the driver was a young man, maybe in his twenties. He was an extra-large size, but not fat, just a big person. He probably played football or was a wrestler in high school or college. He was wearing a plaid flannel shirt and well-worn blue jeans with several grease stains on them. He wiped his hands on the jeans as he approached Dan.

"Who are you, and what are you doing out here?" he asked as he got closer.

"We're two detectives from the Department of Criminal Investigation of Iowa. The one on the ground is my wife and partner. She is bleeding internally. She needs medical attention right away," Dan told him.

"How did you get in such a bad shape?"

"We were kidnapped and the people who detained us were criminals. The leader was a lady and she was diabolical. She not only ran a prostitution ring, but she claimed to be a cult leader. She dipped me into a vat of scalding water and then proceeded to inject the same water into my wife's lower internal organs via an enema syringe. My wife was scalded internally. You've got to help us!" Dan pleaded.

"My name is Trent Hammon. I live just three miles from here. Stay right here. Don't move. I'll get my cell phone. It is inside the cab. Then, I'll see how I can be of help."

Trent ran around to the opposite side and climbed back into the cab. He fumbled around to find his phone. He held it up for Dan to see. He started to climb out, but he stopped. He grabbed his coveralls and a hooded sweatshirt. As he hurried back, he dialed 911. He handed Dan the coveralls.

"Can you get these on? I'm sure they'll be big enough around, but they might be short."

Trent helped Dan walk to the tractor, so he could lean on the fender. Dan gingerly pulled the coverall on over his fiery skin. The cloth rubbed him a bit, but the warmth and the covering of his bare body was comforting.

A voice spoke on the phone, "Emergency, how may I help you?"

Trent answered, "This is Trent Hammon from Oakville. I have two people with me who need medical attention. They claim to be detectives for the DCI. They are badly burned. I'll let you talk to the man. He is in better shape. He can tell you the details. I have to attend to his partner."

"Wait, where are you?"

"Oh, I almost forgot. I'm four miles south of Oakville on Highway 99, turn left on 250th Avenue until you come to Five Mile Creek Road. It's about a mile. Follow Five Mile Creek to the end. I'm about a quarter of a mile from the river."

Trent handed the phone to Dan. He walked over to Bobbi, who was still sitting on the ground.

Reaching her, he asked, "Can you stand?"

Bobbi tried to stand, but her legs wouldn't hold her. Trent knelt beside her and helped her stand up. He put his arm around her shoulders and held her. He could tell Bobbi was in a daze.

"I brought this sweatshirt for you to put on. It will keep you warm."

He slipped the shirt over her arms. It was very big. His hands trembled as he zipped the zipper on the naked woman. It covered Bobbi all the way to her knees.

She whispered, "Thanks," and then collapsed again.

Trent caught her and lifted her into his strong arms. She

weakly threw her arms around his neck. Trent placed her on the wide fender alongside Dan.

"I explained the situation to the dispatcher. The Oakville Fire Department is on its way. I also pleaded with her to call Iowa City and ask for a Medi Vac helicopter. She told me she doesn't have the authority to ask for a helicopter. The fire chief or head medic is responsible for the call, but she would put in an alert to the helicopter crew. Next, I told her to call Captain Stender of the DCI in Des Moines. She is having her assistant call. It seems like there has been a lot going on in the area, law enforcement-wise. She asked me to stay on the phone until the medics can get here. Would you like to talk to her?" Dan asked.

"Yes."

Trent took over the phone conversation.

"I'm going to load this couple into my tractor cab and drive to the road. There's a wide spot in the road about one-half mile away. The helicopter can land there. How soon will they be arriving?"

"Firemen in about fifteen. The helicopter could be there about thirty minutes after they are notified by the fire chief."

"We'll be waiting. Is there a possibility they can launch the copter earlier? The lady is in a very bad way."

"We're checking into that request."

Trent handed the phone back to Dan and said, "Man, your feet are bloody. Let me give you my socks."

Trent sat on the rubber track and removed his shoes and socks. He handed his socks to Dan and put his bare feet back into his shoes.

"You keep in contact. I'll help you climb into the cab. You sit in the buddy seat next to my seat. I'll lift your wife up to you.

You hold her until I get seated. Because of your condition, I'll hold her on my lap as we cross the field.

"Can you do that?" questioned Dan.

"Oh, yeah, I've held many of my kids on my lap while I'm driving." Then he smiled and said, "I used to hold my wife on my lap when we were dating. It's amazing what you can do with one hand when you're driving slowly."

Dan smiled back. He could imagine the petting that might have gone on. Slowly with Trent's help, Dan climbed into the cab. Trent lifted the barely conscious Bobbi up to Dan. He climbed in. Dan helped Trent position Bobbi on his lap. Dan held Bobbi's head on Trent's shoulder.

He kept repeating, "Hang in there, hon! We're going to be all right."

Trent fired up the big engine. The noise was deafening.

"Oops!" he said. "I forgot to shut the door. Can you reach the handle, Dan? I can't with your wife on my lap."

Dan stretched forward, grabbed the door handle, and pulled the door shut. The noise level dropped dramatically. Trent slowly speeded up the engine. At half-throttle, he put the tractor in reverse. As he released the clutch, he also raised the implement he was pulling. As soon as it was out of the ground, he switched to a forward gear and throttled up. The tractor leaped ahead, causing Dan to hit his head on the cab glass. Trent didn't notice. He was busy trying to operate the machine with Bobbi on his lap. He turned toward the opposite side of the field and let the implement down into working position.

He commented to Dan, "If I let this thing out of the ground, we would bounce clear across the field and probably break an axle."

Dan rubbed his head and said, "What do you call this implement?"

"It's a field finisher. It's a disk, field cultivator, and harrow all in one. Once I pass over this field, it will be ready to plant. It's forty feet wide, so I can do about twenty acres per hour."

Dan was amazed at Trent's skill, especially with Bobbi lying on his lap. They approached the drive where the pickup was sitting. Trent slowed and raised the field finisher. Once out of the ground, he stopped. He pulled another lever back and the wings of the finisher folded up straight. It was now about fourteen feet wide.

Trent announced, "I usually pin the wings tight for road travel, but today, we will let them bounce. We need to get to the combine pass as soon as possible."

"Combine pass?" asked Dan.

"Yes, it's a wide spot in the road where two combines with wide heads are able to pass each other. It is just a convenience we farmers have built for ourselves. The helicopter and the fire truck will meet us there."

Sure enough, as they drove down the gravel road, Dan could see the flashing lights of the emergency vehicles. They arrived at the combine pass at the same time. Trent let the finisher down on the roadbed and shut off the engine. One EMT, who introduced herself as Tanya, was opening the door before the motor died. She took one look at the detectives and called for a stretcher. It took Trent and two other men to carefully remove Bobbi. Tanya quickly inserted an intravenous needle into Bobbi's arm. She had one of the men hold the bottle while she checked Bobbi's vitals. She unzipped Bobbi's sweatshirt to check her heart. It was then she realized Bobbi wasn't wearing any clothes. She lifted the bottom of the shirt and could see that Bobbi was still passing blood.

"Hank, bring me a blanket and someone call for a copter. This lady is going into shock. We need to get her to a hospital and quick," she said.

A fireman brought a blanket. Four firemen carried Bobbi

away to the side of the road.

She looked at Dan and said, "What's your problem, Red?"

Dan slowly crawled out of the cab and stood on his blood-soaked stocking feet. He slowly unzipped the front of the coveralls. He stopped when he reached his waist.

Tanya pulled the zipper down a little further before she exclaimed, "Holy geez! You're no better than the lady. Get me another stretcher! This guy is going with the lady."

"Hank, where is that copter?"

"About five minutes away. The pilot says he sees our lights and warned of the dust his rotors will kick up. He said the copter crew was notified by a Captain Luther, an associate of Captain Stender, of the Department of Criminal Investigation of Iowa to leave early. He suspected the couple you have are the agents who have been missing for several hours."

Tanya barked out orders, "I just found out these two are DCI agents. They've been missing for several hours. We better take good care of them. Cover up both patients completely. Everyone else hide behind the trucks. I'll stay with the lady and hold the bottle."

Hank shot back, "I'll hold the bottle. You hold the blankets."

Soon, they could hear the whomp-whomp of the helicopter blades. It settled down in the middle of the road after stirring great clouds of dust. Two people emerged from the copter. One of the persons was a doctor, the other was a trauma nurse. The doctor quickly examined Bobbi. He determined her condition was very critical. After he checked Dan, he hurried back inside the copter and immediately was on the radio calling the hospital to be ready when they arrived. The nurse guided the firemen to where the stretchers would be placed. He asked if someone could come along and help. Tanya volunteered immediately. She gave the thumbs-up as the copter lifted off. Someone else would drive the emergency truck back to Oakville. Later, her husband, Hank, would drive to Iowa

City and pick her up. Trent looked at his watch. It was five minutes to two. He sat on the tractor track and sighed. He pulled a big red handkerchief out of his pocket and wiped his brow. He looked a little pale.

"Are you going to be all right?" someone asked.

"I'm just a little shaky. My wife will never believe that I found two naked cops in our field. Truthfully, I thought I was seeing a pair of aliens from outer space standing in my field. They were naked and bald. His skin was bright pink. She was dirty from falling in the field. I had to think a minute before I got out of the cab."

"Why don't I follow you home?" asked a Des Moines county deputy. "I'll explain everything and I need to ask you some more questions anyway."

Chapter 21

The raid was not a success. Yes, the feds found a few illegal
aliens, but not the busloads they had anticipated. Less than 10
percent of the workers were detained. They delayed the second shift
by thirty minutes, and then left with their detainees. Captain Stender
and his crew found little evidence that there was anything going on
in the plant other than killing cows. The Temple of Truth was intact
with its luxurious furnishings. The women's quarters were empty
and looked as though everyone had left in a hurry. He did find one of
his employee's handguns which indicated they were here at some
point in time. The room where the cleansing took place was clean
and sterile as it should be. They even failed in finding two young
agents. The worried captain had no knowledge of where his
investigators were. The truth was Bobbi and Dan were about to be
dumped into what was supposed to be a watery grave at the mouth of
Two Mile Creek.

The captain decided to regroup back at the sheriff's office.
He let the feds and the state police finish their investigation. He
knew the sheriff and the Wapello police were not excited about

raiding the plant. They had friends and family working there.

In Sheriff Cramer's office, the DCI agents, plus the chief of Wapello police, and the sheriff sat around a table in the back room.

Captain Stender spoke first.

"To make this meeting less formal, my name is Cal. We are working on the same project, and I would like to have everyone on a first name basis. Is this okay?"

Everyone nodded affirmative.

"Good! Right now, the following people are missing: three DCI agents, a bus load of young women, and the manager of the plant, who I am told, is Jacob Johnson. The electrician who found the woman named Melanie, told me her last words were, 'The girls are at Jake's place.' He also told me it was close by. Does anyone know anything about this place?"

There were snickers and chuckles from the other law enforcement officers.

Randy spoke up, "Everyone in Louisa County knows about Jake's playhouse. He has wild parties there. We're told it was built to mimic Hugh Heffner's Playboy mansion, inside and outside, including a pool with small rooms to each side for extra-curricular activities. We heard the water is always heated and no swim suits are allowed, especially on the women. We've all been called there once or twice to investigate, but either he shuts everything down before we get there, or he pays the fine and continues on. We know there is prostitution going on there, but we can't prove it. So, we are just waiting for him to do something really stupid. It looks like this may be it. I have some aerial photos of the place. If you looked at them, it might help you get to know the layout."

"Yes, I'd love to see them."

Randy left and brought back some roll-out photos of the expansive home.

"You see, Cal. There is only one road in or out. The river borders one side, and it is high this time of the year. There are thick woods that lead to the next door neighbor's property. I'm told, he has some vicious guard dogs. Are there any questions?"

Cal was silent for a minute as he looked over the map. He looked at his watch. An office assistant came into the room.

"Is there a Captain Stender here?" she asked.

"Yes, I'm Captain Stender."

"Captain, I just received a call from the Burlington General Hospital that a man named Ron Puck has been admitted. He is in the operating room as we speak. He was severely injured in a car wreck near the Acme Plant. The doctor said he is in serious, but stable condition. His injuries are not life threatening. He would like to speak with you."

"Thank you, and may I know your name, Miss?"

"Mrs. Joan Devale."

"Thank you, Joan. Tell the doctor on the phone I'll be there in two minutes."

Cal turned to the men around the table.

"Gentlemen, I believe we have a reason to search the big mansion. Randy, can you get us a court order to search the place? I think we should grab a bite to eat and meet back here at 12:30. Chief Frost, I'd like to have your assistance. Your men may not be needed, but I have a hunch, you will be. The larger force we show may quicken the arrest. Everyone agree?"

Everyone agreed.

"Good, I'll see you back here in one hour. I hope I find my two missing agents at the Johnson home. They are young capable agents, and I hope they are okay. Now, I have to check on one of the three who were missing."

Sheriff Cramer and his deputies headed for Gramma Emma's Café.

As they ate, Emma approached Sheriff Randy and asked, "Randy, have you seen Melanie today? She was supposed to be here at eleven. I wonder if something is wrong, because she is almost never late for work."

Randy's face turned white.

He looked up at the older lady and said, "Sit down for a minute, Emma. I have something to tell you."

"Something has happened to Melanie, hasn't it?"

"Yes, I'm afraid it has. Melanie was found alongside the road by Two Skunk Creek. She was badly bruised and beaten up. It looked as if someone had pushed her out of a moving vehicle or something. Tyler Koen found her. She died in his arms. I'm sorry."

"She's dead? Oh, my goodness! I'm so sad! How will I get along without her?" Emma sobbed. "She was like a daughter to me, since my daughter died two years ago from cancer. She doesn't have much family. Just us here in Wapello."

Randy patted Emma on the shoulder and gave her a hug.

"Emma, we're going to get the person who killed Melanie. If we're lucky, we'll have him this afternoon."

At 12:15, Cal returned. He asked for a sandwich and coffee.

"Gentlemen, this is the plan. We will go to the Johnson place immediately. Does one of the departments have a tranquillizer gun?"

Chief Frost said, "Yes, we do. How's your man?"

"Thanks for asking. The doctor told me he is in stable

condition. He had to amputate his left foot, because it was crushed beyond repair. He has a broken arm and several cuts. The bad part is I just hired him for this case. He was a private investigator and a Marine veteran," Cal replied.

Then he explained his plan.

"We'll try to quiet the dogs the humane way at first. If it doesn't work, we shoot to kill. Understand?"

Cal continued, "First, I'll ask for a surrender. Randy, do you have the search warrant?"

"Yes."

"If he or they refuse to surrender, we will try to negotiate. We would like to be able to have the girls, who are now hostages, released. If we start to hear gun shots from inside, we charge the doors. My men will take the front. Sheriff, you take the west side and south side facing the river. Captain Frost, your men cover the east side. I want no lights or sirens. This is to be a surprise, I hope. Evidently, we didn't surprise them at the plant."

* * *

The entourage of law enforcement vehicles headed north on Highway 61. They turned on the blacktop leading to the Johnson residence. Captain Stender stopped at the iron entry gate. He opened his car door and stepped out. Two big German shepherd dogs bounded toward the gate. Chief Frost loaded his tranquilizer gun with a double dose. He fired point blank at one of the dogs. The dog didn't seem to be phased. They waited a few seconds for the medicine to work. Nothing!

Captain Stender aimed his revolver and shot. The animal dropped in his tracks. The second dog started to retreat. Stender fired again. The threat was over. A deputy climbed over the gate and cut the hydraulic hoses which ran the gates. Another man pushed open the gates and walked in on the lawn.

"Stop right there, or I'll shoot!" came a voice from the house.

The squad cars from the various departments fanned out across the lawn and formed a barrier to hide behind. Some of the deputies went to the south and west side of the house. Wapello policemen ran around to the east side.

When Captain Stender was assured the building was secured, he grabbed his bull horn and responded.

"This is Captain Stender of the DCI. We would like to come in."

"Not by the hair on my chinny chin chin," was the answer.

"Sheriff, there are three persons with cell phones in the house. We should be able to get one of them to answer. Start with Mr. Johnson. If he is smart, he'll answer. I'll let you start the conversation, because he knows you."

Randy punched in the phone number he was given at the office. The phone rang and rang. He hung up. He tried the house number with the same result. Lastly, he punched in Rosa's number.

"Hello," a woman's voice answered.

"This is Sheriff Randy Cramer. Is this Rosa Mendez?"

"No, this is Bonita Ramez. I answered Rosa's phone, because she is with Mr. Johnson right now."

"Can you tell me how many women are with you?"

"Thirteen, counting the housekeeper, Tillie, and fourteen, if you add Rosa."

"Are you in danger?"

"I don't know. We are locked in the changing room near the pool. There is a way out, but it is through the swimming pool. There are steps which lead into the water from here. They were the steps we women had to use to enter the pool when we were entertaining the male guests. We could swim under the wall to get outside. Mr. Johnson had it built this way so we women could enter the pool wet and naked for the gentlemen."

"Do you think you could swim out now? I have several deputies on the pool side to help you out to freedom."

"We'll have to hurry. I'll try and bring Tillie with me."

"Leave the phone on, so I can hear if someone is coming."

"Okay, here we go."

There were some muffled voices and splashing of water.

The sheriff heard, "I'll help you, Tillie. Just hold your breath."

The escape seemed to be working until Randy heard, "Stop! The rest of you!"

There were a couple of screams and some heavy footsteps.

A deep voice bellowed, "Git upstairs! Everyone to the laundry room."

Sheriff Cramer spoke on the phone and his voice got the deep voiced person's attention.

"This is the sheriff. I need to talk to Jake."

There was swearing and grumbling. It sounded as if clothes and equipment were being tossed around.

"Where's the goddam phone?"

"Right here!" said Randy.

244 • Iowa Exposed

He wanted whoever it was to find the phone and maybe take it to Jake.

Finally, the voice answered, "Who is this and how did you get this number?"

"I repeat, this is Sheriff Randy Cramer of the Louisa County Sheriff's Department. I would like to speak to Jake Johnson. Who is this I'm speaking with?"

"This is Lobo. You are on Rosa's phone. I'll take it to Jake."

The phone went dead. Randy looked at Cal. Had they lost their connection? Did he throw the phone in the pool? There was a commotion coming from the pool side of the house. Randy's body radio crackled.

"We have five very wet young women coming out of the pool and one older lady. They seem to be okay. We need some blankets and towels."

"Can they walk?"

"Yes."

"If they can make it to the front area, I'll have the blankets ready. They can get into some warm vehicles also."

In a few minutes, the six women led by Deputy Laurie Rains, the only woman in the department, appeared around the north side of the mansion. The five younger women were soaked, but their mini-skirts and thin tops were already drying. It was Tillie in her cotton housedress, who was chilled and bedraggled. The men had retrieved all the blankets from their car trunks and handed them to the women. Laurie led them around behind the department's van to dry off.

Randy heard her say, "Let's get you out of that wet dress, Tillie."

It was followed by a terse, "No! Not here with all these men around."

"Listen, I'll stand guard on the other side of the van and keep everyone away. Bonita, you help her change and wrap up."

"Okay, come on, Tillie. No one will see you. See, I'm down to my underwear already. As soon as your dress dries, you can put it back on. Why don't you sit in the van while we wait for our clothes to dry?"

Randy heard the van door open and then close. Six hostages down and seven to go. The phone buzzed.

"Sheriff, this is Jake. I want you to leave my property."

"I will when all the girls are released. If they are not released in ten minutes, we will start shooting. I'd hate to see this beautiful house shot up. Why don't you be reasonable and give up?"

"I'll think about it."

"Ten minutes!"

During the wait, Cal walked back to the van. He wanted to see if Bobbi and Dan were inside the mansion.

He tapped on the side of the van to get their attention inside. The back window opened.

"Is everyone decent? I'd like to talk to you. I'm Captain Cal Stender of the DCI."

"Yes, we are all covered."

Cal opened the front door and climbed into the driver's seat. He turned to see the passengers. Their hair was uncombed and they were shivering.

"Would you like me to start the engine and turn the heater on for you?"

"Yes, please."

"Are my two agents in the house with Mr. Johnson?"

"No! Do you mean the young woman and man who were trapped by Mrs. Ping?"

"Did the man have reddish hair?"

"Yes."

"They were DCI agents. Do you know what happened to them?"

"The last we saw them, Mrs. Ping was going to take them to the cleansing room."

"The cleansing room? What's that?"

"About the worst torture one can imagine. If you survive it, you make sure it doesn't happen again. You'll do anything for Mrs. Ping. That's how she controls us."

"And what do you do for this Mrs. Ping?'

"We entertain her gentlemen guests and sometimes her women friends."

"So you are prostitutes."

"No! We are pleasure girls. We give massages, baths, and entertain the guests. We may have to go to bed with the men now and then, but sometimes they are women. You do what they want."

"Do you have sexual intercourse?"

"Sometimes, yes, but a lot of married men refrain. Some men are so fat, they can't even see their peepee. It is just a job. We are trapped so you make do."

"Another question. What is this cleansing?"

"Mrs. Ping claims she is a priestess of some religious cult who demands everyone tells the truth. If she catches you lying or trying to escape, you are cleansed."

"And?"

There was a collective sigh.

"You are taken into the cleansing room and made to drink some terrible tasting stuff. I think it is a powerful laxative. Then you are strapped to a chair and Willie shears off all your hair. Your stomach begins to feel terrible. You vomit in the room's only toilet bowl. Next, she stands you over a big floor drain. You are ordered to disrobe. If you refuse, Freddy cuts your clothes off. You will remain naked for the rest of the ordeal. A cold shower douses you as you stand over the drain. I mean, it is so much water you can barely breathe. You stand there shivering trying to hold yourself, because by now your bowels are about to erupt. She lets you go to the toilet, which is sitting in the room without any partitions. There is no privacy. You feel like you want to die. Everyone is watching you take a crap. After you have emptied your bowels, Rosa leads you to a table and you are tied bending over with your legs spread apart. Mrs. Ping administers the final dose. She has an enema syringe, which she fills with tap water and shoots it up your butt hole. You feel you are about to explode and finally you do. You are a mess, but guess what? She has Freddy spray you with high power water. You are now cleansed. You are cold, naked, can barely walk, and your stomach wishes it was somewhere else. Mrs. Ping allows you to walk to your room if you can. Otherwise, you crawl. No one is supposed to help you. Not everyone makes it. A couple of girls have died. I do know we heard some terrible screams coming from the cleansing room right after we were forced back to our room. I'm afraid they might have been from one of your agents."

"Thank you for your information. I hope we will have the rest of your friends out shortly."

There was some noise coming from the south side. The captain exited the van and hurried to the side entrance. Four women emerged from a basement door. They ran as fast as they could away from the house. In the group was another older woman. Captain Stender asked her name.

"Lily Thomas."

"She's not Lily Thomas. She's Rosa Mendez, our warden. She makes us do what Mrs. Ping wants," came a cry from the girls.

"Rosa Mendez," Captain Stender repeated, "you are Rick Sanchez's girlfriend. You helped him kill Mrs. Hellzer. He claimed you stole Mrs. Hellzer's undergarment right off her body while she was tied to a table. You are under arrest for murder. Deputy Rains, read Rosa her rights and book her. Make sure she is separated from the others."

Rosa stared at the captain and screamed, "I didn't murder anyone. It was Rick and Freddy. They put her on the tracks. You can't pin that on me!"

"But you didn't intervene at any time and I understand you covered the car windows with cardboard. I'm sure the fingerprints we found on the window glass will match yours. Now tell me, how many girls are left inside the mansion, and who is Mrs. Ping and Lobo?"

Rosa was silent.

"Okay, we'll find out soon enough, and I'll testify you were not a willing suspect. I'm sure the judge will consider that in the sentencing."

Rosa quickly spoke, "There are four more girls in the mansion. I don't know what he is going to do with them. Lobo was tying them up. Lobo is the former Sergeant Keith Waters of the Muscatine Sheriff's Department. Mrs. Ping or Mrs. Boss is really Jake's mother, Rita Johnson, wife of JJ Johnson. She is not here, because she has to be in Burlington for her husband's debate. That is all I know."

"Thank you, Rosa. You have been very helpful."

Captain Stender returned to the group of officers at the gate.

"Have you heard anything from inside? I learned there are four young women still in there. Try Mr. Johnson again. This time, give him five minutes. I'm worried about the remaining four women. Rosa said he was tying them up, but didn't know why. I don't think we can wait much longer."

Randy punched Jake's phone number this time.

"I hear you, Randy. I've got four beautiful young women in here with me along with Lobo. If you follow my orders, they will not get hurt."

"That depends what your orders are."

"I want the three cop cars blocking my driveway moved, and I want all cops to back 100 feet away from those cars. I want no one to follow me for five minutes. Understand?"

"When do we get the girls?"

"Right after I clear the end of the drive, you can have two of them. The next two will be left on the road before I get to the highway. Okay?"

"Okay."

"I will open the garage door in five minutes. Tell that top cop from Des Moines his two detectives are probably talking to the fishes in Five Mile Creek and Drainage Ditch. I hated to kill the woman. She was really cute."

Randy relayed the message to Cal. He immediately radioed the Des Moines County Sheriff. He said he would send a patrol out to check. It was five minutes on the dot, and the garage door started to open. The drive had been cleared. All personnel moved back one hundred feet, but they still had their guns drawn.

A gray Porsche with a red racing stripe down the middle emerged. There was one woman lying across the hood with a rope tied to her middle and extending into the sunroof; another woman was lying across the trunk next to the rear window. A rope went from her to the sunroof. Finally, there were two women walking, at this time, alongside the car. They were positioned by the front windows, so no one could shoot the driver or the passenger without hitting the women.

They each had their hands tied behind their backs and a noose was tightly secured around their necks. The rope of the nooses also fed into the sunroof. One bad step and they would hang themselves. The car moved slowly forward. The runners kept pace easily. The lawmen just had to watch and do nothing.

The car gained momentum. The girls started to run faster. Soon, they were going as fast as they could run. The vehicle reached the end of the driveway, and the driver pushed his foot to the floorboard. The tires squealed. Both women fell and rolled to the side of the road. Their nooses had tightened. They were gasping for breath.

Two men dashed forward and worked the ropes loose. One girl blacked out. She soon recovered. The two were severely cut and scratched by their fall on the blacktop. The Porsche sped on with the two girls tied to the hood and trunk.

About a block away, Jake applied the brakes and swerved to the right. Lobo released the rope. The girl on the hood slid and rolled into the ditch and down a steep embankment. Jake then stopped the car for a second before he floored the accelerator again. The tires squealed and smoked on the dry pavement. Lobo released the last rope. This girl fell from the top of the trunk and rolled along the edge of the road.

It was only seconds before the law officers reacted. They

were on the scene administering first aid to the victims. They were badly scratched and bruised, but their injuries were not serious. The pair had made a successful getaway.

Cal heard his radio talking. He hurried to his car. It was the Des Moines County Sheriff.

Cal answered, "Captain Stender."

"Captain, this Jim Sloan, Lieutenant Deputy of the Des Moines County Sheriff's Department. I think I have good news for you. A farmer near Oakville found a man and a woman in his field. They were both bald and naked. The woman was bleeding internally. The Oakville Fire Department answered the call. They immediately called for a helicopter to transport the pair to the burn unit at the Iowa University Hospital in Iowa City. The last report I received was the man was doing okay, but the young woman was in intensive care and in a coma."

Cal breathed a sigh of relief. His agents were all accounted for. He thanked the lieutenant and told him he would be in touch later.

Due to transporting the women, plus Rosa, and assisting the four injured women, it left only one officer to chase the escaping Porsche. It was one of the DCI agents. He was a mile away when a voice from a Louisa County Deputy called over the radio that a gray and red sports car had just passed the L & M High School. The high school was located just off Highway 61. The deputy usually was at the high school when it dismissed for the day.

"This is Deputy Gomez of Louisa County. Should I pursue?" he asked.

"Yes, but don't put yourself in danger. This is Lieutenant Holmes of the DCI. I'm in pursuit about a mile away. The car is being driven by two suspects in a double murder and kidnapping in Louisa County. They are armed and dangerous. It looks like they are heading for Muscatine. I'll notify the Muscatine Sheriff and Police."

"I'm on my way. I will do my best."

The chase was on. Just north of the school, the highway becomes a four-lane expressway. Jake floored the Porsche. He was doing more than one hundred miles an hour. Jake had three options as he entered Muscatine County. He could continue across a flat truck crop area called 'The Island' on 61 at his high rate of speed and hope to beat the cops to the stop light south of town where they probably would set up a road block, or, he could take the blacktop road to Fruitland and catch the Grandview blacktop back to Louisa County and continue to his parent's home north of Washington. Or, he could choose a curvy blacktop road called Bluff Road along the edge of 'The Island' and sneak into town on a two lane road. His goal was to get to Gary Dawson's Classic Car Shop. If he could get there, he could quickly trade cars or steal one if Gary wasn't there. Jake chose the Bluff Road option.

The Muscatine Police did set up a blockade at the stop light. It wasn't long before they saw the pursuing squad cars and the flashing lights. The bad thing was there was no one between them and the charging cars. In minutes, the pursuing cars were screeching to a halt at the blockade.

The Muscatine police chief hurried to the first car and asked, "Where is this car you were chasing?"

Lieutenant Holmes replied, "I don't know. He just disappeared when we came over the hill. Are there other routes into town he could have taken?"

"Yes, Bluff Road, but it's slow and dangerously curvy."

"Not for a sporty Porsche! But is that the only road?"

"He could have driven through Fruitland and used Steward Road, or he could have turned south toward Grandview."

"Doesn't that road connect to 92 and go to Washington?"

"Yep!"

"His folks have a plush home just north of Washington. Maybe he circled back to get there or at least change autos. Let's have someone over in Washington County check the Johnson place."

"Okay, will do," said the police chief. "We'd better check his other option on Bluff Road. I wonder why he headed this way, anyway."

"My first guess is because his partner, the former sheriff's deputy, is familiar with the town, and they can hide for a few hours," Holmes replied.

* * *

Once Jake hit the city limits, he slowed down to the posted speed. He didn't want to attract any attention. He reached Front Street and drove slowly past the hotel. Gary's shop was located in the next block. The shop had been a car dealership for years, but when the downtown area dried up for business, they moved to the outskirts to be where the businesses were located. It spanned a half a block.

Jake pulled into the shop's building, which previously had been used as bays for the mechanics to work on cars. As luck would have it, Gary was putting the finishing touches on a blue Chevelle 350 Super Sport.

Jake pulled up next to where Gary was working, rolled his window down, and asked, "Hey, Gary, you got any fast cars for sale?"

Gary recognized Jake from the many car shows he had attended.

"I've got a couple good ones, including this car. The guy who owns it bought a Camaro to restore and doesn't have room in his garage to store it. I also think his wife is putting some pressure on. My other one is a 1998 Corvette. It's mine, but I've already got four. I've had this one for a while, but when I purchased another beauty in Phoenix, I decided I didn't need five."

"Is the Chevelle ready to go?" asked Jake.

"Sure is. I have a customer coming from Davenport to look at it late this afternoon. I have it fueled and washed. I hope he is on time, because my wife and I have a 3:30 tee time at the country club. Do you want it?"

"I might. What are you asking?"

"Fifteen Grand."

"Wow! That's pretty steep."

"They don't make 'em like this anymore."

Jake got out of his car to look at the Chevy. The passenger side door opened and Keith crawled out.

"Can I trade my Porsche?"

"Sure, but then I'd owe you money. What do you want?"

"Ten grand. Cash. "

"Who's the guy with you?" Gary asked trying to buy a little time to think.

"This is my bodyguard, El Lobo. That's not his real name, but that is what the Mexies at the plant call him. He's been around the area."

Gary shook hands with the big man with the mustache. He would swear he had seen him before, but he couldn't place him at the moment.

"Do you mind if I look around?" Lobo asked.

"No, go right ahead," Gary answered.

Gary's phone rang.

"Excuse me a minute."

Gary went into his office to speak in private. Lobo casually walked over, stood by the door to his office, and listened.

He heard, "Yes, I understand. How about four tomorrow?"

Lobo heard the conversation end and Gary redialing.

"Honey, we can go to the club a little earlier. The guy from Davenport can't make it. Say, do you remember a big man with a mustache? He used to stop in once in a while and check on me. You know, he worked with Sheriff Joe. Really? Yes, I'll be careful. I'll try to delay them. I'll call the police if things get hairy."

Lobo smiled as he walked away from the door. He quickly returned to Jake and informed him of the conversation.

"We'd better get going," answered Jake.

"Sorry for the inconvenience, Jake. Sounds okay, but I don't have that kind of money just lying around," Gary told Jake when he returned, trying to stall the deal.

"What have you got lying around?"

"Maybe five, I'd have to go to the vault and check."

"You have a vault?"

"It's not really a vault. It's a fireproof room where the former dealership kept records, titles, and money."

"If you have five thou', you've got a deal."

At this point, Gary started to become suspicious. Jake and Keith seemed to be very anxious to close the deal. He also realized Karen was right. Lobo was really Sergeant Keith Waters. He was wanted for several charges associated with the Sheriff Department scandal. Once in the vault, he decided he would call 911.

Gary asked, "Is this car hot? Are you guys running from someone or something? Maybe I should check with my attorney first."

Jake replied, "You don't have to do that, Gary. We're legit. You'll find the title and registration in the glove compartment. My name is on both."

Gary was now watching Jake and his body language. He actually forgot about the big man Keith, as he told the cops later. Keith pretended to be looking at the photos of some classic cars hanging on the wall behind Gary.

All Gary heard was, "Sorry to have to do this to a friend," before it was lights out.

The big man had grabbed one of the many trophies Gary had sitting on a file cabinet and slammed it alongside Gary's head.

Lobo dragged Gary into the vault. He quickly looked on the shelves and found a bank bag and some twine. He stuffed a rag in Gary's mouth and tied his hands and feet. He slammed the vault door and both men ran for the blue Chevelle.

"Do you know how to drive a stick?" asked Jake.

"Sure do. I used to dream of driving one of these babies."

Lobo fired up the engine. The car literally rocked when the motor idled. She was ready to go. He eased the car out of the garage.

"Which way?" he asked.

"East and over the bridge to Illinois. We'll travel the two lanes. The cops will be checking the interstates," said Jake.

Jake then looked at Lobo and said, "I guess you already know there are some guys in Lombard who will put us up for a few days until this all blows over, right?" Lobo nodded.

They met a cop car at the stoplight before the bridge. He just smiled at the fancy car and drove on. They crossed the bridge and headed east on 92.

"How much money did ol' Gary have in the bank bag?" Lobo asked.

"I don't know. Let me see," Jake replied.

He dumped the contents on the seat between them. There were a few checks and a lot of cash. Jake counted out $6,000.

"Wow! This is great. We won't have to use credit cards for a long while, which means the cops won't have a card trail. By that time, my mother will have things under control."

The pair took the bypass around the Illinois Quad Cities and continued east on 92 toward Mendota.

Chapter 22

While Jake and Lobo escaped, Captain Stender let the others chase them. He turned his attention to his two agents who were taken by helicopter to the burn unit in Iowa City at the University Hospital. He showed his credentials to the receptionist. She gave him directions and asked him to check with the attending nurse. When he reached the waiting room, two people were already sitting there. He introduced himself. They were Bobbi's parents.

Bobbi's mother, Millie, asked, "Would you like to see Bobbi? We can go in for a few minutes. They have her in an induced coma, because of the pain in her lower intestines and colon. Whoever did this has to be a maniac. Who would ever force scalding water and acid into another person? And Dan has half of his body burned. He told me they dunked him into the tank with the hot water. He is recovering two rooms down from Bobbi."

"Can he talk?" asked Stender.

"Oh, yes, but he is in a lot of pain. He wants to see Bobbi, but the doctors and nurses feel the trauma of seeing her would be too much for him to handle right now."

"Let's go see Bobbi, and then I'll talk to Dan."

The captain and the Strouds walked into Bobbi's little cubicle. Cal was shocked by what he saw. Bobbi was quietly lying in the bed with many tubes and wires leading from her. Her bald head was covered with a skull cap for warmth. Her eyes were closed and her breathing was shallow.

Millie whispered, "The doctor said her insides were severely burned. He had never had a case like this. They are keeping her sedated for three days, and then they will check her colon again. If it shows progress, they will awaken her. She may have to wear a colostomy bag. They don't know for sure right now."

Cal remained silent. He wanted to see Dan. He left the Stroud's and headed to Dan's room. Dan was awake when he entered.

"Hi, Captain Stender," he said as the elder entered the room.

"Hi, yourself, Dan. Can you tell me about this?"

Dan started to recall everything he remembered from the time they entered the plant until the farmer found them. The captain wrote down some notes.

"The one thing you are not going to believe is the lady or witch who dunked me and burned Bobbi was not Mrs. Boss or Mrs. Ping, but Mrs. JJ Johnson or Rita. She not only runs a prostitution house, but she has this cult where if you don't tell the truth, she, as the head priestess, can cleanse you. She has every one of the girls in her control. So much so, that if she says jump, they jump. If she says strip, they strip everything off right there. She proved it by having one girl strip right before us. I mean, not just her outer clothes. She had to take off everything. It was terrible. She stripped Bobbi and sold her clothes. After humiliating her, she proceeded to inject hot water and acid into her lower bowels. It was diabolical. I was bound with handcuffs and could do nothing. I believe this lady has murdered several young women through her torture tactics."

"You are so right, Dan. One of the men who put Mrs. Hellzer on the railroad tracks has confessed in Paris, Texas. I'll have an extradition order to bring him back to Iowa. When you feel up to it, we'll have a court stenographer take a statement from you. Right now, you take care of yourself and get better."

Cal was about to leave when Dan asked, "Have you seen Bobbi?"

"Yes, she is sleeping."

"Could you help me get to see her? My mom will be here soon, and I would like to see her before she comes."

Cal peeked out through the curtained room. The nurse at the desk must have been busy with another patient. He spied a wheelchair across the hall from Dan's room.

"Do you think you can stand the pain?" he asked.

"My biggest problem is moving with all these bandages."

"I'll help."

Dan and the captain slowly maneuvered the chair into the room and alongside Dan's bed. He grimaced as he sat down. Cal took another look in the hall. The coast was clear. He pushed Dan down the hall and into Bobbi's cubicle. He opened the curtain and rolled Dan in so he was positioned next to her bed. Then he left them alone. Cal met the Stroud's in the waiting room.

"I just took Dan to see Bobbi. He's in there now. It is all right. Dan told me everything. I know who the people are we must catch. I promise the person who did this to your daughter will be in custody before the day is over. We already have two in custody. They are confessing about the others. I pray Bobbi recovers fully. The department will cover all charges and therapy. I'll call you as soon as I know more. Oh, blame me for taking Dan to see his wife. I don't want you to get into any trouble."

Mr. Stroud thanked the captain and wished him luck, for his daughter's sake.

Chapter 23

When Gary woke up, he was in the vault, bound, and gagged. He had a severe headache. The vault door was closed, and it was pitch black inside. For a moment, Gary lay on the floor and tried to figure out his next move. The only thing he could remember was his wife, Karen, was coming to pick him up, and they were going golfing at 3:30. Waiting was probably his only and best option. When Karen arrived, he would kick the file cabinets or door to get her attention. He was sure when she recognized his cell phone was going unanswered, she would come earlier. He did wonder what was happening with the two men who had just assaulted him.

Karen entered the parking lot behind the Classic Car Shop. She waited for Gary to come out. She impatiently honked the horn. Finally, she got out and stomped into the building.

"Gary! Gary! Where in the heck are you?" she called.

She entered the office. It seemed okay except for a cell phone lying smashed on the floor. No wonder he hadn't answered his phone, she thought. Then, all of a sudden, she heard a noise coming from what seemed like inside the vault. She ran to the vault door. It was locked.

She ran to Gary's desk and searched for the extra set of keys. Then, she remembered Gary telling her he had hid the extra set under the bench in the shop. Karen wasn't too pleased about crawling under a dirty shop bench in her new golf outfit, but she would have to do it. Gary must be in the vault. He was right. The keys were hanging on a nail in the greasiest corner of the bench. Karen ran to the vault and unlocked the door.

"Gary!" She screamed when she saw him lying on the floor, tied up and bleeding. She pulled the rag from his mouth as she held his head in her lap.

Gary whispered, "Two men came in and wanted to trade cars. One guy was Jake Johnson. I didn't know who the other one was until I talked to you. When you told me about Keith Waters being wanted for drugs and other charges, it hit me. Keith was standing right outside my door. I was about to call the cops, but he hit me alongside my head with something hard, and the next thing I knew, I woke up here."

"I'm taking you to the emergency room right away. You're going to need stitches."

Gary interrupted her, "First, we have to inform the cops that they should be looking for a blue Chevy and not a gray and red Porsche."

* * *

Jake and Lobo were cruising along Highway 92 just east of Walnut, Illinois.

Lobo announced, "I hate to break your bubble, Jake, but we need to trade cars again. Gary's wife has most likely found him by now, and the cops will be looking for this car. What do you want to do?"

"I don't know. Where can we trade cars around here?"

Just as he said that, a pickup with a man and a woman pulled out of a farm yard and were headed west. They passed the two men in the blue Chevelle. Lobo slowed down and kept watching the pickup in his rearview mirror. The pickup disappeared around a corner. He let the Chevy coast and drove into the farmyard.

"What in the 'H' are you doing?" Jake asked.

"I'm trading cars. With a little luck, the farmer we just met has a car sitting unlocked with the keys in it in his garage. Let me check."

Lobo got out and entered the garage walk-in door. Soon, the big garage door opened and Lobo backed out a big Mercury Grand Marquis. He motioned for Jake to come. Jake shut off the Chevy and hurried over.

"Now, we're talking luxury," beamed Lobo, "and look, there is a road map of all the local roads in here. We can go all the way to Chicago without even driving on a state road. Here, you run the maps, and I'll drive."

Lobo pulled the big Mercury out on the road. He smiled. This was his kind of car.

Jake studied the map. There was a county blacktop just north of 92. It ran along an interstate railroad track. If they followed it, they could get all the way to the outskirts of Aurora. Once in the city, dodging the police would get simpler.

Lobo pushed the old car to eighty miles an hour, well past the posted 55 MPH limit. They passed a sheriff's patrol car sitting in a drive. Immediately, he pulled out and turned on his lights in pursuit. Lobo pushed the car faster. He had been a cop at one time, and he was a good driver.

A mile ahead, the road crossed a set of railroad tracks. There were no crossing arms, just warning lights. They began flashing.

Lobo knew if he could get across the tracks, the pursuing car would have to wait. It would be close. He floored the big Mercury. The train engine sounded its horn.

Jake screamed, "Don't try it! Lobo! We won't make it."

Lobo didn't seem to hear him. He roared ahead. The train was speeding at fifty miles per hour, the car at eighty. They came together with a horrible grinding crash. The speeding car disintegrated. Lobo was thrown out because he didn't like driving with a seat belt. He died instantly when his head hit a railroad tie. Jake was trapped in the car. The gas tank split open. It burst into flames when the fuel hit the red hot catalytic converter. He was burned beyond recognition.

The train screeched to a halt about a mile down the track. The pursuing sheriff's deputy had already called for emergency help. By the time the train engineer got there, it was not a pretty sight. It took several minutes before Keith Waters was identified from his driver's license. His name was run through the files, and he was identified as a wanted man in Muscatine County, Iowa. The man in the burned-out car was probably his boss, Jacob Johnson. He had just been placed on the fugitive list that morning.

Captain Stender received a call from Des Moines informing him of the accident and deaths of Jake and Lobo. A feeling of satisfaction entered Captain Cal's mind. According to Rick Sanchez, there were eight people involved in this prostitution group. They now had accounted for five—Melanie, Jake and Lobo, aka Keith Waters, were dead. Rick Sanchez and Rosa Menendez were in custody.

The Des Moines County Sheriff was on his way to pick up Willie Hamilton in Mediapolis. By six, Fast Freddy Rodriguez was spotted in Galesburg. Instead of going to Peoria immediately as told, he decided to pay one of his lady friends a visit. He made the mistake of leaving the blue and yellow, number 66 wrecker sit outside. The Galesburg Police caught Freddy in the bedroom with his pants down, literally.

The only one left was Mrs. Rita Johnson. Cal knew she would be at the Burlington Civic Center attending her husband's political debate. The debate was supposed to begin at eight. Cal arrived with several officers at 7:45. He had contacted the Burlington Police ahead of time and found out the police chief would be attending the debate also. He would be sitting in the front row with the candidate's wives. Cal asked one of the policemen who were there for security reasons if they would please ask the chief to meet with him at the back of the room.

When the officer went to the first row, the proceedings were about to begin. There was some commotion and debate to get the chief to move. When he was informed it was the head of DCI eastern division, he changed his mind. He apologized to the wives and followed the officer to the back of the room.

"What's this nonsense about making me leave the debate?" he huffed as he approached Cal.

"Chief Sampson, I have a warrant for the arrest of Mrs. Rita Johnson."

"On what charges?" asked the flabbergasted chief.

"Running a prostitution house, torture of an officer of the law, ordering the murders of those same officers, suspected murder of four other individuals, plus tax fraud including the Department of Agriculture of Iowa, and on top of those charges, she is dealing in human trafficking."

By this time, Chief Sampson was shocked. He quickly changed his mood when the captain presented the warrant for Mrs. Johnson's arrest.

Cal continued, "I'd like to arrest Mrs. Johnson after the ceremonies. I assume there will be a press conference afterwards, and most of the public will have left. Is that true?"

"Good thinking, Captain. I'll make sure she is detained backstage. I must say this is the most unbelievable arrest I will ever witness. I would have never guessed the nice Mrs. JJ Johnson would be a criminal."

The debate was cordial with each candidate answering the moderator's questions. At the end of the debate, the families joined the men on the stage. Johnson's opponent had his wife and three children beside him. JJ had only Rita.

"Where's Jake?" he whispered to Rita.

"He is at the plant. Some kind of equipment problems," she answered.

The crowd began to leave after some handshaking and well-wishing. JJ and Rita walked back on stage. Chief Sampson approached the Johnson's. At his side was Captain Stender.

"Mr. and Mrs. Johnson, I would like you to meet Captain Stender of the Department of Criminal Investigation of Iowa," said the chief.

Captain Stender shook hands with JJ and then turned to Rita.

"Mrs. Rita Johnson, you are under arrest for running an illegal house of prostitution, human trafficking, suspicion of murder, and fraudulent reporting of taxes."

Rita was shocked to say the least. A woman DCI agent stepped forward to handcuff Rita. She read her, her rights. Rita stood quietly for a minute, as if in a daze, and then she exploded.

"Get your filthy hands off of me. I had no part in thothse murders, and I do not run a houth of Prothtituiothn. They were call girls."

Captain Stender calmly said to her, "We have one of your former employees, a Ricardo Sanchez, who has confessed to several murders ordered by you and helping with your call girls as you call them. We have your call girls in custody. Several are illegal aliens. They claim they were bought and sold by a dealer in Guatemala.

They are your slaves. You are involved in human trafficking which I believe is your expertise."

"Continue to handcuff her, officer," ordered the captain.

JJ finally asked his wife, "Is this true, Rita?"

"Yes, some of it, but I can prove my innocence on most of the charges."

He then asked, "Why, Rita?"

"It was because you were so occupied with your dealerships and politics, you forgot about Jake and me. Jake loved his women. When he and I went to Cancun, Mexico, I met a nice gentleman who supplied Jake with all the women he needed. We had a visit with him, and he indicated there was big money in call girls. He would supply the girls for 40 percent of the profits. The packing plant provided a prefect cover. It has been great for the last four years, and you were too dumb or busy to figure it out," Rita replied.

Mrs. Johnson turned toward Captain Stender and with a smile said, "At least that sexy little cop you sent to stop me won't be able to testify. She and her homely husband should now be down river a couple of miles. I must say captain, the women you hire are very sexy. I'd like to have a couple of them in my group."

Captain Stender smiled when he replied, "I must inform you, Mrs. Johnson, both of my agents, Bobbi and Dan Dorman, whom you tortured, stripped naked, then dumped them and their truck into a drainage ditch to drown, survived. They were saved by a farmer working the field next to the ditch. Agent Stroud is still in a coma as the result of your actions. Mr. Dorman is recuperating from his bad burns. He is the one who will be able to testify against you and your employees. I suspect his testimony, as well as many others will lock you up for several years. These are serious charges, Mrs. Johnson. I suggest your husband find a very good lawyer."

"Captain Stender, where will you take my wife?" asked JJ.

"The Burlington City Jail. She'll be booked and will be detained by the Burlington Police."

"I'm not wearing one of those orange jump thuits," Rita screamed, as her lisp was getting worse.

"Oh, but Mrs. Johnson, we have the perfect one just for you. It has prisoner written across the back. I got it straight from Saks Fifth Avenue," said Chief Sampson smiling. "We'll even give you a pair of new shoes."

As the police led Mrs. Johnson away, JJ called after her, "I'll find a lawyer as soon as I can, dearie. I'll get you out."

Captain Stender confronted Mr. Johnson again, saying, "Mr. Johnson, I hate to continue to be the bearer of more bad news, but my office has reported to me within the last hour that a car-train accident near Mendota, Illinois might have involved your son. He was riding in a stolen car with Sergeant Keith Waters. Mr. Waters was thrown from the car and killed instantly. We believe your son was trapped inside the car and was burned to death. We will need your permission to get his dental records for identification. One of the officers has the proper papers from the court."

"I understand, Chief Stroud. I will do anything and everything you ask within the law. I'm sure my attorney will be in contact."

Chief Stroud looked at his watch. The little square on the side of the dial told him it was April 26. He thought, "Today, April 26, is exactly one month since the homicide of Karen Hellzer. What started as a suspected homicide had developed into cleaning up a crooked sheriff's department, discovery of a human trafficking-prostitution operation, plus several more murders." He shook his head and tried to remember when he had worked an investigation which yielded so many different endings.

Chapter 24

On April 29, the attending doctor for Bobbi and Dan prescribed another colonoscopy for Bobbi. The results were favorable. He decided to bring Bobbi out of her induced coma. Dan's burns were healing. Only his feet and legs were still bandaged. The nurses rolled him in a wheelchair to be at Bobbi's side when she awoke. Her parents stood at the end of the bed.

Coming out of her coma didn't happen quickly. They waited. Slowly, Bobbi turned her head. It seemed to hurt her. She grimaced. Dan gently held her hand. One eye opened, then the other.

She looked right at Dan and said, "Hi, Danny boy. Are you ready to make a baby?"

Dan's face turned red as a beet. Bobbi's parents, the two nurses, and the practitioner-on-call, all laughed. Bobbi's mind was fine. It would still take two weeks before they would release her. She would have to remain on a liquid diet until her intestines and colon had completely healed.

Chapter 25

May 10

Sheriff Joe Ward, Don Larson, and Alvin White appeared before the judge in Muscatine County Court. Don and Alvin pleaded guilty. They both were given suspended sentences and three years on probation, plus they would forfeit their retirement pensions. This really hurt Alvin, because he was almost sixty-five. Neither of them could ever work in law enforcement again.

Sheriff Joe was being charged for tampering with state's evidence, racial profiling, illegal strip searches, sexual harassment, dealing in illegal drugs, and bribery. He protested the bribery charge until he realized if he cooperated with the investigation, he might receive a lighter sentence. He admitted to receiving bribes, not only from Mrs. Johnson, but from other prominent businessmen and politicians in Muscatine County. His testimony would affect many in

274 • Iowa Exposed

the area. He was appointed a public defender to represent him, and his trial was set for September 29. He would not be imprisoned, but he would be under house arrest and required to wear an ankle bracelet. He accepted the judge's decision.

Ricardo Sanchez was extradited back to Iowa to face charges of manslaughter, along with helping run a human trafficking operation. Rosa was charged the same.

Freddy Rodriguez was brought back from Galesburg, Illinois. He was charged with murder, money laundering, and running an illegal house of prostitution, among other minor charges. Their cases were to be tried in Louisa County.

Willie Hamilton, the lagoon manager, made the mistake of staying home instead of going to Las Vegas. The Louisa County Sheriff picked him up easily. He confessed to helping bury Mike Herera and three or four others. Mike was the only man. He didn't have any knowledge of who the others were or why they were buried there. He knew they were all young women. He just did as he was told. He cooperated with the sheriff's office and showed them where to dig. The sheriff exhumed five bodies—Mike Herera's and four young females. They drained the lagoon and quickly found Mike's big Harley.

Mrs. Rita Johnson's case would be tried in Des Moines County where Burlington is the county seat. She did have her expensive attorney, Sam Chasem, present. He pleaded on behalf of his client, but although she had ordered some of the deaths, she was not directly responsible. She did plead not guilty to the human trafficking charges, because it gave her lawyer time to work on the case. The judge relented after much begging to put her on house arrest and because Rita had just been informed her only son, Jake, had been killed in a car-train accident. The judge ordered her to wear an ankle bracelet, and she would not be able to leave the state of Iowa.

Although Rita mourned her son, a vacation to Paris, France with her bridge group seemed more important to her. As soon as she entered her home, she called her best friend, Alma Hackett, who had a law degree, but she seldom used it. Her husband, Luther Hackett, was a partner in a large firm in Iowa City. Alma assured Rita she could get the restrictions reduced by using her husband's law firm's name. Rita would not have to cancel her plans, and she would be able to go with the gang to Paris. One week after her court appearance, she and Alma petitioned the same judge. They met late in the afternoon in the court room.

"Your Honor," said Alma, "my client is credible. She works diligently for several charities in Washington and Iowa City. She has been an outstanding citizen of the community. Her attorney, Sam Chasem, is with my husband's firm of Hackett, Cuttin and Chang. I'm sure you know my husband, Luther. I am representing Mrs. Johnson in lieu of Mr. Chasem, because he had other obligations. I am seeking a special variance in Mrs. Johnson's restrictions so she can fulfill her dreams of a vacation in Paris. She would not try to leave Iowa except she has had this trip planned. I, personally, will see she returns to face all charges. I trust you will rule in favor of my client."

The judge sat quietly for a moment. She eyed the two women dressed in expensive pant suits with matching high-heeled shoes. They both had their hair recently set and combed, their nails were manicured, diamond earrings dangled from their ears, and on their hands were several gem-encrusted rings. She imagined they had driven to Burlington in a Cadillac or BMW.

The judge leaned forward on her desk and said, "Counselor, I respect your husband's status in the world of law. He is a fine attorney as is his group. I sympathize with your client over the loss of her son. I also realize the expense of having to cancel plans while waiting for the courts."

Alma turned to Rita and winked. The judge was softening.

The judge continued, "But, if for one moment you and your client, Mrs. Johnson, think you are better than the common man, you are mistaken. Just because you have money and social status does not give you special legal privileges. Being a suspect in several murders, plus human trafficking, and running an illegal house of prostitution puts your client as a high-risk suspect. If you think you can come into my courtroom and flaunt your expensive clothes and big money, you are mistaken. I will not rescind my court ordered house arrest for your client. In addition, if she tries to bend the rules one iota, I will have her incarcerated immediately. Do you both understand me?"

Alma spoke before Rita could say a word, "We understand, Your Honor."

"Now, you two get out of my courtroom and do not bother me with any more of your trivial wants and trips to Paris."

Rita was shocked. Alma had not gotten her restrictions reduced. She would not be going to Paris with her club.

As soon as they were in Alma's Mercedes, Rita exploded, "That thon of a bitthch of a judge. I'm going to have JJ, when he is elected, have her removed. Who does she think she is? I'm going to report her to the media."

"I wouldn't do that, Rita. It might backfire. JJ is in enough trouble, politically, as it is," Alma answered.

Alma drove up the long drive to Rita's mansion. They sat quietly for just a minute before Alma spoke.

"Rita, don't do anything foolish. I know you wanted to go to Paris, but under the circumstances, maybe you should put it off. Maybe if you keep a low profile, JJ may still win this primary, and you will get to go to Washington, D.C. Think of the future, not what's happening right now. I think our friend, Thelma Riess, would love to go to Paris. Maybe you could sell her your reservation."

The statement enraged the already steaming Rita.

"I will not give up on my trip to Paris. I deserve it, and I will not sell my spot to that hussy Thelma Riess from Oregon. She may be your friend, but she is not mine. She's just waiting for someone to quit our bridge club, so she can join. How could you even suggest her? She's only a wife of a bank vice president. What kind of money does she have? She can't afford a pot to pee in. Have you given up on me?"

Alma was very quiet and stared at Rita. Her friend was in deep trouble, and she didn't realize how deep. She thought her money and social status would rescue her. Alma knew different.

"Rita," Alma started, "you have been a dear friend for many years. Before you get out of my car, I'm going to be very frank with you. You are in very deep trouble with the law. The charges against you are very serious. You could be imprisoned for a long time. I would not, if I were you, do anything to anger the courts, or you *will* jeopardize your ability to clear yourself from those charges. Plus, it would cause JJ to have to withdraw from the race, if that scenario hasn't already occurred."

Rita opened the car door and turned to Alma.

"Well, my friend, I didn't think you would bail out on me. I guess I was wrong. I will do this on my own. I will, in spite of your predictions, see you in Paris. You can tell Thelma Riess, she can go to hell! Good-bye!"

Chapter 26

Today, Bobbi was scheduled for her final colonoscopy during her hospital stay. She dreaded the process of fasting and drinking the cleanout fluid. The worst was this was the first time she would have any knowledge of the doctor running the test. After what Rita had done to her, she was paranoid. She requested Dan be allowed to stay in the room with her during the procedure. Under the circumstances, it was allowed.

The scoping showed a little scarring but no inflammation. She could be released if Bobbi and Dan had someone present to take care of them. Within six weeks, however, Bobbi must agree to the doctor performing another colonoscopy. Bobbi's mother suggested the couple come to Maquoketa and rest at the Stroud farm. She could take care of them, which included feeding Bobbi only soft foods for two more weeks. Millie promised she would make Bobbi stay true to the diet. The farm would be a quiet place where they could recharge and heal. Bobbi had lost twenty pounds since entering the hospital. She was quite thin.

* * *

At the farm ten days later, Bobbi entered her mother's kitchen wearing her pajamas and fuzzy slippers. Her dark hair was growing back. It stuck out like a bristle brush because it was still too short to comb.

"Good morning, honey," greeted Millie. "How was your night?"

"Oh, fine, sort of," was the answer.

"Didn't sleep well?"

"Yeah, I just couldn't shut my mind off, and then I'd have to go to the bathroom. This soft diet is horrible. How many days before I can eat normally?"

"Another three, and then we'll have to keep you away from the good stuff like French fries and greasy hamburgers. What else is puzzling you?"

"Well, I guess I can tell you. Two nights ago, Dan and I tried to have sex. It didn't work. We tried again last night with the same result. He just can't get an erection. He's really concerned that we won't be able to have any children."

Millie hugged Bobbi and consoled her, "I wouldn't be so concerned. Dan had a part of his anatomy really traumatized. It may take a while. You could always go to a specialist. I'm sure they have medicines which will help. Just be patient. Say, by the way, where is your dashing young prince?"

"He's checking in with Des Moines. They would like our expense accounts and hospital costs. I really think Captain Stender is wondering when we can return."

Dan appeared just minutes later. He apologized for being late for breakfast.

"You, at least, get food. All I get is mush," quipped Bobbi. "Did you get a hold of Cal?"

"Yes, he was wondering if you and I are strong enough to come to Des Moines. They would like us to give them some statements plus other accounts. We could take our time driving. He would also like us to check in on Ron Puck and his friend, Phil. Ron is recuperating at the Veterans' Hospital in Iowa City. He lost his foot and two fingers in his ordeal with the end loader. They say he'll be out in a month after his therapy. Phil had his jaw unwired and is doing fine. He's at home in Walcott. I told him we could do it. I think if we stick to Interstate 80, we will always be close to a rest stop, just in case you have an emergency."

"Sounds like a plan. I think I can handle it. When do we leave?"

"As soon as you are off the soft diet and your mother thinks you can go."

Millie chimed in, "In three days, I think Bobbi can go. She can't stay here forever."

"One more thing," continued Dan, "Cal wants us to attend an honors ceremony for Betty Winters and the Gomez sisters. Remember, she was the deputy who exposed Sheriff Ward of Muscatine and then had a terrible accident. She tried to sue Toyota for negligence. Toyota had their experts check her car and found someone had cut the brake lines and altered the steering system. Later, former Deputy Alvin White confessed to the automobile tampering committed by him and Sergeant Keith Waters. As a result of the accident, she sustained multiple leg fractures plus a broken arm. The impact also caused her to lose her hearing in one ear. She'll be on permanent disability. Tonight, she is receiving a medal of bravery and a key to the city. The Gomez sisters' tape of the sheriff's misconduct brought the great Sheriff Ward to justice. Captain Stender would like us to be there representing the DCI. I told him one of us or both of us would be glad to be there. Millie, you and Bill are also invited."

"I think that would be great. I'll bet Phil might be there, too," added Bobbi.

Bobbi was excited. It would be the first positive event she would attend in more than two weeks. It also meant the first time she felt comfortable being away from a bathroom for more than thirty minutes.

They arrived at the high school auditorium thirty minutes ahead of the ceremonies. Bobbi and Dan were ushered backstage. Bill and Millie found good seats in the audience. The DCI agents were introduced to Betty. She was resting in her wheelchair and was surrounded by reporters and friends. As soon as the media discovered the arrival of the tortured DCI officers, Bobbi and Dan were also being interviewed. It was five minutes before the program when Bobbi spied Phil and Sherry Robbins. She barely recognized Phil. He had dropped forty pounds. He still wasn't a solid muscular he-man, but he looked nice.

"Hi, Phil," she called. "You look terrific."

"I did lose some weight. You know you can't eat fattening foods when your mouth is wired shut. I even worked out a bit. Believe it or not, Sherry has lost twenty pounds, too," he replied.

"Great."

"You look like you lost some pounds, too, but you didn't need to."

"Yeah, I lost twenty. I couldn't eat anything for ten days and everything was through the tube. After that period of time, I could only eat soft foods for two weeks. I have two days left, and then I get to eat some solid food. I'm counting the hours."

"When I had my jaw unwired, the doc said I could eat solids but not anything that required tough chewing for a couple of weeks. Sherry is becoming an expert cook at preparing hamburger recipes. I should be able to have a steak on Memorial Day weekend."

An official cut off their conversation and led them to their respective seats on stage. Several officials spoke and told Betty's story. The surprise of the evening was the governor appearing to present the awards. Betty sat at the edge of the stage in her wheelchair as Anita and Juanita Gomez received their awards. When Betty was to receive her award, her husband handed her a pair of crutches. She slowly arose from her chair and walked to the center of the stage. Everyone stood, applauded, and cheered for nearly five minutes. The Gomez sisters came forward and hugged her. Betty's and the Gomez sister's courage brought down a very corrupt sheriff's department. Because of their courage, Muscatine County was a much safer place to live.

Two days later, Bobbi and Dan visited Ron in Iowa City. He was in good spirits, but still had a long way to go. Of the four law enforcement members, Ron had received the most extensive injuries. He was lucky to be alive. As the Dorman's left, they met Julia Herera in the hall. Evidently, Ron's injuries hadn't dampened her affection for Ron Puck.

Bobbi and Dan spent a week in Des Moines. Even though they enjoyed the farm, being in their own apartment was more relaxing. Bobbi applied for the desk job, and Dan put his name on a list for another team. The soles of his feet were still tender, but by wearing extra stockings, he could walk comfortably. Millie called and wondered if the pair was still coming home for the Memorial Day weekend. Bobbi assured her they were.

* * *

It was nine in the evening when the young couple arrived at the farm. Millie surprised Bobbi by telling her, her sister, Carol and her husband, Tom, were coming for a visit on Saturday. It meant the two sisters and their husbands would be sharing a bathroom. It wouldn't be a problem except Carol was very pregnant, and Bobbi still had spasms and needed the facilities in a hurry. It could be interesting.

Saturday morning Bobbi was the first to arrive at breakfast, and she was still in her pajamas. They hung on her thin body like clothes on a line. Her mother noticed Bobbi's thin hands sticking out of the sleeve. As Bobbi went to the refrigerator, Millie could see her daughter's legs were just sticks.

"Are you feeling all right?" asked Millie.

"Yeah, Mom. I'm just a little hungry."

"Do you want some eggs and bacon?"

"Yes, they'll go good with my yogurt and probiotic drink. My doctor said the acid Mrs. Johnson injected in me killed most of the good bugs in my intestines. I don't digest things completely. I'm always hungry, but I don't gain any weight. Doctor Sam told me it probably will take me six to eight weeks to fully recover. He assured me I'd recover. I just have to be patient."

"But, you're so thin."

"I know, but don't worry. I'll be all right."

"Okay, but you be careful."

Dan arrived with a fuzzy red beard and short hair. He was wearing a T-shirt and shorts. On his feet, he wore special socks, because the bottoms of his feet were still very tender. They were like a newborn baby's feet. It was all new skin. He padded over to Bobbi and kissed her. Millie smiled.

"Two eggs and bacon, Dan?" Millie asked.

"Yes, Millie," Dan replied smiling as he had remembered to call her by her first name.

Millie got out a dozen eggs from the refrigerator.

She asked, "Why don't I just scramble a dozen? Bill will be in shortly, and he'll be hungry."

She was right. Her husband entered shortly after checking the cattle.

"Going to be a nice day. Dan, do you want to go out to the fields to check the corn and beans with me after breakfast?" Bill asked.

"Sure."

Next, Bill suggested Bobbi and Dan visit Bobbi's grandparents.

"Sure," said Bobbi. "Is one of them ill?"

"No, but I think it would be nice before Carol gets here."

"Okay, Dad, we'll go as soon as I dress. Do you suppose Grams will be surprised by my hair? It is a little longer and beginning to lay over."

"I showed her several photos of you when you were in the hospital, so she won't be surprised."

Bill gave Dan a quizzical smile. Evidently, his daughter had forgotten about farming. Her traumatic experience in Wapello had erased her thoughts about coming home. He smiled at Millie. His daughter and her husband were going to be surprised when they visited Millie's parents.

"Why don't you go about ten? I'll be sure to have Dan back in time for a shower," Bill chuckled.

After finishing breakfast, Dan hurried and dressed in some old jeans and a denim shirt. He put on an extra pair of socks, because he had to wear sandals until his feet healed. Bill picked him up in his Prowler UTV. Dan waved as they sped out of the farmyard.

Bobbi helped her mother clear the table and headed to her bedroom to change. Millie followed her a few steps behind. She stood outside the door and knocked.

"May I come in, Bobbi?" she asked.

"Sure, Mom."

Millie walked in and watched her daughter lay some clean clothes on the bed. It seemed to her Bobbi was going to stall until her mother left.

"Do want me to leave while you dress?" she asked.

Bobbi didn't answer.

Millie set her jaw. This time, she was going to be adamant.

"Bobbi, I don't' know what the problem is, but I'm going to find out. Take off your pajamas. You're hiding something from me, your own mother. Do you have a skin problem or something?" she inquired.

Bobbi stood by the bed and faced her mother. She slowly unbuttoned her top and slipped it off.

Millie gasped. Her daughter was super thin. Her collar bones stuck out. Every rib could be easily counted.

"How much do you weigh, honey? You're like a walking skeleton."

"I'm down to ninety pounds, but I've gained five back."

Bobbi continued to undress. As she slipped her bottoms off, her lip began to quiver like a little girl, and she began to cry. Bobbi's hip bones stuck out like a fashion model's. Her thighs were atrophied. Millie rose from the bed and held her daughter.

"What's the matter, honey? Is it something with Dan?"

"No, no, Mother, it isn't that. You just wouldn't understand."

"Try me?"

Bobbi sobbed on her mother's shoulder. Millie pulled a blanket from the unmade bed and wrapped it around her naked daughter.

Bobbi tried to stop crying. She began to speak between her sobs.

"Oh, Mommy, it was terrible what she did to us."

"Who's she?" her mother asked, knowing her little girl hadn't called her Mommy for years.

This had to be serious.

"Mrs. Rita Johnson."

"Isn't she the wife of the man running for congress from the first district who was just arrested?"

"Yes, she is, and she was arrested, but the judge felt sorry for her and didn't put her in jail. She let her go free, but she has to wear an ankle bracelet. It isn't fair."

"Tell me all about it, Bobbi. Maybe it will help."

Oh, Mommy, Dan and I were instructed to delay the suspects until our captain could organize a raid on the plant. We arrived at the office and asked to see the manager. He didn't want to see us, so we used our badges and barged into his office. He escaped out a hidden door in the rear of the building. We followed him. We saw him disappear behind another door. It was marked, "Do Not Enter." We pulled our weapons. We were welcomed inside the room. Once inside, we were tricked and they disarmed us. This lady everyone called Mrs. Ping greeted us.

"After a demonstration of her power over her girls, she had Dan removed from the room. She continued to interrogate me. When she was unsuccessful, I, too, was taken to the room. I found Dan, his head shaved, in a harness and he was tied up. Ping continued to question me. I refused to answer.

"She had Dan stripped and dunked into a tank of hot water and acid. When that didn't work to make us talk, she started on me. She had my head shaved, and then she made me stand in the middle of the room with everyone watching. She sold the clothes right off my back, piece by piece. She didn't stop until I was naked. The last was the worst. A big man made me take off my bra. He claimed he wanted to give it to his girlfriend. Then he made me strip and give my panties to him. I had to turn around several times so he could get a good view.

"Mommy, it was so embarrassing standing naked in front of all those people, especially the men. I could feel their eyes searching me. The worst was she made me drink a terrible tasting fluid, and I vomited and had diarrhea. I had to sit on the toilet which was in the room, but it was exposed. Everyone watched me vomit and pee.

"She dipped Dan into the hot acid-laden water a couple more times, and he was burned severely. He couldn't help me. They tied me to a table and the witch gave me several enemas from the vat of hot water and acid. I thought I was going to die. I guess they thought I was dead, because they wrapped me in a canvas cloth and put Dan and me in the back of his pickup to dump us in the river. If it wasn't for a pair of side cutters in Dan's tackle box, he couldn't have gotten loose. We escaped the pickup while it was underwater. I had so many cramps, I couldn't walk. Thank God, the young farmer showed up, or we would have been names on the obituary page."

Millie held her trembling daughter close and said, "It okay. You're alive. Dan loves you, your dad and I love you, and you are going to be fine. I promise. Now, dry your tears and get dressed. Do you want me to help?"

"Yes, Mom, thank you for listening, but Mom, now I hate to undress in front of Dan. Really, I hate to undress in front of anyone, even you. When I take a shower, I lock the door. I change clothes in another room. When we try to have sex, I keep my top on, and I never leave the bed until Dan has left. What am I going to do?"

"Oh, Bobbi, my child, I think it will all work out. It may take some time, but God will help. You just keep praying. Now, let's get you dressed. Dan will be back and ready to go to Grandma Miller's," her mother replied drying her own tears.

Dan and Bill returned. Dan was all excited about what he had learned. He noticed Bobbi's red eyes and knew she had been crying.

"Is something wrong?" he asked.

Before Bobbi could say anything, Millie butted in, "Bobbi and I had an unpleasant conversation about your ordeal. We both got fairly emotional. We're okay now. Isn't that right, Bobbi?"

Bobbi shook her head, yes.

* * *

Dan and Bobbi drove to the Miller's. Grandma and Grandpa Miller were waiting for them.

"Do you want some coffee and cookies?" Grandma Edna asked.

Bobbi knew she had to say, "Yes." It was a good thing Grandma Edna's cookies were always good. They sat in the kitchen around the table and talked. Bobbi filled the older couple in about their jobs, but she left out the bad parts. She also knew Grandma Edna didn't approve of her being a cop. That job was for men. Grandpa Henry just listened. When the conversation wound down, he spoke.

"I hear you two would like to try farming," he said.

The statement surprised the younger couple, because they had completely forgotten their wish to farm.

"Yes, I guess...so," stammered Dan.

Henry smiled and continued, "Mom and I would like to retire. We are looking for some young couple to take over. Bobbi, your Uncle Ken had and never will have a desire to farm and your mother is already farming. I know Dan, you're a greenhorn as green as you can get, but your father-in-law said he would help you out and guide you. Are you interested?"

Dan replied, "Yes. We're interested. I'm flabbergasted. I'll work as hard as I can, Mr. Miller."

"Farming does include hard work, but in today's world, it is also involves management. It's bookkeeping and watching every penny. I must also say, it does take a little luck, but we think you will be fine."

"But we don't even know where to start," Bobbi blurted out. "We have some savings, but not that much. I know it takes a lot to start farming."

"Let me tell you my plan," Grandpa Henry continued. "I realize one of you or both of you will have to get a job in town for a while. Grandma would like to see you be a stay-at-home mother, Bobbi, so it means Dan would have to work elsewhere. Your dad has already helped me several times with his equipment. I think he will continue to help you young folks. You will have a year to work things out, because this year has already begun. I plan to have our farm equipment sale next fall. It will be quite a bit of income. Next, I'll have all this year's crop to sell for next year and no expenses for seed and fertilizer. I, or I should say we, are ready to offer you and Bobbi one year rent free to get you started, because you will have more expenses than you ever imagined."

Bobbi and Dan were speechless. They had smiles as wide as a jack-o-lantern. They were going to be Iowa farmers.

Grandma changed the subject.

"Your mother invited us over for supper. I hear Carol and Tom are coming. I heard she is pregnant, and I'm going to be a great grandmother. This is so exciting!"

Bobbi affirmed Carol and Tom coming for a visit, and then they realized they had better be going. She was supposed to help fix lunch. She hugged both her grandparents and thanked them for their generosity.

The ride home was exhilarating. Both would ride a few feet and then both start talking at once. They'd laugh. Then they'd get quiet. Then they'd start talking at once again. It was that way all the way home.

Carol and Tom had arrived by the time they pulled up to the front door. Bobbi ran to greet her younger, very pregnant, sister. They hugged or tried to hug. It seemed Carol's enlarged tummy kept getting in the way. Carol ran her hand down Bobbi's back.

"My lord, you're thin. I can feel your backbone. What happened to you besides being dumped into a river and being rescued by a handsome farmer?" she teased.

Bobbi snapped back, "I was forced on a crash diet and forgot to quit. I got down to ninety-pounds before the doctor put me on a special high protein, high vitamin, and probiotic diet. I've gained back five pounds since then. I eat but have a difficult time digesting the intake."

"Well, you better get fatter. Thin heifers have a hard time getting bred, you know."

They laughed and kidded each other for the next ten minutes. They were two sisters who loved each other.

Grandpa and Grandma Miller came after lunch and rejoiced in Carol's pregnancy. Dan grilled hamburgers, chicken, peppers, and potatoes for supper. His expertise with the grill amazed everyone but Bobbi. She claimed that was why she married him. Grandpa Henry was the one to announce he had new renters, and he was going to retire.

"Is it anyone we know?" asked Carol.

Henry smiled, "I think so. I just rented our farm to Dan and Bobbi. Grandma and I both think it will be nice to have a young couple continue to farm our ground and not some big corporate farmer who already has thousands of acres."

Carol looked at her beaming sister and said, "Well, Buttons, you always said you wished you were a boy, so you could farm. Congratulations! Does this mean I can bring my kids for a visit, and they can stay to play with their farmer cousins?"

"You betcha," Bobbi answered, "and if they're girls, I'll take them skinny-dipping in the quarry."

"Well, this one is a boy, so I guess it won't work," Carol shot back.

"Heck, we'll take him anyway. He might as well get used to his girl cousins, if he has any. It's a good time to learn about the birds and the bees."

"All right, girls, that's enough!" butted in Millie. "We have a few years to worry about that. Let's clean up the dishes and join the men on the deck. We can visit a little later."

The night went by fast. It was past 9:30 when the grandparents left. The air was getting chilly so they retired to the family room. Bobbi and Dan chose the love seat, Bill, his big leather lounger, Millie, her favorite swing rocker, and Carol and Tom, the couch. Carol leaned on Tom because her huge tummy needed support and the little one inside was waking up and beginning to kick.

She sighed, and remarked, "I'll be glad when the baby is born. Maybe then I'll get some sleep."

Millie burst out laughing,

"Get some sleep? The only time you'll get any sleep is when

the baby is at our house. You won't get a good night's sleep until he's married and becomes someone else's baby."

Bobbi looked at the clock. She was so tired. Her thin body just didn't have any extra to give.

"I'll think I'll go to bed," she announced. "You coming, Dan?"

"I believe I'll stay for the news, and I want to talk to your dad some."

"Tom," said Carol, "I need help getting up. I need to go to the bathroom."

"I'll have to use the half bath in the hall. Bobbi will be using ours."

Tom helped his overloaded wife to her feet. She headed for the hall. Millie followed.

"Could you come to the kitchen when you're finished?" she whispered to Carol.

"Sure, Mom, I'll be there in a jiffy."

The men stayed to watch the news. Millie waited for Carol at the kitchen table.

"What's up, Mom?" she asked.

"It's Bobbi. She is so thin and now she is scared."

"Scared of what?"

"Scared of undressing in front of Dan or anybody."

"That's not unusual, but maybe for Bobbi it is. We used to skinny dip all the time in the quarry. I didn't think she had a problem. When did you find this out? Did Dan say something?"

"No, I found out today. I followed her to her room to have a talk and she seemed reluctant to change her pajamas. I confronted her and scolded her. I told her she was hiding something from me. I told her to take off her pajamas and let me see. As soon as she took off her top, she began to cry. She told me about her ordeal. She was forced to stand naked in front of all kinds of people. Now, she's afraid to even shower without locking the door. They can't even have sex naked. She has to wear a top and doesn't get out of the bed until Dan leaves. He also has a problem, but I can't cure that one. Do you think you could help?"

"It sounds serious, Mom. I'll have a talk with her later, after she has napped. I'm up several times during the night, you know. She told me she still gets up during the night. If you hear us talking, just know we are okay."

Later that night, the two sisters did meet in their common bathroom. Carol asked Bobbi about her ordeal, and she tried to encourage Bobbi to try just some simple things like wearing only a towel for a few minutes after a shower. Maybe she could work around the house in her robe with nothing on underneath. Bobbi said she would try.

Carol suggested, "Tomorrow night, let me help you get started. You meet me here early in the morning. I want you to agree to do what I am going to do. Okay?"

Bobbi answered with a tentative, "I guess so."

At the breakfast table Sunday morning, they decided not to attend church. Carol just didn't think she could sit that long. The conversation was mostly about the new grandson coming in June.

"Do you think you and Dan could watch the farm around Father's Day? Dad and I want to help Carol for a few days," asked Millie.

"How many days are you talking about, Mom?" quizzed Bobbi.

"Three or four days, and we could make it over a weekend."

"I think we can get off. We've taken quite a few days now, but most of those will be sick days and recovery from a job-related injury."

Bill changed the subject and said, "I saved this issue of the North Scott Press for you, Buttons. It was written by your friend, Phil Robbins. It tells all about the revamping of that packing plant you and Dan investigated."

Bobbi stopped eating for a moment. Her face flushed. She coughed and took a drink of coffee. She sat looking down at her yogurt for several seconds. Dan reached over, put his hand on her knee, and patted it as if to say, "Are you all right?" Bobbi reacted by placing her hand on the top of his and rubbed it. She'd be okay.

"I'd like to read it, Dad. We were wondering what happened to the plant," she replied.

Bill continued, "I probably should let you read it, but I'll tell you what I got from the article. The plant operated under a court authorization for four weeks. A group of cattlemen and the Wapello State Bank decided the plant needed to stay open. The bank stated the number of jobs it created and how it helped the economy of Louisa County and the surrounding area. The cattlemen told how the plant was one of a kind and a place to dispose of cows, which had outlived their usefulness. The nearest facility doing the same was in Norfolk, Nebraska. The cattlemen formed a co-op and bought the plant.

"They sold shares and anyone selling cows who is not a member would be assessed a small fee. They hired the present manager, because he had managed the plant for the Johnson's, who merely provided the money when the plant first went bankrupt. The best idea was they included all the workers in their plan. Each employee was included in the dividend payout according to the time they had worked there. They also have bi-monthly staff-employee meetings. According to Phil, it is working out very well. The plant should survive and be a great asset to the county and to the state. You can read the details of who is running the plant and who is on the board of directors, etc."

Dan smiled at his wife, then at everyone else before he spoke.

"Bobbi and I have fond memories of that place, don't we, Bob?"

With that statement, Bobbi punched her husband in the shoulder.

"Your memories may be fond, but mine aren't."

The rest of the day was all family talk. Everything was discussed from the new baby boy's name, to what equipment Dan would have to have to start farming, and how much it would cost. The evening meal was provided by Dan again. He grilled some steaks and chicken breasts. His sides were grilled beets, carrots, and potatoes in foil. Millie furnished her fresh strawberry pies for dessert. Everyone was stuffed. Carol and Bobbi continued their routine of an early bedtime.

They were both in the bathroom when Carol asked, "Are you ready to try my idea tonight?"

Bobbi paused for a moment, "I guess so."

"Listen, if you don't think you are ready, we can wait."

"No, no, I've got to face this now, or I'll never have any children. If I don't hear you, you come and wake me."

"I'll wait until early morning, so you will have a good night's sleep."

* * *

It was five in the morning. The sun was just rising in the east.

There wasn't a cloud in the sky. Carol made her usual bathroom run. After she had finished, she waited for Bobbi. She peeked into Bobbi's room and could see she was sound asleep. She tiptoed over to her bed and tapped her on the shoulder. Bobbi opened one eye and pushed her away. Carol persisted.

"Come on, Bobbi. You promised."

Bobbi rolled out of bed and followed her sister into the bathroom.

"Now here's what we are going to do," Carol ordered. "We are going to strip naked and go outdoors on the deck. Nobody will see us. We are going to embrace the morning sun and hurry back to our beds and our husbands."

"And?" Bobbi asked.

"Get in bed naked with them."

"And?"

"Stay naked."

"Right."

"But what if Dad wakes up and sees us out on the deck?"

"I already told Mom. She'll make sure he stays in bed." Carol smiled as she continued, "She thought it was time for a little loving for herself, if you get my drift. Okay?"

"Okay, but how do we get out of here? We have to go through our bedrooms. What if Dan or Tim wakes up and sees us?"

"Boy, you do have a problem. It doesn't bother me who sees me naked. I've been naked so many times in the doctor's office. I almost feel I should just wear a robe when I go there. It sure would save time. Most of the women are parading around from room to room in those little gowns with their butts exposed anyway. You just get used to it. Let's go through your room."

"Okay."

"Then off with the clothes. Let's go and greet the morning sun."

Bobbi tiptoed through the family room while poor Carol waddled. Bobbi slid the sliding door open and stepped outside in the awakening sunshine. The sun had a golden glow and skin tones were darker and richer. Bobbi jumped up on the picnic table and stretched her arms to the sky. She was trying to be brave.

"Ah, the freedom of rural living!" she whispered to herself.

"Do you remember when we did this as teens?" Carol asked.

"Yeah! And when we saw Dad's light in his bathroom flick on, we knew we were trapped. We had to run around the house and hide in the bushes until he left for chores. Mom was sure surprised when we ran into the kitchen with nothing on."

Carol looked at Bobbi, who was shivering, and she said, "Aren't we the pair? You're as skinny as a rail and me as fat as a pig, with my belly button sticking out like a mole mound on a pink hill. I can't wait until this baby is born."

"Are you sorry you are pregnant?" asked Bobbi.

"Heavens no, I'm as happy as a coon in a sweet corn patch. This is the best thing ever. Just think, I'm giving life to a new person, and then I get to nurse him, raise him, and watch him grow up. This huge belly and my oversized breasts are just part of the plan. If it wasn't for women, there wouldn't be any people. I told Tom I want three or four kids," Carol answered. "Now let's get inside before we freeze."

They hurried back inside and quietly closed the sliding door. Bobbi led the way. She stopped outside her parent's bedroom door. She motioned for Carol to come and put her finger to her lips to indicate quiet. Inside, they could hear a sigh and then a moan. Finally, they heard the voice say, "I love you."

"We'd better get out of here," whispered Bobbi.

Because the outside air was cool, Bobbi was freezing, but it made snuggling up to Dan much nicer. Carol was a genius. Dan ran his fingers up Bobbi's thin leg. He smiled with his eyes closed. He rubbed her chilly back and pulled her close. He loved the feeling of having her breasts push against his chest. This was like old times. Now if he could just function.

The next morning, Millie sent Bill down to Casey's to buy a dozen and a half donuts. It was a treat for everyone. The morning news announced JJ Johnson was withdrawing from the Congressional race. He had too many family issues to continue. He wished his opponent the best of luck, and he said he would support him in the general election.

The visit was over too soon. Bobbi thanked Carol for her help. Hopefully, she could put her ordeal at Acme away forever. At least, she didn't mind sleeping nude with Dan anymore. In fact, she whispered to Carol, she and Dan were going to try only wearing pajamas around the house and not in bed. Maybe it would change if she got pregnant, but right at the present time, this was the plan.

Both sisters and their respective husbands had a three-hour drive ahead of them. Lunch was leftovers. After a few tears and hugs, Bobbi and Dan headed for Des Moines. All the way home, they talked about what they would do once they were farming. Bobbi already had her mind made up. She was going to raise meat goats and maybe a few lambs. She had read goats were the hot item and fairly easy to raise. It would be something she and the kids could handle, if she became a stay-at-home mom. Dan said on his first day off he was heading to the Iowa State Extension Office to gather all the information he could find on farming in Eastern Iowa.

Chapter 27

Rita Johnson's friends began to dwindle. Her friend, Alma, pumped her husband, whose firm was handling Rita's case. She found Rita's defense was going to be a tough one. The trip to Paris with the bridge club was still on. Despite Alma's urging, Rita was not changing her mind. She was determined to travel to Paris, regardless of her situation.

To top off Rita's anger, Thelma Reiss had put her name on the waiting list for the same tour, and she was rewarded by another cancellation. She would be on the airplane with Rita. Alma told Rita the airport security would stop her before she got past the first check point. She told Rita her ankle bracelet would be a dead giveaway.

Rita decided to try to outsmart the court system. She would cancel her ticket at the Cedar Rapids Airport and leave from the Quad City Airport in Moline, Illinois. Certainly, the courts in Illinois were not updated on her status. She thought if she removed her ankle bracelet and left it at her home, it would indicate she was still in Iowa. Once she arrived in Chicago and was seated on the plane destined for Paris, she assumed she would be safe. She made sure she traveled on a different airline than her friends from the bridge club.

She chuckled to herself, "Won't the girls be surprised when I show up at the tour's first organizational meal."

June 15 was the Paris departure date. Rita called Alma and told her she had taken her advice and withdrawn from the trip a couple of days prior. Alma told her she had made the right decision.

Rita kept her real plans a secret. Her flight from Moline was to leave at seven in the morning. JJ was not going to be there to take her to the airport. He assumed she had given up on the trip. He was in Moline, all right, but at a two-day, major John Deere conference, which meant he wasn't home to stop his conniving wife.

She cut her ankle bracelet off and laid it on the kitchen counter during the night. This would be a test if the authorities could detect whether she was wearing it or not. Boy, it felt good to get rid of that horrible looking thing. She slept soundly that night, because she had everything covered.

She drove her BMW to the airport, parked in the long-term lot, and passed through the security line. She made it with ease. Her flight was easy, and she would have a two-hour layover at O'Hare Airport in Chicago. She would be in the air before her bridge club even landed in Chicago on a flight from Cedar Rapids. Her flight was called. Rita always rode first class. She didn't seem alarmed as she approached the check-in desk and found three security personnel standing by the desk—two men and a woman.

"Mrs. Rita Johnson?" inquired the airline person.

"Yes," Rita answered.

"May I see some identification?"

"Yes, is there a problem?"

The agent at the desk showed the security woman Rita's identification card. The woman reacted immediately.

She moved over to Rita and took hold of her elbow.

She said, "Mrs. Johnson, will you please follow me?"

Rita reacted by pulling away and asked again, "Is there a problem? I won't miss my flight, will I?"

Rita started to resist the officer. The two male officers moved forward and each one grabbed one of Rita's elbows.

"Please, Mrs. Johnson, come with us."

"Why?" she screamed.

"You are under arrest for breaking a court order in Iowa, and you have illegally removed a tracking ankle bracelet. We are ordered to detain you until the proper authorities can process your case and extradite you back to Iowa."

"What about my luggage?"

"Your luggage will be removed from the plane before it leaves. We will make sure your husband or close relative receives it."

Rita struggled a bit, but soon gave up. She realized she was not going to Paris or anywhere else. The Burlington Jail was probably her next stop. She knew the kind judge who had given her freedom would not look kindly on her planned escape. The strong demanding Rita Johnson had tears running down her face as they walked to the security office. Her life as she knew it was about to change drastically.

Chapter 28

Tuesday morning back in Des Moines, Bobbi was assigned to a desk job, which she expected because she was still very weak. Dan partnered up with Dick Sprouse. They were to investigate a police shooting in Ankeny. The first night home, Dan was already complaining. Dick was a smoker and a divorcee. He didn't smoke in the car, but as soon as he stopped, he had to have a cigarette. His breath and clothes smelled of smoke. Dan figured unless his former wife also smoked, it was the cause of their divorce. The men had nothing in common. Dan was twenty-eight and Dick was fifty-four. His children were far away and because of the divorce, he was lonely. He talked and bragged about his conquests of the bar women he had met.

Bobbi's desk job was also boring. She loved the outdoors and the excitement of investigating. She would apply for a permanent desk job only if she had children. She wanted to be home every night. The desk job Captain Stender had promised became open June 15. Bobbi applied, but found others in the department were also interested. She knew most of the women had much better computer skills. The job was not a sure thing. Bobbi's best hope was she'd get strong enough to go back being a detective with Dan. It would be a long time until January 1 of next year.

Carol had her baby boy on her due date. Grandmother Millie was anxious to help her and see her new grandchild. It was a three-hour drive to Bolingbrook, Illinois. She called Bobbi.

"Is it possible for you to come over Father's Day weekend?" she asked.

"We could be there Thursday night late."

"Good, we'll leave the key under the flower pot on the front porch. I want to be at Carol's by five. Tom is picking her up at the hospital around four."

Bobbi and Dan were very tired when they arrived at the farm. Bobbi went straight for the flower pot and dug out the key. Once inside, she headed for the refrigerator knowing her mother had it well-stocked.

"I'll fix some supper while you carry the luggage in. I see Mom left us some meatloaf. How do you feel about eating some meatloaf sandwiches?"

"Never had one," Dan replied.

"What? You never had one? Well, Danny boy, you're going to eat the best meatloaf sandwich you'll ever taste," she answered.

Bobbi seemed to be full of spirit. She and Dan were home on the farm and no one was there to bother them. The biotic medicines and drinks seemed to agree with her. She had gained another ten pounds. Her hair had grown out enough for her to be able to brush it. Next week, she was actually going to a hairdresser to have it styled. They would go visit her grandparents, the Millers, on Friday evening just so they could have the whole weekend for themselves.

A June cold front blew through Friday afternoon. Dan

marveled at watching the thunderheads build up and the pounding rain. By 8:00 p.m., the storm was over and the sky cleared. The late evening news promised a rare June day. Although it was a cold front which passed through, it was a Pacific air mass and not a Canadian one. It was to be in the 80s with low humidity.

Saturday morning, Bobbi suggested they have breakfast on the deck. Dan set the table and poured the coffee. Bobbi said she had to go to the bathroom. When she reappeared, she was wearing a see-through short nightgown with no undergarments. Dan's eyes bugged out. Bobbi purposely turned sideways so the sun would shine through the very thin fabric. Although still very thin, the outline of her body was quite sexy.

"You like?" she coyly asked.

"Very much!" Dan answered. "Why did you even put it on? You realize there is nothing left to the imagination."

"That's the idea," she replied with a sexy smile. "How's about a little R&R after breakfast?"

"I can try," Dan said.

They basked in the warm morning sun. After collecting the dishes and putting them in the dishwasher, Bobbi led Dan to the bedroom. As much as Dan tried, nothing worked. This was getting serious.

"It's all right," Bobbi assured him. "We have to be patient. The doctor says there's nothing wrong, and it's just a manner of time. Let's take a nap and go check the cows later."

"Okay!"

"Say, have you ever been to the quarry?" Bobbi asked.

"No, but I've heard you talk a lot about it."

"I suggest we go on a picnic at the quarry after we check the cows."

"Sounds like a deal," Dan said, "but first let me take a nap."

Bobbi awoke before Dan. She packed some sandwiches, a few chips, cookies, and some Iowa wine. She backed the UTV up to the deck and loaded it with an air mattress, air tank, a small folding table, two empty five-gallon pails, a towel to sit on, one to use for a tablecloth, and an old quilt. When she was all finished, she awakened Dan.

He opened one eye and was greeted by a beautifully thin wife wearing a pink top and denim short shorts. Her toenails were painted a bright red. He smiled and wondered what she ever saw in him, a tall, rangy red-headed Irishman. She bent down and kissed him.

They headed out to the pasture and found the cows lounging in the shade just a couple hundred yards from the quarry. The quarry was closed decades ago. It was water filled and clear. Several springs which flowed into the pit kept it fairly free of moss until late summer. It was hidden by five acres of white pines, part of a government re-forestation project. The pines were some twenty-plus years old and stood forty feet high. Bobbi and her sister had helped plant some of the trees when they were children.

Bobbi drove the UTV across the creek. She waited for Dan to open the gate and drove through the pines to her private piece of heaven. She stopped on a flat spot just north of the quarry pond. It was treeless because of the lack of topsoil. This is where they would picnic. Behind them was a wall of yellowish gray limestone. It was the beginning of the quarry years ago. The good stone ran out, therefore, the pit was dug. The pit was only twenty feet deep at its deepest.

Bobbi hopped out and said, "Follow me."

She led Dan to the edge of the quarry.

"See those steps in the stone over there?" she said, pointing to her left. "That's where you enter the water. You follow a narrow ledge for about twenty feet to that little cedar tree. Right there is a drop-off. Dad believes there was some poor stone there, and it slid into the deeper water. Now look about ten feet along the shore, and you can see another ledge. It extends out forty feet. It varies from two feet to four feet deep. That is where Carol and I learned to swim.

"The water tends to be warmer on the ledge. Beyond the ledge is the deep cold water. When we were young, we always had one of our parents come with us. They trusted us as teenagers, if we came together. Sometimes, we brought some friends. They all had to promise there'd be no horseplay or diving.

"One time, Carol let some boys come with us. They almost ruined our fun. They dove off the side with the cliff, and one of them got a big gash on his head. Dad said no more parties. The only ones who could swim there were just Carol and me. We loved to come out here and sunbath or just talk.

"We got fairly brave after a while. When we knew Dad was working, we would come out here and go skinny-dipping, then sunbathe nude on our towels. We thought we were really daring. We told Mom about it one time. She just smiled and told us a secret. She and Dad had skinny-dipped there a couple of times when they were young. We couldn't believe our folks ever did such a daring thing. Any questions?"

"Yeah, when do we eat?"

"Do you always think of food?"

"No, I think of sex sometimes."

Bobbi punched him and ran back to the UTV.

"You blow up the mattress, while I set up the table and food," she instructed him. "I suggest you put it halfway into the shade. I might want to sunbathe everything except my head. We'll eat in the sunshine and find out how hot it is. This old cliff reflects the heat."

They ate the rest of the meatloaf sandwiches, some chips, and finished off with some homemade chocolate chip cookies. The sun didn't seem too hot, so they pulled the pad out into the sun.

"Aren't you going to take off your shirt, Danny boy?"

"If I take off my shirt, I'll burn bright red without some suntan lotion," stated Dan.

"Don't worry. I brought some 50 SPF for your tender skin. Now take off your shirt, and let me cover your back with lotion. You can do your legs later."

Dan stripped off his shirt and Bobbi applied the goo. He applied some to the front of his legs as she worked on his back.

"Now me," she exclaimed as she pulled her top over her head.

Dan willingly obliged. They lay down on the old quilt and air mattress.

"If we didn't have this mattress, we'd be lying on rocks. That's why I brought it. Now close your eyes and listen to the birds and the wind as it tries to find a way through the pines."

It took twenty minutes before the sun was no longer just a little warm. It was hot. The little breeze they had, died. They both became hot and sweaty.

"How about moving this further under the tree?" he asked.

"I agree. It's hot now. You drag it back. I've got to go to the bathroom."

"Where's that?" he asked.

"Boy, you are naive. You just walk back into the trees and do it. I'm only going to pee."

Bobbi rose, grabbed a napkin from the picnic basket, and disappeared into the trees. Dan got up and dragged the mattress into the shade. He had his back turned away from the way Bobbi had gone.

"Hi, Danny, my lover boy, he heard from a female voice behind him.

He turned and there was Bobbi in her underwear. She smiled with an impish smirk, as if she was doing something daring.

"I didn't want to ruin my bikini lines, so I thought I'd lay with you in just my bra and panties. You don't mind, do you?"

Dan smiled back, and said, "Definitely not. You'd look good in nothing at all."

"I was hoping you would say so."

In a quick motion, she reached back, unhooked her bra, and let it fall. Next, she slipped off her panties. She gave him a sexy pose.

"I think nothing at all is better and you should do the same," she suggested. "We could enjoy nature together."

He wasn't as quick. She unbuttoned and unzipped his shorts to help him undress. He stood there a second not really ready to go all the way.

"Oh, come now, Danny boy. It's just you and me. I won't take any pictures."

He slid his undershorts down and stepped out. As he reached to pick them up, she patted him on his bare butt.

"You're a good looking piece of man," she teased as she eyed him up and down.

Dan responded by giving her a muscleman pose, and then he

tried a Tarzan yell which was pitiful.

Bobbi laughed.

They hugged and kissed.

"Want to go for a walk?" she asked.

"Where?"

"Just out among the trees. There's nobody here but you and me, Danny boy, and maybe a couple deer, woodpeckers, and rabbits, but they won't tell."

"Like this?"

"Yep!"

"Well, I've got to wear my sandals."

"Okay, I'll allow that. Nothing else though."

She took his hand and they slowly walked through the white pine trees. The pine needles were soft on the forest floor. They covered all the small stones and twigs. It was late spring and the white pine shed their old needles. Bobbi led him up a slight incline to a small clearing. They were on the top of the cliff. She stepped out into the sunshine.

"Look, see how far you can see from up here? You can see all the way to the Maquoketa River. See that tree line over there?" she pointed her finger. "That's the south ridge of the river."

Dan wasn't so enthusiastic about his exposure. He looked around, but was more concerned about who or what might be watching.

"Come on, silly. There's no one even close. This is what I enjoy about rural living. You don't have to worry if the neighbors are watching. You can sit on the back deck in your pajamas, or walk around inside your house with the shades up in your birthday suit. Or, you can go to the back corner of the farm and sunbathe nude and no one cares. Just like Adam and Eve in our own little Garden of Eden."

"Well, God can see us, so don't eat any apples," he quipped.

Bobbi began to dance in circles around Dan. She trailed her fingers on his body as she danced. He caught her and they embraced. Her body against his made him forget where they were and that they were nude.

Bobbi, sensing something was working, at least, she was losing her fears of be naked with her husband, said, "I'll race you back to the mattress," and she took off running down the slope through the pines.

Dan followed, but at a much slower pace. He had to duck under some of the lower branches or get swatted. When he finally caught up to her, she was kneeling on the mattress. He flopped on, but the mattress slid on the slick needles. He slid right off the other side. Bobbi piled on top of him, laughing, and giggling. He wrapped his arms around her, and they rolled a couple of times in the soft needles.

When they stopped, they were lying on their backs looking up through the branches. The sky, what they could see, was blue with a few puffy clouds starting to appear. Their bodies were covered with pine needles and Bobbi's hair, although short, was full of the tan needles. They held hands while looking up. Bobbi closed her eyes and listened to the sounds of nature.

Suddenly, she awoke from her swoon and said, "These pine needles are poking me, and I'm getting itchy. Let's go for a swim."

She popped up and pulled Dan along. They walked hand in hand to the shore of the quarry.

"The water may be a little chilly, but all I want to do is wash off."

She entered the water first. It was not as cold as she imagined. Of course, she was only up to her knees. Dan followed close behind. He purposely placed his hand on her behind as she walked ahead of him. She turned.

"I don't want to get lost," he told her.

They reached the cedar tree and the gap. Bobbi jumped toward the opposite ledge and reached it easily. Dan slipped into the water more slowly and crossed the gap. The water on this side was surprisingly warm. The sun reflecting off the submerged ledge warmed the top layer of water. They splashed into waist deep water and washed each other's itchy backs. She dipped her hair and vigorously washed out the needles and other debris. Dan's hair was much shorter. Since his shaving at the plant, he decided to keep it short for the summer.

They splashed and played in the shallow water.

"I'll race you to the middle," challenged Bobbi.

"You're on."

They waded to the edge of the ledge.

"One, two, three, go."

Bobbi splashed ahead. She could swim, but her form was not great. Dan just lay over on his back and began to do a backstroke.

He was well past the middle when she hollered, "Stop!"

She quickly turned and headed back. Dan did a swimmer's flip and soon caught up and passed her with ease. He stopped when his hand touched the shore rocks. He was puffing as he sat on the bottom. The water here was only two feet deep. Bobbi stopped as soon as she reached the ledge. She stood in waist deep water and glared at him.

"Since when did you learn to swim like that?" she asked.

"Since high school."

"I thought you were a basketball player, not a swimmer. You're pretty tall for a swimmer."

"Yeah, I know," he answered, "but in high school, I was a six-foot-four scarecrow. I had no body whatsoever. I tried basketball, but I knew I'd be riding the pines all the time. I had a buddy who was a diver. He encouraged me to try swimming. The school had a great coach. He made everyone feel important. When he saw my long arms, he told me I was a backstroker. I did all right. My senior year, I made state. There I came in tenth."

Bobbi stared at her husband and replied, "Well, I thought I knew you, but this is a surprise, Danny boy. My husband, a great swimmer, I should have brought you out here long ago. You could have saved a damsel in distress."

She waded close to him and sat astraddle his legs. She looked into his blue eyes and rubbed his short reddish hair.

"I love you, Danny boy. I love you with all my heart. If we never can have children, we'll adopt. Don't ever feel you are less of a man because of what happened to us. I just want you to be happy."

She pulled herself close to him and kissed him. Her tongue searched inside his mouth. They clung together for a long time.

Finally, he broke the clinch and whispered in her ear, "I'm getting chilly. That flip I did out in the middle took me into the deep water. That stuff must be forty degrees down there. Let's go lie down and sunbathe again."

She let him up and had him turn around. She wanted to check his butt for mud and moss. Even though it was clean as a whistle, she pretended to splash it and give it a good rub. They walked hand in hand to the gap. Bobbi went first again. He followed. She was about six feet ahead of him as they waded to the limestone steps. His eyes followed her every movement. He couldn't believe what he was watching. Even though they had been married for two years, it was like he was seeing her for the first time. He marveled at the way the water trickled from her wet hair down her bare back. When she ascended the steps, her every movement captured his senses. Her legs, her back, her shoulders, and her head glistened in the sun. She was covered with tiny diamonds of water.

"I brought a couple of towels to dry with," she said.

He smiled and thought to himself, "She had this skinny-dipping swim all planned ahead of time, the little snipe. But I loved it."

She dashed over to the UTV and pulled a cloth bag out of the back. Inside were two older towels.

"They're not the best, but they still will dry," she kidded and walked over to the mattress.

They both toweled off. Dan watched her every wipe. She finished by drying her hair. She looked at her husband gazing at her. She stared back and gave him a very serious look.

As she came closer, she said in a quiet calm voice, "I need you, Dan. I need you now. Hold me close. Don't ever leave me. You're my hero."

Dan held her and caressed her. She pressed against him and sighed. All of a sudden, she felt a push on her tummy. She slowly reached down and touched his erection.

Bobbi whispered as though not to scare it, "Our friend has awakened. I knew he would."

She knelt and gently held Dan's erection, then she kissed it right on the tip.

Dan cringed and also whispered, "We must hurry. I don't know how long I can hold on."

Bobbi lay down and he stretched out on top. She guided him

in to insure the act of love. Dan felt little shock waves emitting from his groin area all the way up to his neck. He had had them before, but not at this intensity. These were almost taking his breath away. He wondered if Bobbi had the same feelings. After all, women are different.

He rose up on his elbows and opened his eyes. She was lying with her eyes closed and her mouth slightly open. He heard her sigh. It wasn't long and it was over.

Bobbi opened her eyes and whispered, "Don't leave me. Stay in!"

She wrapped her legs around his and held him tight. He rolled her over and put her on top. She continued to press him in and lay down on his chest.

"I love you so much," she said.

"I love you, too," he answered.

Finally, she released his legs.

"That was wonderful. It seems so long ago since we had sex. Let's just lie here for a little longer before we dress and go back."

They lay on the mattress for another thirty minutes. Then it was time to go. The day would be one they would never forget. The probability of it happening again was small. There would be very few times when the combination of a blue sky in June, the low humidity, the temperature in the eighties, a secluded, private Garden of Eden, and time alone would happen in the near future. She suggested they not wear their underwear home, because they would have to shower right away anyway. It was a good ride to the house. They showered together.

"Let's go to town and eat at a restaurant tonight," suggested Dan.

"Okay, just as long as it is not Chinese," she answered smiling.

* * *

The sky was just becoming light, when Bobbi nuzzled her sleeping husband. She played with him until he awoke. He opened his sleepy eyes and smiled at his beautiful naked wife lying next to him.

"Hi," he said.

"Good morning, Danny boy. Want to try again?" she cooed.

It didn't take long and they were making passionate love. When finished, they lie exhausted beside each other.

Bobbi asked, "Would you like to go to my church this morning? I'd like to see some old friends."

"Sure. I might as well meet your friends, since we're coming here next year."

Dan drove out to check the cows in the UTV while Bobbi fixed breakfast. They arrived at Bobbi's home church early. The minster greeted them. At the end of the service, the minister and the board chair passed out little wooden crosses to all fathers. When she came to Dan, he said wasn't a father. The minister looked at Bobbi and winked.

She said, "But you'll be someday, won't you?"

Bobbi couldn't help but giggle a bit.

Chapter 29

Iowa City

Ron's sister, Sue, picked him up at the Veteran's Hospital in Iowa City. Ron had finished his rehabilitation. His severed foot was replaced by a prosthetic one. The injuries to his arms and hands required him to relearn how to take care of himself.

On the way home, Ron kept telling his sister, he could take care of himself. He insisted he was quite capable of being on his own. Sue just smiled and listened quietly. She changed the subject and told him about the farm. He asked about the Little League Baseball in West Liberty. She told him it was going well. As they pulled into the drive to his little house, he noticed another car in his drive.

"Whose car is that?" he asked.

"I have no idea," Sue answered with a smile.

They pulled up to the side door of his little house and

stopped. Out of the door stepped Julia, smiling. She opened the car door.

"Welcome home, stranger," she cooed.

Ron was shocked, and asked, "Why are you here?"

"I figured you needed some help for the first few days. I have my folks taking care of little Mike. I can't stay right now though. There's a big celebration at the ballpark. Do you feel you could come?"

"I guess so, but I can't drive yet."

Sue winked at Julia and said, "Travis and I will see he gets there. It's around seven, isn't it?"

"Yes. I'm sorry I can't stay. Maybe tomorrow, it's Saturday."

Julia gave Ron a peck on the cheek and got into her car and left. Sue helped Ron inside his little house. Julia had cleaned it from top to bottom. All the dishes were put away. The bed was made, which was something Ron never did. All the towels were hanging properly in the bathroom. There was a note on the top of his chest of drawers which read, "I love you, Ronnie." It was signed, Julia H.

"Tonight, why don't you eat with us at our house? Tomorrow, I'll take you grocery shopping," Sue told Ron.

He didn't refuse. After an early supper, Travis, Sue, Ron, and Nathan, Ron's nephew, drove to the West Liberty Ballpark. The place was packed.

"I wonder what's going on tonight?" asked Ron.

"I haven't a clue," replied Travis. "It must be really special."

As soon as they entered the parking lot, a man came up to Travis and motioned him ahead. He had him park a few feet from the right field fence. Several men came to greet Ron and helped him out of the car.

"Do you need a wheelchair?" they asked.

"No, I can make it to the stands with my cane. I'm just a little slow," answered Ron.

"You're not going to the stands, Mr. Puck. You are the guest of honor. Your seat is right behind home plate."

Just as planned, Julia and little Mike appeared. She gave him a big hug and kiss. Mike just gave him a hug. They slowly walked to the home plate area. On each base line, there was a little league team standing proudly in clean uniforms. Because of Ron's efforts, there were four teams in West Liberty.

Ron looked down the baselines. There were Latinos with their brown eyes, black hair, and olive skin. There were local boys and a couple of girls with blond hair and blue eyes, and even a pair of redheads with freckles. There were boys with slanted eyes and light brown skin, and there were a pair of boys with dark brown skin and kinky hair. Because of the processing plants in West Liberty and Columbus Junction twenty miles away, West Liberty had become a melting pot of nationalities and cultures.

The master of ceremonies was the Mayor of West Liberty, Jim Wilson.

He stepped to the microphone and announced, "Tonight, we are here to honor, one of our own, Ron Puck. To start the ceremonies off, we will first have the National anthem sung by the Gomez twins, Anita and Juanita. Will everyone please stand and men, please remove your hats as they sing. The pair of young women stepped forward, each gave Ron a hug, and then they sang a wonderful rendition of the Star Spangled Banner.

The mayor came back to the microphone and said, "Everyone, please be seated. I would like the four teams to be seated also. The Sox and the Braves go to the dugouts, and the Giants and the Royals, please find your seats in the stands. I would like the captains for tonight from each team to run out to the new scoreboard. Would each one of you grab a rope hanging on the board covering?"

The four ball players hurried out to the center field scoreboard and each found a rope.

"Now, on the count of three, everyone pull the rope. One, two, three!"

The cover slid to the ground.

"As mayor of West Liberty, Iowa, I and the town council have declared this ballpark be named "Ron Puck Field." Ron has been the master of organizing the Little League ball program here. He also has helped many of us out. His generosity and teaching skills are remarkable. Through baseball, he has taught our children fair play, sportsmanship, discipline, and character. He taught the boys and girls to win without bragging and to lose without crying. We are so fortunate to have him here tonight. Thank you, Mr. Ron Puck."

The crowd rose and gave him a standing ovation. They applauded and cheered for several minutes. Ron was in tears. He whispered something into Julia's ear. She retrieved his wheelchair. The length of time he had been standing and the emotional event were weakening him.

The mayor continued, "Tomorrow, we will have a Little League Tournament called the "Ron Puck Invitational." Our four teams plus four teams from the area will compete in a double elimination tournament. We have gotten permission from the other teams to have two, three-inning exhibition games tonight. The innings will not count for our pitchers. The real tournament will start at eight o'clock tomorrow morning. We hope Ron will be able to present the trophies at the end of the day."

Ron answered, "I'll be here even if they have to carry me in on a stretcher."

The exhibition games were played, and by 9:00 p.m., most of

the families had left. Just well-wishers and friends stayed to talk to Ron. It was past 10 o'clock when Ron and his sister finally got home.

"Could Nate take me for groceries, tomorrow? I don't think I'll arrive at the games until later in the afternoon. I need to go to the bank, also," Ron said.

"Sure, Uncle Ron, I'd be glad to take you. You bank in Durant, don't you?"

"Yep! I can get my groceries at Jeff's Market. Can you take me all the way to West liberty, too?"

"I can't do that, because I've got to go to work over at the Wilton Pool, but maybe Mom can take you."

"Sure, Ronnie. Do you think you can find a ride home?"

"I'm sure Julia or someone will drive me home."

* * *

Ron made it to West Liberty by 1 o'clock. He found out the men had rigged up a lift to raise him to the announcer's stand. He had the best view in the park. The day was very warm and the wind picked up, causing the dust to blow around on the diamond. The last game was between West Branch and West Liberty. Both teams had lost one game, so the winner would take home the trophy. Fortunately, for West Liberty, the West Branch team ran out of pitchers of any quality. During the fifth inning, West Liberty scored eight runs. West Liberty held the other team scoreless and won by the ten run rule, 12-2. Ron was lowered out of his perch and was able to present the trophies. It had been a great day.

"I'll take you home, Ronnie," cooed Julia. "Little Mike is sleeping over at his friend's home."

Ron hobbled over to her car. His leg was really tired and sore. They were only halfway to Atalissa, a little town about five miles out, when Julia looked over at Ron and saw that he was asleep. He didn't awaken until she turned onto the gravel road to Ron's house.

He opened his eyes, looked over at Julia, and said, "I guess I wasn't much of a conversationalist, was I?"

She answered back, "That's all right, honey, you were very tired. I think I'll stay over tonight to make sure you make it to bed. I can sleep on the sofa. I brought some extra clothes."

It was after 10:00 p.m. when Julia and Ron arrived at his home. Both were tired and dusty. Ron was revived a little by his nap, but the day's dirt and grime were getting to him.

"I need a shower," he said.

"I'm sure you do. I'll get your towels and clean clothes. You go on in."

Ron didn't protest. He was too tired to say anything. He sat on the first kitchen chair he came to. He pulled up his pant leg and unharnessed his artificial foot. Now he needed his crutches to maneuver around. He hobbled into the bathroom and sat on the stool. He studied the shower. His was a tub shower combination, which meant he would have to step over the edge to get in. At the VA hospital, they had rails and bars for support and no tubs.

He thought to himself, "This is the first home improvement project I'll have to get done."

By using the top door track, he lifted himself over the edge with his good hand. His other hand was frozen into a claw. He had only his thumb and index finger which worked. He leaned on the wall for support and turned on the water. It felt so good. When he finished showering, he tried to repeat the process, but his good foot slipped and down he went. It was a slow descent, but a noisy one.

Julia rushed to the door and screamed, "Ronnie, are you all right?"

"If you call lying on the floor with my head in between the toilet and the sink all right, then I'm fine. I could use a little help."

Julia rushed in, and she literally picked Ron up and sat him on the stool. She finished drying him off before he could speak.

"You're a very strong woman for your size," remarked Ron.

"Listen, I work at the nursing home. I pick up old people all the time."

"So you think I'm old," he answered back with a smile.

"Oh, no, honey, you're not old. You just need someone to look after you."

Julia helped him into his bedroom and got him dressed.

"I made some lemonade and brought some cookies. I'll help you out to the porch. It is nice and cool out there."

She got Ron settled into his rocking chair and put his lemonade and cookies on a plate beside him.

"Now, I'm taking a shower. See you in a few minutes."

Ron sat and rocked. He reviewed the events of the day. He hadn't expected such an honor, but it was nice to be recognized. He had his eyes closed when Julia opened the screen door and stepped out. She tapped him on his shoulder. He opened his eyes and gazed at the beauty standing there before him.

She was wearing a light blue nightgown with a deep neckline. Her wet hair shone in the moonlight. She was barefoot. Although she was not a tall woman, she was well-proportioned. Her ample breasts held the gown away from her tummy.

She could tell Ron was pleased by what he saw. She turned away, stood in the moonlight, and began to brush her long black hair. Ron shuffled his foot and tried to get up.

"You need something, honey?"

"Yes, I do, as a matter of fact. Would you please get me the brown paper bag I left on the counter?"

"Sure," she said.

Julia disappeared into the house and soon returned. She handed the bag to Ron. He fumbled around inside the bag with his good hand.

"May I be of help?" she asked.

"No, I can get it."

She turned again to brush her hair. The next thing she heard was Ron talking to her.

"Julia, I want to say something to you."

She turned around and found Ron on one knee. He held a little box in his hand.

"Julia, I thought about you all the time I was in the hospital. I hated to have you leave when you visited me. I love you, Julia Herera. I know I love little Mike, and I'll try to be a good father like his real father, Mike. I know I'm a cripple, but I will be able to drive someday. I figure I could sell security systems or something. So my big question is: Will you marry me?"

Julia stared at the man on his knee and said, "Oh, yes, yes, I'll marry you. I love you. I love you. I love you with all my heart."

She bent down and kissed him. Her gown gapped and Ron received the best view on the porch.

He asked, "Now, will you help this old man up? I have to go to the bathroom."

She helped him stand and handed him his crutches.

"I'll be waiting for your return, my honey."

Five minutes later, he returned to find Julia standing in the moonlight. Ron hobbled over and touched her shoulder. She turned and held him tight. She rubbed against his chest. Ron tugged at one little cap sleeve and slid it down her arm. It seemed the natural thing to do.

She pulled her arm free and she helped slide the other arm free. It wasn't difficult once the gown was over the top obstacles. It was an easy drop. He hopped away on his one foot and leaned against the porch post to admire his Mexican beauty. Her olive skin glowed in the moon's light. Her black hair cascaded around her shoulders.

She smiled at him and touched his good hand.

She lifted it around her shoulders and quietly said, "Come, my old man, let me help you to our bedroom. I'll show you some moves you never dreamed of. We Mexican women are great lovers."

With his arm around her shoulders, he limped into the house. This would be a night to remember.

Epilogue

The year passed slowly for Dan and Bobbi. Grandfather Miller had his machinery sale in December. He and Grandma moved to Maquoketa. The bank worked out a line of credit for the new farmers. The loan included enough to buy twenty does and a buck goat. Bobbi found a local breeder of Boer meat goats, who helped them get started. Dan found a job as an insurance adjuster for a local mutual insurance company. The job gave him the freedom to have flexible hours. Bobbi worked part-time at the local bank. They had been trying unsuccessfully to get pregnant.

Easter was early this year. The temperatures were still in the forties feeling nauseous for the last three mornings. Dan told her he'd do the chores. He hurried outside. He knew he'd have to shower before leaving, because the goat odor clung to his clothes and skin. Bobbi was to shower immediately. She undressed and sat on the stool.

Reluctantly, she decided to try another pregnancy test. She had done it many times with no positive results. This time, it was different. She couldn't believe her eyes. The tester indicated a positive for pregnancy. She jumped up and ran to the back door. She pulled on one of Dan's hooded sweatshirts and ran out the door.

She was about ten feet from the door before she realized it was chilly out and all she was wearing was a sweatshirt and her fuzzy bunny slippers. She turned and dashed back inside and pulled on her chore coveralls. She slid her feet into her cold yellow knee boots. She grabbed her stocking cap and pulled it over her ears.

She ran outside again and called, "Dan! Dan!"

Dan heard her screaming. He thought something was very wrong. He opened the barn door just as Bobbi was reaching for the handle. The swinging door almost knocked her down.

"What's the matter? Are you hurt?" Dan asked excitedly.

"No! No! Nothing like that," she answered.

She reached into her pocket, pulled out the tester, and held it up to his face.

"Look, Danny boy, we're pregnant! We did it! You're going to be a dad."

Dan grabbed Bobbi, hugged her, and swung her around and around. He put her down gently.

"You'd better rest," he said.

"Don't be silly. I'm okay. I'll be okay for a while yet. We won't even tell anyone because it is very early. What a wonderful Easter this is!"

* * *

Ron and Julia were married later that summer in August. He received permanent disability for his injuries sustained from the Jeep accident. Easter proved Julia meant what she claimed—Mexican women were great lovers. She was six months' pregnant with a little girl.

* * *

Rita Johnson's trial was delayed several times through legal maneuvering. The problem was they didn't know which charge the prosecution should try. The murder of the young woman found in the meat tub seemed to be the easiest to prove. In January, Rita was convicted of second-degree murder and sentenced to fifty years in prison with the possibility of parole in twenty. Rita would be seventy-nine before she could petition for parole.

The employees of Rita's 'Mrs. Ping's Girls' were given varying sentences from five years' probation for the lagoon manager, Willis Hamilton, to 10 years in prison for both Ricardo Sanchez and Fred Rodriguez. Rosa was sentenced 15 years, because her involvement with Rita. The slave girls were returned to their home countries. Two of the girls applied for political asylum and were accepted. They are on track to become citizens of the United States.

Finally, the most important person in this story was Phil Robbins, the mild-mannered reporter from the little town of Walcott, Iowa. Even though he was not a prominent character in this event, without him, there would be no story. If he had not been the good friend of Darren Hellzer, who contacted Phil out of desperation, Ron Puck would not have been involved.

Ron's expertise led to Bobbi and Dan Dorman of the DCI, which, in turn, led to the investigation of a corrupt sheriff's department, a prostitution operation in Wapello, and several unsolved murders.

If it hadn't been for Phil, Mrs. Rita Johnson would probably have become a congressman's wife, and she could have moved her business to Washington, D.C., where the clientele are more numerous and rich. Melanie might be still alive. Phil's friend, Ron, would have all his limbs. To end this tale, we honor the newspaper reporter, Phil Robbins.

Finally, Sherry, Phil's wife, did receive her $2,000.00 from the DCI, which she promptly spent on a new digitalized sewing machine.

The End

About the Author

Bob and his wife, Jane, live on the family farm which was established in 1868 by his great grandfather. The farm has grown since its beginning from the original 80 acres to 640 acres. Bob was raised on the farm. He worked and played there all his life. The pastures and corn fields are featured in his stories. Bob and Jane raised three sons and taught them the rewards of diligent work. After farming for 48 years they retired in 2008.

Bob started writing as a hobby. He had written some small essays before and some church skits, but never a novel. If fact, his first novel "The Nightgown" started out as a short story, it just grew and grew.

It was Jane who encouraged him to publish the book. To his surprise, he discovered readers actually liked his prose. He continues to write using the thoughts from his many hours in the tractor or combine cab. His writings give a different perspective on the lives of rural America. His stories take the reader on a trip which reveals not all rural living is drudgery and heart ache, but there are many fun and romantic times involved.

The second novel, "The Fourth Generation" is about the children of the couple in "The Nightgown". It tells of rural children working and playing together from small children to adulthood.

His third book "Call Sara" is a sequel of the first. It tells of the main character, Sara, and her life after a tragic accident takes the life of her husband. She finds many people still need her. She also discovers another love to carry her through t heresy of her life.

This fourth novel is Bob's first venture into the cops and robbers genre. Again he draws from his eastern Iowa roots to weave his tale. "Iowa Exposed" is about the fictional packing plant and the sinister elements existing within its walls.

Made in the USA
Columbia, SC
15 September 2021

45534671R00207